To: Stephanie

NEW WAVE

THE ISLANDS OF ANARCHY BOOK ONE

JENNIFER ANN SHORE

2019

D1153718

To: Stephan

Ebook ISBN: 978-1-7326083-0-6

Print ISBN: 978-1-7326083-1-3

PROLOGUE

MY ARMS AND LEGS DRAGGED, growing heavier with each movement. I pushed forward, unsure why I felt the weight of my own body in addition to everyone else's as I continued upward. The sky, a beautiful, tranquil shade of blue, was almost too peaceful to witness this chaos.

The ship rocked violently. The metal was cold beneath my fingertips, but my palms were sweaty and hot, making it difficult to grip the ladder. I had three, maybe four, rungs left until I reached the top to fight back or they started firing again, tearing through my delicate skin as I tumbled to my death. I wasn't sure what would happen first.

Expletives carried up from the fight below me, just as common to my ears as the steady clanging of firefight. I panicked, realizing the sound wasn't just from our guns — the enemy resumed their side of the fight, and a few bullets zoomed past me. I pressed my body against the side of the ship, climbing the last few arduous feet.

I pulled myself up toward the steel wall, and a bullet cut through my chest. I keeled over, falling behind the thick barrier. I screamed from the impact, not prepared for the searing white hot pain, then succumbed to the encroaching blackness.

1

_____

THE FIGHT against sand is futile. Everyone native to the island knows it, which is what makes it so easy to spot an outsider. I didn't think there was anything wrong with being from here, of course, but most people preferred not to be. Still, the sooner a person can accept the ever-present grains of sand in shoes, pockets, food, and everywhere else imaginable, the better.

The grit in my hair was as natural to me as breathing, and the billowing dust clouds caused by the rickety trucks driving across the island ensured my clothing would never truly stay black. I secretly loved the way it looked like fireworks splayed across random parts of my body, leaving a tinge of light-brown dust. Not that I had any experience with fireworks, but from what I heard, it was pretty spectacular.

I wore it with honor, a reflection of my upbringing. My mother said the sand and dirt were the perfect remedy for many of life's ailments, and I believed her wholeheartedly. She also invented funny breathing tricks for curing headaches and hiccups. She created coconut milk mixtures for sunburns and herbal remedies for the most trivial things, but above all else, she'd always said the grime was an important part of life.

Not everyone shared her views, though. On a rare occasion, we'd see someone try to battle the elements. We'd take bets on how long it'd take them to give up. My mother was always right. I still kept up the little game, even though she'd been gone for years.

"Thirty seconds," I sighed, passing a tall man who was cursing the sun for beating down so strongly.

His clothes were wrinkle- and hole-free, with the white of his shirt still bright and the blue pants still dark, which meant he was likely a visiting member of the Authority. The Guard members, decked out with their heavy vests, shields, and firearms, flanked by his side were also a dead giveaway. They watched him, wordlessly. He balanced on one foot to pour the sand out of his shoe then repeated the motion on the other side.

I took a hard right into a bank of trees, and I could feel a small smile forming on my lips at the thought of him realizing the sand from his shoes blew around and covered his entire backside.

My walk to visit Luca was usually uneventful, but I was glad for the distraction. All morning I allowed apprehension to grow to full-on wobbly kneed nervousness. I wished I could drink some chamomile tea, like my mother used to make, but no one on the island received the little white flowers in their rations for years.

I rubbed my eyes, trying to shake the thought of her brewing up some concoction in our tiny kitchen. I didn't need to stir up any of those memories today. I needed to talk to Luca.

He preferred not to be interrupted at his Placement. His

supervisors didn't mind if he took a lunch break or stepped out for a few minutes, but he truly preferred to sit silently for hours on end, diligently working and completely enthralled in projects.

Everyone, including me, marveled at his dedication to sitting at his desk, which was usually covered with balled up pieces of paper, small screwdrivers, rulers of various sizes, and pieces of broken electronics. Those weren't unique to his workspace, though. Almost every memory I have of Luca includes one of those components.

He's always been the productive one out of the two of us. I'm a dreamer, and he's a doer. Even with our nearly identical upbringing, his personality seemed so different from mine. He always knew what his path would be, despite the fact that his future was, is, and will always be in the hands of the Authority. Not in mine, in his, or anyone else's, regardless of our opinions on the matter.

Long before Luca got the results of his Placement at age eighteen, we both figured he'd be in a mathematics-heavy job. His brain was wired to solve puzzles and obsess over numbers. He didn't want adventures or time outdoors or anything else his colleagues talked about during the day. He liked to have a real, tangible problem to solve — or his mind would create one.

We were relieved that the Authority recognized his abilities and placed him on Island Seven as an Engineer in the big lab. I felt a little uneasy about giving credit to the Authority, but they did well.

I forced myself not to worry about what would happen to us if he was transferred to another island or put in a Placement that didn't align with his passion. But once he marched home, described the nervousness of all the other 18-year-olds waiting for the Placement results, and got confirmation he would remain here with me, I released a breath I'd been holding for months.

We were happy for a few hours, letting relief wash over us, allowing ourselves to smile and talk about the changes ahead, but then when the horn sounded for curfew, the elation snapped out of us. Worry flooded in. We told each other that Julian probably went to his own family to share his news, and he'd come by the next day.

We found out days later that he'd received Placement elsewhere, and we were devastated.

The void his presence left felt familiar to us. We went through the same rollercoaster of depression and anger when we got the news that our parents died. Only, this was worse, in a strange way. He was still living and breathing; we just didn't get to witness it.

In the months that followed, I became the top student in Education, making such remarkable improvement that a few educators mentioned I was finally beginning to rival Luca's accomplishments. In his Placement, he found his own version of solace by pouring hours into repairing the systems and machines on Island Seven. Most of those around him felt limited by their tools and available parts, but Luca enjoyed the challenge. He pushed through assignments in half the time allotted, baffling his peers.

It took Luca completing his third assignment earlier than even the first one was due, his superiors moved him onto special projects. Those took a lot longer to solve, which made it difficult for him to turn off his thoughts at night, but that eventually became second-nature. He was always in a problem-solving, self-inflicted state of stress, and I was always worried about his problem-solving, self-inflicted state of stress.

These days, he barely slept. He tried to hide it, not

wanting to let it add to the burden in our lives. But when you spend your spare hours with only one person who has been attuned to your emotions your entire life, not much slips by.

It wasn't until he stopped eating a few weeks ago that I really started to worry. I watched Luca bite his nails night after night while trying to think through some missing piece or a new approach. I began to resent him for pulling so much out of himself for the Authority, for his Placement, for anyone who wasn't me.

Typically, Luca gets up at dawn, chugs a cup of luke-warm coffee, goes to his Placement earlier than anyone else, ventures home after dusk, sleeps, then repeats the cycle all over again. The hours and days and months were so repeti-tive that they were becoming blurry.

We desperately needed a new routine, which coincided almost too perfectly with my Education wrapping up a few weeks ago. I guessed the Authority decided since I'd taken all the tests for Placement, there was no need to try and teach me anything until the next round of Authority servi-tude was doled out, falling shortly after my upcoming eigh-teenth birthday.

This time gave me something I'd never experienced — freedom. To choose my own schedule. To enjoy my time. To decide when I would wake up, eat, run, whatever. It was exhilarating.

I wandered around the island, uncovering hidden paths and abandoned beaches. After several hours of purposely getting lost one day, I walked by the big lab, and that's when I decided if Luca wasn't willing to make a change or take ownership of his own neglect, I would do it for him.

Now, each afternoon, after spending the morning boxing, lifting weights, or doing other training I picked up from Julian years ago, I would bring Luca lunch. At first, he was annoyed by my presence each day. Actually, I think, to some degree, he was still annoyed, but I persevered.

Maybe he discovered some degree of adequate nutrition was actually important. It did make our rations go by a lot quicker, but life's about trade-offs, and I'd rather have Luca alive, healthy, and stressed than any other alternative.

I pushed through the doors of the lab, clutching the sandwich wrapped in banana leaves. I ignored the usual stares from the Engineers in their identical faded blue shirts and made my way to the back where Luca's station was.

He glanced up at the large, digital clock on the wall, probably feeling my impending arrival. He leaned back against the hard metal of his chair, raising his arms above his head to stretch his stiff back and shoulders. I dropped his lunch in the middle of his desk and ran my fingers over some of the electronic parts.

"Mol, cut it out," he said while swatting my hands away.

"What are you working on?" I asked, hopping up on the three-legged stool next to him. I sat on my hands to stop them from picking up some of his more interesting pieces. My black boots hung a few inches from the ground, and I tapped them against one of the legs.

"Let me guess," I teased. "It's top secret? You can't tell me? It'll take too long to explain?"

His stone facade relaxed slightly. "Am I that predictable?'

I pursed my lips, pretending to mull it over. "A little bit, but I find it endearing."

"That's all that counts, anyway."

I smiled at him and flicked his shoulder. "So serious, Luca," I chastised, wearing my best fake pout, which was sparingly successful when I was younger.

He reluctantly grinned. "Tell me about your day, Mol."

I nodded toward his sandwich, which he began to pick at, and told him about the outsider and some of the training I did earlier. I appreciated this time with him. After all, life could be totally different after I receive my Placement in a few weeks. Despite my recent high marks in Education, I wasn't set up to be an Engineer or most of the other duties on Island Seven — maybe a Foreman job in one of the facilities or something.

The Authority typically didn't put women in those types of jobs. We're more suited for logistics or paperwork, apparently. It was infuriating. They governed the Network of Islands with rigor, setting forth suffocating rules and guidelines. Even with our important contributions, a few years ago I overheard one of the visiting Authority members say we have the worst living conditions. Apparently Island Two maintained paved roads. No dust fireworks for them.

Each island produced some quantity of food and specialty service or trade. Island Five produced the bulk of the rice supply, but some of it also came from Island Two, which also grew herbs and other small plants. Island Four worked with metal and other building materials, and of course, Island Seven manufactured goods, clothing, and whatever Luca did all day.

In Education, we were taught to appreciate the balance of the Network. Every person has a part in contributing to the overall good. By adhering to the rations, the Placement, the Authority's rules, we're a part in setting up success for society.

When I was younger, I bought into it. No one told me not to.

My parents shielded me from their struggles, but after they died, reality slapped me pretty hard. I quickly understood why they were so strict about portions, curfew, and the other matters that once seemed so meaningless. It didn't take long to uncover the contrast between what was taught and what was true.

I ignored the rows of fruit trees picked by those in that Placement and shipped off to the other islands as Luca and I shared cups of rice to stretch the week's rations. I didn't think twice about the Authority members, roaming freely at all hours. I overlooked the Guard members pacing in the sun, always prepared for some nonexistent but apparently imminent threat. I carried a ration of clothing, a true rarity, back home.

"We are setting up for prosperity." My educators reiterated that endlessly. "This is the most fair way to exist. We all have a purpose, a Placement."

It's funny how you go along with life's rules, unquestioningly, until you discover that they should be dragged through the dirt and tossed in a garbage pile.

I was brainwashed. We all were — and most still are. I learned to accept it, pushing away my desire for something more, something I could choose for myself. There was no well-known alternative to the Authority's suffocation.

Luca was watching me carefully. I unknowingly created a silence between the two of us, unsure of when I stopped speaking and my mind started wandering.

"I have an errand to run," I blurted out.

He hated when I said that, the code we established. He made a face and threw away his sandwich crumbs before turning his attention back to the project in front of him. I glanced around to make sure everyone resumed working. They all seemed too preoccupied or busy staring off into space to pay attention to us. Still, I dropped the volume of my voice a little lower.

"It's time, Luca," I said, my voice barely above a whisper. "They would understand."

He paused for a minute, eyes darting while his brain processed. "I don't agree," he said, almost choking on the words. I could feel the dread through his syllables, but tonight was a big night for us.

A few years ago, during one of my early morning runs, I came across an underground market in one of the abandoned buildings, hidden from the Guard on patrols around the island. There were dozens of people there trading rations for other supplies. It was a beautiful picture of discretion and volition. I didn't even notice the tears that formed into my own eyes until I ran home, faster than ever, to tell Luca what I found.

I went back the next day, observing the process of trading, and eventually, I started pawning off our possessions. At first, my inexperience with the market and the types of people that frequented it created a learning curve for negotiation. I traded some items for a lesser value, just excited to get some additional coffee beans and rice, but I learned from my mistakes.

It added some assistance for a while, but now, we were getting desperate again. Bitterness rose up in my throat every week I collected the "generous" and "fair" rations from the Authority. They regulated housing, rations, and almost every aspect of our lives, but there were some items we could live without — old tools, small pieces of wood, scraps of fabric.

It was easier to negotiate when the faces became familiar and trust grew. Almost every day I'd visit the man with no teeth who sold bread and the elderly couple who mended fabrics just to exchange pleasantries. I'd even grown to appreciate the children who tried to pickpocket.

I learned that the morning was the best time to trade — some of the more rough-around-the-edges crowd woke up after noon. Mavis, harsh, strong, and somewhat terrifying, fell somewhere between approachable and those I typically avoided, but I was told that she was the one suitable for my latest errand — my last errand. After that, Luca and I would have to figure something else out.

"When do you leave?" Luca coughed out, refusing to meet my gaze.

My hand moved to the jacket pocket that contained my mother's gold necklace. Selling illegally grown herbs or fabric was fairly straightforward in the market, but trying to sell gold — the most valuable item in the Network — was no easy feat. Apparently Mavis excelled at difficulty.

I looked up at the clock on the wall. My precious time with Luca was over for the day, and a wave of nervousness hit me. In a few hours, I'd be at sea, then on a different island — both new experiences. I put my hand on Luca's shoulder, and he immediately tensed.

"Now," I breathed. "Well, Luca, you keep the Authority happy with whatever it is you do, and I'll see you later at home."

He already tuned me out, pushing himself back into work. He didn't respond, so I lingered for a minute, hoping he'd confirm that he'd heard me. Or wish me luck. He didn't. Some sort of reassurance would have been nice, but sometimes you need to be your own source of optimism.

I tried to think of anything but the uneasiness I felt in making the trek to the west end of the island. The most logical way to get to each side of the island was through the main road, but there were too many Guard members on patrol, so I took a hidden path through one of the coffee plantations.

I made the decision that the next few hours would be enjoyable, a rarity up until recently, when I started to grow accustomed to the time by myself. I would miss it, nearly to the level I missed Julian and my parents, but a part of me, growing bigger each day, was eager to see what my future would be.

It didn't matter if I became a janitor or a seamstress or any other job in the factory. I just wanted to stay on Island Seven with Luca. Leaving him would be miserable — even more so than staying here.

After our parents died, we were caught in waves of grief for months, but we carried on. Julian was a big part of that. He was the person who pulled us from our sadness and back to normal. We spent afternoons challenging each other, debating, bickering, and laughing, but everything changed the day they got their Placements.

We didn't know where he was transferred to or what he was doing, but it wasn't anywhere on Island Seven. For months, we didn't talk about it. The wound was too fresh and too deep. Eventually, I started to bring up jokes Julian told or remind Luca of a fight he broke up between the two of us.

Eventually, we found a way to be content with what we were given — until life on the Island worsened.

I noticed it first with the coffee. We ran out of grounds days earlier than usual, so we had to drink smaller cups with more water. And then the rice bag became lighter. I pretended the weight seemed to decrease due to my expanding muscle mass, but we started going to bed hungry.

If Mavis came through, it could drastically improve the quality of our lives. That was what drove me and my wavering confidence to approach her. I showed her the necklace, and she instructed me to arrive at the abandoned dock at sundown today. Mavis would collect her payment on the return route, once "the goods are successfully transferred." It seemed legitimate enough.

At the dock, I waited with a handful of people, some of whom I recognized from the market. I assumed Mavis and I were traveling alone, given the risk, but when Mavis and the motor boat crashed to a stop at the dock, we all filed in, one by one, slightly rocking the boat with each step. I jumped in and scooted over to get some form of self-inflicted seclusion, barely having time to get settled against the damp wood when we pushed off the dock.

The wind was warm, and it picked up quickly. The smell of the sea was sensational — so was the breeze. The boat rocked with the waves but managed to plow through, splashing warm water into the boat.

My long, blonde and somewhat straight hair whipped between my face and back, almost guaranteed to be a knotted mess once we stopped. My mind flickered to a vision of me, hair huge and wild, getting so many coffee beans and other essentials for the necklace, that I laughed aloud. Paired with the strange thrill of watching Island Seven grow smaller and smaller across the water, I was a little punch-drunk. I'd never tasted moonshine, but I was willing to bet the effect was similar.

I rested my head against the edge of the boat, watching the waves move back and forth, trying to reel in my giddiness. I loved the idea of being surrounded by open air and sea with nothing but opportunity. Everyone stays in one place, with so much complacency and sadness, when there's a possibility of adventure — if only things were different.

Mavis, sitting in the back, rotated between staring at what was ahead and the people she was transporting. I wondered how Mavis ended up in this position. Did she even have a Placement? How did she get this boat? When did she find the route to the other islands?

I pictured her, clad in raggedy clothing and rubber boots, stepping up in front of a panel of Authority members and getting assigned to transport people illegally between islands by way of a very old motorboat.

"I've never seen hair that color." I exhaled, trying to quell the nausea that arose at the man's gruff, deep tone.

I'd never exactly blended in on the island. The majority of people were tanned and dark-haired. Although there was some variation, Luca, my mother, and I were the only people with a combination of fairer skin, blue eyes, and light hair.

I reluctantly turned to see who made the comment and saw the three greasy men huddled together a few feet away staring straight at me. Grime was good, sure, I agreed with my mother on that principle, but these men were in an unclean category of their own.

"Do you think it's that color everywhere?" The skinniest one made a lewd gesture, and they all laughed.

I took a deep breath and did a mental checklist of Julian's preferred defensive maneuvers. It was a bit super-fluous at this point — everything was ingrained in me now.

I spent weeks watching Julian and Luca practice — or rather, watching Julian try and teach a hopeless Luca how to correctly take down an opponent. After Julian deflected Luca's punch for the twentieth time, I jumped up off the patchy grass and said I wanted a shot.

At first, Luca and Julian laughed at my request to join their sparring. It was calm and sunny that day, but I vividly remember my body flushing hot with anger. I vowed that men would never laugh at me like that again — at least, not without consequence.

Julian obviously planned to humor me, but after I caught him with an elbow to the face, kneed him in the groin, and tackled him to the ground, he embraced it. From them on, Julian would entertain my questions on best defenses or knife skills for hours, giving Luca the opportunity to sit off to the side with some old scrap metal and wires.

We found a weird sense of happiness, and I clung to it.

"Always have something you can use on you," Julian warned long ago. "Whether it's a pencil, a rock, or your hands. You always want to be ready."

I was wearing my favorite thick boots, suitable for landing hard kicks on their dirty faces, and my go-to black pants were stretchy, so that wouldn't prohibit any movement. My jacket, which once belonged to my mother, was probably a different shade of green at some point. It was practically covered with pockets — more than any other jacket on Island Seven. One held the necklace and a few assorted scraps of paper took up the others, but the one right by my left wrist contained my pocket knife.

"She's nothin', though, brothers," the third man chimed in. "I've been to the big ship and seen them Elite women."

"Yeah, right," he scoffed, voice echoing with disbelief. "Who would let the likes of you on the ship?"

"No, brother, I've seen them," he insisted. "Beautiful. Them women, serving the Commander and Guard breakfast, lunch, dinner, and..." He paused for emphasis. "Dessert."

I turned my head away.

Their conversation likely was nothing different than normal nighttime market happenings, but it made me want to go home, take a good bath, and scrub my skin raw — if there was enough soap ration at home to do so.

They were definitely vile, but these men could be truly harmless — just your average gang of friends colluding in illegal activity and making jokes about women. Another benefit of life under the Authority.

"Hush!" Mavis snarled, and they immediately stopped. "Keep your heads down and shut up!"

Mavis walked the fine line between terrifying and tough, but there was no doubt she was well respected — and feared. I hoped someday I could be the type of woman who could commanded respect like that. Admittedly, I didn't want to adopt all of her traits.

It was strange, though, that Mavis stood up for me. Clearly my request wasn't unique enough to create some sort of bonding experience between the two of us, in her eyes at least, so I guessed she was sick of these types of men and their comments too. Still, I couldn't fight the unease that was circling my mind.

Something felt wrong.

I sat up to get a better look at Mavis, noting her petrified face was fixed in the distance, her eyes wide and mouth open. The waves stopped hitting against the boat, and a chill crept up my spine. I could hear my own breathing heavy in my ears.

As I turned to look at what frightened her so, a bright light swallowed me whole.

2

————

CONSCIOUSNESS FLICKERED in my mind suddenly, propelled from a black hole and pulled back into cognizance.

The pain was all-encompassing. The burning sensation radiated from the top of my skull, the throb of discomfort fanned downward. It was pure agony seeping in from my skin into my muscles and bones. My lungs felt trapped in a container too small to house them, heightened by every intake of air.

It hurt to breathe. It hurt to think about breathing.

I moved my head slightly against a cold, hard surface, and a heavy pulse drummed behind my eyes. The rest of my body slumped over, the pain pumping like blood through my veins. I flexed my hands, testing their tenderness, attempting to find stability. The rocking back and forth made me want to vomit, but I was in too much pain to let it happen.

By slowly counting each inhale and exhale of my own breath, I discovered it wasn't my body that was swaying — it was the room.

I opened my eyes and recoiled at the brightness. Everything was white, too sterile. The floors, the walls, the ceiling, the tables, and the chairs. It was a picture of purity, immaculate and perfectly square — a stark contrast to the uneven floors and mismatched colored walls on Island Seven. A fleeting thought of pride fluttered through my pounding headache. I characterized my home quite well at this moment by being so bruised and disheveled.

I drew strength from that comparison and sucked in a slow, cold, calculated breath, trying to be mindful of my abdomen. I lifted my head and sat upright, wincing, and I gripped the edge of the table.

My head spun, but I fought to stay conscious. The thought of passing out was alluring. How nice it would be to let the pain drift far away, and I felt the pull. My determination to get my bearings overpowered the temptation of relief. I focused on the movement of my mouth and was surprised to find it was my teeth chattering. I wished it was desensitizing, but my shivering only heightened the misery.

I concentrated on breathing again as flashes of being slammed to the ground, getting kicked in the ribs, and looking up to see the butt of a gun driving toward my face streamed through my mind. It felt like my body was tossed around for hours in some sort of a machine.

"Ouch," I whispered. The sound echoed off the walls or possibly just in my head. I couldn't tell the difference.

I ran my tongue over my lips, tasting bitter, metallic blood. I felt the bump on my head and gingerly touched my swollen right eye. I didn't have to lift my shirt, which was splattered with blood that was possibly not all my own, to see the damage. I could feel the bruising forming already. My legs and arms seemed to be generally unscathed, which eased my worry slightly, but it didn't quell the other emotions. I wasn't afraid, necessarily, more uncertain.

A tangible sway threw my dizziness into overdrive. I wasn't bothered by the rocking on Mavis's small boat, but the lurch felt like another blow to the head here. I was likely in one of the rooms on one of the Authority's bigger fleet ships, which were a source of fascination for those on the islands.

People at the market speculated about life at sea, but when I tried to pull some answers from Luca, he either didn't know or didn't want to tell me. It didn't diminish my desire to figure out what was true and what was completely made up over bootleg liquor, so my understanding of the Network was picked up from other people or my own observations. Typical Luca, he always—

"Shit!" I slammed my fist on the table, sending a painful wake-up charge to my damaged body. The immediate rush of shame went well with everything else I was feeling.

Luca never loved my trips to the market, but I ignored his warnings and concerns. We were too helpless to follow the rules. He was frustrated, and I didn't see another choice. His objections ceased almost immediately the first night I smugly dropped the extra coffee beans in front of him. Now, I was sure he was picturing the scene under different pretenses.

I imagined him sitting at his Placement, channeling his resentment into his work while thinking about his sister who got caught underage and out past curfew. His coworkers would stare, knowingly, for different reasons than outward appearance, in fascination of how someone can carry on with the humiliation of being my brother.

The slight reprieve of the additional rations could have been worth it in the end. If I approached Mavis months ago, or if we could actually be in control of our own lives, instead of the Authority, things could be so different. I stopped my brain from feeding into that frustration tailspin. I couldn't spare the room to house that emotion or let self-pity and desperation get the best of me.

My naïveté didn't allowed me to consider the possibility of Mavis's boat getting picked up. I was so focused on trading the necklace that I didn't think through the consequences. Of course, the Guard patrolled regularly, but I assumed Mavis took care of planning for all of that.

I vowed to be better at thinking through the complications, to be more like Luca, and I surveyed my surroundings once again.

The bare room gave no indication of how long I'd been out, and I wondered if the news of the boat's fate made its way back to the island. Sometimes the Authority would make examples of rule breakers and other times, people would simply disappear.

My eyes adjusted to all of the details — I completely missed the door. Of course there was a door. How else could I have gotten thrown in here? If my brain wasn't so foggy or the pain so overwhelming, I probably would have noticed it earlier. I wasted precious time when I could have been thinking out a strategy.

Realistically, the door's odds of being unlocked were fifty-fifty. I needed to try it, regardless of how much physical pain it would cause to get up. I gave myself a mental pep talk and counted down from ten. Nine, eight. I flexed my legs and wiggled my toes. Five, four. I swung my hips to the left and my abdominal muscles grabbed. Three, two. I exhaled, readying to stand, and the door swung open.

Instinctively, my hand shot to the pocket with my knife, but it wasn't there. I couldn't remember if it got lost in the scuffle or if the Authority simply confiscated it. I gritted my teeth at my carelessness. I should have checked for any weapons to use before I even considered trying to escape the room. I could practically feel the Julian of my subconscious rolling his eyes at my oversight.

I looked up at the doorway, expecting someone from the Guard. A burly man with a huge gun or knife or some other form of torture device, ready to make me scream or beg for forgiveness. Instead, a woman walked in, carrying a stack of papers.

Her red hair, something I'd never seen, contrasted beautifully with her skin. The clothing she wore, a slightly blue shade of gray was cut magnificently, emphasizing her small waist and jetting outward at the hips. The woman, like me, stood out in the barren space but for entirely different reasons. If the woman noticed, she didn't let on. Instead, she let the door slam, strutted over to the opposite side of the table, and sat down, not even bothering to look at me.

"So, Mol, let's skip the pleasantries and get right to it, yes?" Her voice was high and hollow, I noticed, and I also knew that wasn't really question, so I remained silent. The woman focused on carefully spreading out small stacks of papers out on the table between us.

"I've been informed of your intentions by the others who accompanied you on the boat. I also have every Network file on you. I have details on your birth, parents, and current circumstances. Additionally, I have the early results of your Placement, which have been very enlightening, to say the least." She briefly paused at this, letting her eyes travel up and down one of the pages. "So, I think we can agree that I know everything there is to know about you."

The pounding in my head was causing me to process this information at a slower than normal rate. The Placement results were of huge interest, and they were right in front of me, in one of the red-haired woman's neat little stacks. She possessed the information on my parents, my life with Luca, and maybe even my parents' death. The thought of getting information on that made me itch.

This woman wasn't going to give me answers. She was here to remind me that she was in control, and I wasn't. I'd never seen a woman like this, so in charge and well put together. She made Mavis's confidence look like child's play.

It was a little unsettling how she brushed off my life in a few sentences, as though lines on paper could encompass everything. The Authority didn't have a clue. There's no way this woman had information on how hard it was for me and Luca to learn of our parents' deaths. It started the moment the Guard showed up at our home, with their hard expressions, firearms, and matching black uniforms, to deliver the official certificate of their deaths. It set forth a daily struggle for Luca and me.

All the resentment I buried quickly crawled into the front of my mind — along with my desire for freedom and the animosity that grew a little bigger each day. I sucked in air between my teeth. It did nothing to suppress the urge to speak up. It's not like anyone else was here to vouch for me.

"I don't think so," I whispered, twisting my fingers together under the table.

Finally, the woman stopped arranging papers and looked up. Her eyes narrowed, and her jaw ticked. I met her glance, ready to face judgment, her picking apart my appearance, my response, my everything.

"Excuse me?" A sneer tugged at the corner of her mouth.

I cleared my throat. "You said you know everything there is to know about me, and I don't agree with that."

I leaned back into the chair, trying to relieve some of the pressure on my ribcage. She interpreted that as a cocky gesture, but really, I was trying to lessen the strain. The woman brushed a non-existent stray hair behind her ear and straightened up another fraction of an inch.

"All right, how about we agree to disagree on that one? Moving on, a different question, which I have no formal opinion on for you to disagree with. Instead, I would like yours. What were you planning on doing if you successfully fought off five of our Guard?"

I didn't remember there being five Guard members. I tried to recollect the details, but the fog was making its way back in, and I tried to clear my head for the rest of this conversation.

I opened my mouth, and the realization that injuries were the result of the fight started to settle in somewhere in my brain. I paused, somewhat at a loss, wondering what this woman expected from me or what would get me in the least amount of trouble. Perhaps honesty would earn some sort of mercy.

"I didn't really have any time to plan; I just reacted on instinct," I admitted, cringing when the words came out. "My memory is kind of questionable, but I'd like to think that if I knew I was going down, it might as well have been fighting."

I felt uncomfortable in my answer, under the woman's scrutiny. It felt like a test I was failing, and I wondered if this was some sort of examination leading up to a sentence or if she oversaw the punishment.

"I see," the woman sighed. "I personally bet on you swimming back to Island Seven like nothing happened. That, or taking control of that sad excuse of a boat to continue on to sell your mother's necklace."

That was not the response I expected, and all the thoughts in my brain swirled together.

"You see Mol, you did something illegal, and instead of

surrendering and asking for leniency, you gave a black eye to a member of the Guard and slashed another with a rudimentary knife while trying to, apparently, 'go down fighting.'"

"And I suppose it is too late to ask for leniency?"

The woman nodded once, sharply, in response.

I rubbed my temples. The misery began to cascade from the physical to the mental in my mind. Well, if there was no room for tolerance, I could be authentic. Say something that I could hold onto for the rest of my life in a cell.

"I believe what I was doing shouldn't be illegal, anyway. The Authority shouldn't have a say in where I go or what I do. You just want me to play by your rules, to be under your control." I tried to keep my voice level, but the acidity overpowered.

"I do very much appreciate your honesty, Mol, really it is quite refreshing compared to the silence I've been getting from most of your companions." She chuckled, but the smile didn't meet her eyes. "But I have other matters to attend to, so I will now dish out some of my own honesty and discuss your retribution."

She began turning the papers around. Our conversation distracted me, and I'd missed out on my chance to see what was printed right in front of me. I lost count at how many times I'd failed at being observant.

"The others aboard the ship are under different circumstances and their discipline will reflect it," the Punisher explained. "But you are a different story. You're underage. Your files are clean."

She pointed to various lines, confirming what she was saying. I skimmed the page quickly, but nothing interesting jumped out at me.

"However, you do have a bit of arrogance and defiance

that I would like to personally keep a close eye on, and so, to make amends, you will be undergoing Placement early."

I let a laugh slip through my teeth, causing the Punisher to glower. My heart pounded, urging me to at least try to not make things worse.

"I'm sorry," I said, the words bitter-tasting but satisfactory in tone. "I didn't mean to disrespect you. I was just surprised."

The Punisher's demeanor cooled to the point of pure ice. "Well, Mol, you might also be 'surprised,' at some of these opportunities that you were chosen for in the Placement. Most of them involve hard physical labor and almost all require you to remain on Island Seven."

I sat up too quickly, but the elation overpowered all other senses, including the pain. This was coming together too well. Getting an early Placement didn't seem like a punishment — depending on what I was placed in — it seemed like a reward for good behavior. They were just speeding up the inevitable. It was kind of a relief, actually.

Whatever emotion flashed on my face didn't please Punisher. She rested her hands on the table and leaned forward. "You will be put on a special assignment, which will seek to remind you of your place here."

Oh, right. The whole "did something illegal and got caught" thing.

"I'm assuming you have heard about how the Authority works but are unfamiliar with all of the details," she said. "You already know the Guard, and maybe even the General and the Commander, but you might not be familiar with the Elite. You will, of course, learn quickly in your Placement here onboard."

This would be so drastically different from the island. I heard it was rare for the Authority members to stay on land for a long period of time, choosing to float away from the truth, but that's not what inspired uneasiness — I'd heard of the Elite. It certainly wasn't from Luca and his vault of silence, and it probably wasn't from Julian or my parents, which unfortunately meant I likely picked it up from the market.

"Someone will be in shortly to fill you in on the details and escort you to your quarters." The Punisher glanced at her watch and gathered up her papers. "Just let me give you one piece of advice since I believe you are able to receive it."

She stood up, creating somewhat of an intimidating advantage over me. It was all about perception with this woman. I looked directly into her eyes, refusing to blink or look away.

"Don't lose your somewhat peculiar brand of charm," she said slowly and carefully. "Your way of thinking will help in ways you cannot begin to comprehend."

It was too much to take in. It felt like weeks ago that I was in Luca's lab, and then my life moved at ten times the normal speed, trekking over to Mavis's boat, ignoring those repulsive men. Recognition snapped like a rubber band, and I choked.

"Them women, serving the Commander breakfast, lunch, and dinner, and dessert."

The Elite. The blood flushed away from my face, and my heart pounded. I wanted to pass out again or throw myself into the water or do something, anything not to be trapped in this room. I gripped my hair with my fingers, shooting pain up to fight the lightheadedness. I was vaguely aware of the Punisher leaving, but I wasn't ready to let her go.

"Wait," I pleaded. "I just have one final question."

I could have begged her for a change in Placement, but I knew that it would be useless. In this Authority-controlled world, that wasn't an option. I couldn't ask for more advice; it would probably just be more vague and confusing than what she offered already. I could ask to speak to Luca, but I didn't want to draw any unnecessary attention to him.

I felt weak and completely out of my element. Instead of the pain radiating through my body, it was terror. I hated myself for being afraid, but without my physical defenses, I felt exposed. This was a cage, and I was trapped.

The Punisher halted when I spoke but didn't turn to face me. Instead of asking a question that I could use to my advantage, one that could bring some semblance of peace or understanding, I simply chose something I'd been wondering during this entire exchange.

"What is your name?" I asked.

That was a simple question, with a direct answer. In her side profile, I could see the ghost of a smile.

"Hope."

3

To say the women of the Elite were gorgeous might possibly be the biggest understatement of my life. They stared at me, eyes questioning my presence, when I arrived to the quarters escorted by the Guard. I could only gawk at their varying shades of gorgeous caramel skin, silky black hair, and curves in the male-approved places, which spurred them into a frenzy of whispers and uncomfortable laughter.

The Guard directed me to my assigned bed, and once left alone, I grabbed the towel and shower items they'd provided and hurried to the bathroom, refusing to look at anything but my own two feet. Giggles bounced off the metal walls and smacked me in the ears repeatedly. I truly didn't blame the women. Growing up on Island Seven was good preparation, where my long arms, long legs, and blonde hair contrasted just about everything.

Here, my fresh bruises, cuts, and scrapes didn't help me blend in any further, especially once I realized how gruesome my injuries looked. My right eye was swollen, decorated with red and purple splotches of bruising. The cuts on my bottom lip and forehead stopped bleeding hours ago, but the wide drops of blood that dried down my face looked mostly horrific.

Women flitted in and out of the bathroom while I stared at my mirrored reflection. An invisible, five-foot barrier stood between us, and they seemed determined to respect the perimeter.

I staggered over to a shower stall, undressed, and basked in the hot water. On the days we could shower on the Island, we'd be lucky if it was lukewarm. The soap was different here, too. I'd never seen it in liquid form or smelled like flowers because of it. Plus, it stung my face and body, which helped me focus on the physical, rather than mental, trauma. Somehow, the burning of my own wounds made it easier to cope with my new reality. The bruises would fade over time, but the cuts would heal to form scars, a reminder that I was the girl who fought back.

I could live with that.

My resentment for the Authority, for my Placement, for the Punisher, rapidly grew each following day, but outwardly, I tried to adapt. I wore the Elite uniform, a white starched shirt with a high collar, royal blue jacket, and skirt — my first time in one of those. It kept most of my injuries hidden while simultaneously serving as a personal torture device. The short, tight fabric alone was enough to drive me crazy, but there were also strict makeup, hair, personal grooming, and behavioral standards to follow.

The plucking, brushing, and lipstick-wearing was a normal for the other Elite women, but it was all new to me. The first full day in the Placement, I tried to ask one of the others in the dressing room for advice on applying rouge. She simply acted like I didn't exist and made a quick exit. I decided to skip that part of the process, and no one said anything to me about it.

Then again, no one said much of anything to me except when explicitly necessary, but the whispers grew into full-on hostility and snide comments in a short time. I refused to let it bother me. I simply didn't allow myself to have the brain capacity to process hate. It was occasionally successful.

So aside from the vanity, things hadn't changed that much from my life on land. Island Seven was friendlier to me, especially alongside the misfits in the market, but I still didn't truly fit in. I wasn't sure if I'd fit in anywhere.

The chores provided me ample time to analyze my circumstances and foster even more resentment for the Authority. I tried my hardest not to think about it, or much of anything, but I spent hours each day silent and committed to my Placement.

I'd never used bleach on the island, but after days of using it, I swore the smell was permanently stuck to me. My lungs burned and my skin was irritated, even with the defense of a towel tied around the lower part of my face and the bright yellow gloves covering my hands and forearms.

Although I wasn't privy to every single task delegated to the Elite, every assignment was some degree of domestic. So far I was subjected to sterilizing already spotless areas, washing dishes, changing bed sheets, and ironing uniforms. Everything was cleaned and sanitized repeatedly on the ship — even the people.

I longed to be unrefined.

After scrubbing the main kitchen floors on my hands and knees for a few hours, I sat back and gave myself a moment of reprieve. My injuries made the process arduous, every moment shot a jolt of discomfort to some part of me, but eventually my body hummed with a mixture of pain and numbness. I figured this behind-the-scenes grace period surely wouldn't last long — the makeup almost completely covered all evidence of my rebellion.

I stood up and rinsed the sponge out in one of the large metal sinks and poured the dirty water down the drain. I returned the products to the correct cupboard and made a mental checklist of what I needed to grab from the laundry closet.

Since I was technically serving a punishment for illegal activity, a Guard accompanied me whenever I left the kitchens, laundry, or Elite quarters for miscellaneous errands. I was eager to explore other parts of the ship, but the Elite were on a tight schedule, and none of the Guard members seemed to want to speak, let alone give me a tour.

As I gathered up a set of fresh sheets under the watchful eye of a Guard, envy set in. I was wearing black-thigh high stockings and wasting away, but for the man next to me, training, physique, and labor was his purpose. Then again, following me up three floors up to do the scheduled daily upkeep on one of the higher-level Guard quarters probably wasn't ideal for him either.

I walked up the stairs with the Guard trailing close. Out of all the people on the ship, I spent the most time with this man, and I didn't even know his name. I didn't know anyone's name except the Punisher, but I decided that I wasn't mentally ready to associate that emotion with someone who handcrafted this awfulness.

In my peripheral vision, I stole a look at my companion. I observed him in the past few days, a desire to speak to him hung off the tip of my tongue. Whenever I found the courage to open my mouth, he sped up his pace.

Like all members of the Guard, he was exceptionally well-built. Apparently everyone in the Authority was attractive and maintained, although I had yet to see anyone in the

Elite do any exercise. My body tingled with jealousy at the thought of the training the Guard went through to keep up with their physiques.

As if he could sense my eagerness, the Guard turned his head to meet my eyes, and I didn't want to let the opportunity slip past.

"I'm Mol." My voice squeaked, and I winced. I couldn't remember the last time I said something out loud.

I wasn't sure if I was allowed to speak to him, but since the other Elite women bragged about their interactions with the Guard and went into plenty of detail, too much detail, it likely was approved on some level. He nodded and turned his focus back on the route.

"I know," he murmured.

My heart leapt. It was pathetic. It was my first true dialogue in days, those two words, and it felt a lot like rejection. I straightened up my posture and picked up my pace.

"Nico," he said, pointing to the name stitched on the right side of his vest.

I could have known at least five other Guard member names if I looked there. It wouldn't really help my situation but getting a grasp on my surroundings would be beneficial for my sanity, at the very least.

A few beats later, we arrived at the correct room, and Nico stood at attention to the left of the door. The rigidness of the Guard took some getting used to. Typically, they would escort me, avoid meeting my eyes, and wait silently outside while I worked then walk me back to quarters or the next task. Getting Nico to acknowledge my existence was a bonus, and I smiled at him. The corner of his mouth pulled sideways into a smirk, flashing so quickly that I almost missed it.

I entered the room and closed the door. The scent of rich

wood and the sound of the ocean was overwhelming, and I jumped in surprise, ignoring the dull pain from my abdomen.

Only Authority members and key members of the Guard were awarded their own private space on the ship, and the lavishness was astounding. Compared to the Elite quarters and some of the other Guard rooms I'd been in, this felt like true luxury. The carpet was gold and thick, matching the fabric accents on all the furniture. The space was already somewhat tidy, which normally made this process quicker and easier. Even with that, I knew this wouldn't take any less time than the others.

The sunshine, a rarity onboard, was distracting. My skin missed the heat of the rays, and I tried to stay in the beams streaming from the window while stripping the bed. My mind went fuzzy, imagining the wood scent was from the trees on the island and the breeze was coming off the water and on to Island Seven's southern beach. I relaxed into the familiarity, allowing my body to go on autopilot. I folded the comforter over the freshly laundered linens.

The sound of running water stopped. My eyes darted over to the window, which was closed tightly, held in place by a black metal latch. The elements were so distracting that it blocked my brain from deciphering that the noise came from inside the suite. This was my allotted time to be here, so I assumed no one else would be.

A prickly feeling of concern crept up my spine. I glanced around for something I could use to defend myself. Eyeing the heavy, golden candelabra from the desk, the logical fear of the unknown overwhelmed all other thought. I hated my circumstances, but it probably could be worse.

I hurried to finish up before the bathroom door opened, gathering up all the dirty sheets. I willed my body to go faster, praising my long legs for their ability to move quickly, and I almost made it to the entryway when the bathroom door swung open.

A shirtless man stepped out into the main room. His dark brown hair paired well his tanned skin, which stretched tightly against the definition of his muscles. His arm muscles seemed too big for his body, protruding out and forming their way up to a set of hard, raised shoulders. His chest led to a solid stomach but stopped at the black pants of the Guard uniform.

I looked up at his soft brown eyes and recognition hit me like a blow to the head. I dropped the linens I was holding, and I threw myself into his arms.

"Julian," I cried. Words tumbled out of my mouth in an indecipherable mumble. He embraced me, enveloping my body in his for a few moments then suddenly released me back to the ground on my own feet.

"Who brought you here?" he asked, his tone sharp — too sharp to associate with the carefree, happy Julian from my memories.

"What?" I sputtered. Being in his presence was doing strange things to my heart. I placed my hand over it, willing the beats to slow.

"Which Guard escorted you here, Mol?" He hurried the question out a second time, and I took a step away from him.

"Oh, um," I swallowed. "Nico did?"

I don't know why it came out as a question or why I felt so uncomfortable, but he immediately relaxed when I answered. I couldn't believe he was here, right in front of me, but there were now years and inches between us. I had grown and changed since we last saw each other, for some reason, I was astounded that he had too.

"Julian, I, um," I stammered, and I hated it. "I mean, Luca and I." I didn't even know where to begin.

"I know," he exhaled, pulling out the other pieces to his Guard uniform from his armoire. "Luca told me."

My jaw dropped open, and he waved it off. "Look, Mol, we don't have a lot of time. I didn't expect you here this late."

"What do you mean Luca told you? And you didn't expect me? You knew I was here?"

I found my confidence within my anger, which grew with each question. I tried to reconcile this version of us, standing here in richness on the open sea, against the months of misery after he received his Placement. I would never be able to count the number of hours I spent worrying about him and wondering where he was. Now that I was here, in his proximity without knowing it, I was completely baffled.

"What the hell is going on?"

He sighed and buttoned up his shirt. "I'm sorry, Mol. I want to answer your questions, but for now, I need you to trust me — and Luca. Can you do that?"

My agitation was making me fidget, and I didn't do well with patience. There's no way he forgot about that.

I chewed on my bottom lip and watched Julian ready himself. He looked taller than I remembered, but my version of Julian still had to be in there somewhere. I clung to it and let the sense of security of being in his presence comfort me.

"Yes," I answered, simply.

"I need you to act like we don't know each other," he said, so gravely that it was almost like a demand. "You'll learn the dynamics we're up against. All in good time."

There was a barrier between us, set forth by him, that I was desperate to break down. I considered asking for more detail, but I somehow knew he wouldn't reveal what he really meant — just like my conversation with the Punisher.

"But Luca knows I'm here, right? Do you think it'd be possible to somehow let him know I'm okay? Sneak him a letter?"

"No letters!" Julian snapped, and he caught himself, forcing gentleness. "Sorry, just, Mol, we're in enough of a bind with you beating the shit out of two of my well-respected Guard members."

"Your Guard members?" I fired back at him, somewhat incredulous.

At that moment, clouds rolled in front of the sun and a darkness overtook the room. My chest constricted — the quarters, his toughness, and his absence clicked into place. My hands started shaking with an emotion I couldn't put a name to.

We spent years together dreaming and planning for things to be different, and here he was, the epitome of the worst. I snapped to attention, suddenly feeling as though he were a complete stranger instead of the man so much nostalgia was tied up in.

"What happened to you, Julian?" I accused.

He ran a hand through his hair. "I don't have time to explain now," he said, quickly.

I kept my emotion closed inside my mouth and nodded. Julian buttoned his shirt and zipped his vest over it. My breath hitched a little when I realized here, in this uniform, I didn't see the Julian I grew up with. The one who teased me for days about my awkward walk after our first workout. The one who rubbed his stubble on my cheek when he was old enough to start growing facial hair. The one who loved Luca and me so deeply that we spent nights looking at the stars, imagining we were the only three people who existed.

He tied his boots and readied himself to get to his station. He stepped closer to me, and I noticed a slight bruising on his cheek. Julian, following my eyes, smiled for the first time since our reunion. He ran his fingers deliberately over the side of his smooth face.

"Nice left hook, by the way," he answered, managing a slight degree of lightheartedness in response to my unasked question. "I'm glad you've been keeping up on your training, Mol. You'll need it."

He opened the door and ushered me out. Julian and Nico exchanged silent greetings then he made an abrupt exit. I stood there, dumbfounded, until Nico elbowed me into walking back to the Elite quarters.

Something very strange was happening, maybe something bigger than I could have imagined. I felt a little betrayed that neither Julian nor Luca clued me into what was going on — or, at the very least, that they were in communication.

As Nico and I approached the heavy steel door to the Elite quarters, finality set in. I would be in almost complete solitude for the next twelve hours with no one to talk to about my thoughts and questions. Nico turned to leave, and I grabbed his arm.

"Nico, wait," I pleaded. "Please?"

The sliver of kindness he showed me earlier was short-lived, demonstrated by the mixture of annoyance and pity on his face.

"Mol, I'm not even supposed to be speaking to you," he sighed. "I really can't give you information."

He was wrapped up in all of this — whatever "this" was.

"Can't or don't want to?" I asked, innocently.

He considered this for a few seconds. "Does it matter?"

"It does to me," I offered. "I'm going to go insane, Nico.

I'm in the dark, in a strange place, with no one to talk to, no one who will look at me like I'm not abnormal, and now, on top of it all off, I was just introduced to a stranger inhabiting the body of one of two people I care about in my pathetic life."

I sounded like a toddler having a meltdown, but his face was apologetic enough, so I pushed my luck.

"I need to know what's happening here, Nico," I asserted. "I need to figure this out. I can't be in the dark, or I'll go crazy."

Nico turned to push past me, and I grabbed his arm again, harder than I'd intended.

"Nico, I'm—"

"That's your problem, Mol," he growled, wrenching my hand off of his arm. "You're only thinking about yourself. You don't know anything, but you're making demands without any understanding of the consequences."

He took a step toward me, so our noses were almost touching. A less angry version of myself probably would have felt intimidated by his stature.

"I get it. You're confused. You want to know what's happening, but you're not going to get it without a price right now, so just go along with it. I already put my ass on the line for you today, so show a little gratitude."

Shame bubbled up inside me. We only formally got introduced today, but he could have been helping me for who knows how long. I should have pieced together that Nico was a part of my reunion with Julian, but I was so wrapped up in myself that I failed to see the bigger picture, even if it wasn't a complete one.

Luca and I were on our own for so long, taking up all my concern and planning, but I could no longer let that be an excuse. I couldn't afford to be so narrow-minded any longer.

I didn't have any friends on the ship, but I needed to get some allies or I'd be even more miserable.

I didn't want Nico to be mad. I didn't know how, but I wanted to fix this. Julian and I would always physically fight out our problems, and Luca and I rarely disagreed on anything, so I couldn't pull from those experiences. I reached forward and placed both hands on Nico's arms. The affection felt odd in this setting, but it seemed to soften him.

"I'm really sorry, Nico," I said, forcing him to meet my eyes. "I was stupid for not realizing how unaware and selfish I was being. I'm very grateful for the kindness you've shown me, and I hope you can forgive me."

He gave me a small smile, revealing dimples on his cheeks. I hoped that meant I was forgiven, but I didn't get to hear his response because the door to the Elite quarters opened.

I dropped my hands and groaned as three women joined us in the dimly lit hallway. Out of all the Elite I observed, these women were some sort of cruel clique. Every awful thing I overheard about myself, and subsequently tuned out, was from them. They said horrific things about the other Elite members and were the least quiet about their Guard conquests and extra privileges.

"Oh wow," one of the women piped out.

"Well, excuse us for interrupting," the other said, laughing.

I wasn't sure what caused them to have such disdain me, but it seemed my mere presence threw them down a rabbit hole of mean-spirited name-calling.

"Nico, I thought you had better taste," the tallest one said, clicking her tongue. She was the ringleader of the group, perpetuating the negativity.

I glanced up at Nico, eager to gauge his reaction. I

wondered if he was one of the conquests she so often bragged about. His eyes were daggers, and she seemed to take in his anger with fits of giggles. I failed to see the humor.

The sound of their laughter pulsated in my ear drums. My breathing quickened, my lungs slamming against my battered rib cage. My inner monologue urged the rest of me to calm down repeatedly, but it wasn't helping. I was frustrated, and this was not the best timing. Nico put a hand on my shoulder, a gesture of solidarity that caused me to stand down.

The door opened again, and this time, the Punisher stepped out, surprised by the scene in front of her. It took a few beats for the silence to break.

"Do I look like a dirty dish or unkept bedspread?"

"No," one of the women answered, visibly puzzled. Clearly a person didn't have to have high intelligence marks in the Placement exam to get into the Elite.

"Then get back to your duties," she called, the clicking of her heels following her down the hall.

4

I FELT the burden of my presence each time I passed Julian and he avoided me, which was now becoming more frequent. In the weeks since our reunion, I was still reeling with confusion, trying to work out the dynamics of the Authority and his place in it. Resentment sometimes seeped in, too, but sentimentality usually triumphed.

The years of suppressing old memories caught up with me. It was almost painful when they resurfaced, a stinging reminder of all the days lost between us. It was a weird, sick twist that brought me back to Julian. I was humbled by the circumstances, which felt like a punch in the gut on most days.

It was infinitely worse when I thought of Luca. The more time I spent on the ship, the guiltier I felt. I suffered the devastation of losing my parents at a young age, but I considered myself lucky to have pseudo Guardians in Luca and Julian. I didn't do the best job of repaying them.

Even with the uncertainty of my Placement, Luca and I always planned for a future where we'd stay together. At the beginning, we dreamed of finding Julian and making some sort of life, but one day, after many days of frustrating false hope, we agreed to stop thinking of things never to come. I felt trapped by decisions I didn't make and would never get to make.

My frustration with the Authority grew while my body recovered from the injuries. By the time I could take a full breath without wincing, I progressed in both my Placement and indignation. I dropped off extravagant, hearty meals to Guard quarters. Instead of washing and cleaning, I was given more opportunities to silently serve tea or liquor, depending on the time of day, at meetings.

I tried desperately to pick up any and all snippets of information. I was still on thin ice, so I didn't push my luck by lingering to eavesdrop. Mostly the men discussed supply chains, labor, agriculture numbers, and, occasionally, members of the Elite or women they met from the islands.

Most days I was dismissed with a wave of a hand, which made me want to scream at these people, with their finely made clothing and arrogance. They were born into different circumstances, but that didn't mean they were more worthy of respect than me. I doubted we shared the same views.

As I spent my days in servitude, I turned from apathetic to outright bitter. The Elite, the Authority, the ship, everything, was outrageous. I was serving hot dinners with complex ingredients to men who knew nothing of what life was really like on the islands. They merely popped in and out for observations. They took every step to ensure the safety net they created would continue for themselves but not for those on the islands. They have no voice or choice in their lives, but these men are here living in excess and making life-changing decisions without any awareness of the implications.

But keeping my promise to Julian in mind, I stayed

under the radar. Occasionally, I'd catch the Punisher keeping a watchful eye on me. She and Julian walked and ate together quite often. The thought of them working together made me a little queasy, but there wasn't a thing I could do to change it.

I shook off the thought and checked the daily schedule. Normally, I'd glance at the poster quickly then head off to bathe and prepare for the day, but when I saw the date, my eighteenth birthday, along with a new routine, I huffed in surprise.

I'd be serving at a large dinner tonight with a handful of women in blue uniforms who were equal parts beauty and venom. One year ago, I was with Luca, talking about our past birthdays with our parents. I channeled happy thoughts of home to push away the negativity.

"I can't believe she got picked! What is she even doing in this Placement? It's embarrassing for us."

Recognizing the voices, I sighed and double checked that the curtain in the private changing area was closed tightly.

After the run-in with Nico, that woman made every effort to remind me I didn't belong here. I agreed with her, of course, but I ignored her. She was clearly one of the more experienced in this Placement, although she didn't seem to be that much older than me. None of the Elite women were.

"It was months before I got my first glimpse at the Commander," she pouted. Flanked by her followers, she was never without a platform to complain or boast, depending on her mood. "She doesn't even know how lucky she is!"

"Don't get too upset, Emilia," one of the other women said. "You know there are always other opportunities."

"Remember how you made a few of the Authority men

very happy at the big dinner last month?" another woman chimed in.

"You're both right," Emilia said, sighing loudly. "But I'm hoping for the Commander. I think it's time one of us got in to see his private chambers, don't you think?"

The three of them began to whisper excitedly, just below the level I could hear. Why did the Commander, out of all people aboard the ship, not have his washing and cleaning provided for him? Surely some of the Elite go into dust and pick up his laundry at the very least.

"If you had to guess... how big do you think it is?"

I quietly chuckled. If this was the type of stupid questions they asked each other in conversations, I definitely wasn't missing out on female friendship. Everyone knew the Commander's residence was on a secluded part of the ship toward the top. There were only a few rooms surrounding it, so it was probably rather large and probably infinitely nicer than Julian's.

"Probably at least seven inches, judging by his confidence," Emilia said, nonchalantly. "By my experience, the two go hand in hand."

Another fit of laughter from the girls caused my face to redden with embarrassment. I felt the heat gather on my cheeks. I didn't think that's what they meant by "private chambers." Elite etiquette probably didn't approve of their conversation, and I lost all desire to listen in. I tried, unsuccessfully, to push the conversation out of my mind.

The Authority members carried somewhat of a different set of values than I grew up with on Island Seven. They simply didn't have to follow the strict rules they set out for other people, which obviously bothered me. At first, I was annoyed with these little reminders of how spoiled these people were, but now, especially after listening to the carefree chatter of the Elite for hours on end, being here grew into a full-fledged irritation. Not just with the Authority and the Elite, but with every single task I was assigned — and tonight was the biggest one yet.

It was a waste of time and energy to spend an entire day cleaning an already pristine room, polishing silverware, washing glassware, and setting out gaudy place settings. The kitchen staff's white uniforms blurred in a frenzy against the royal blue Elite uniforms. I opted to remain silent and simply did whatever was instructed.

At 1800, the Elite and I remained in the room, and the dishes slid through a small alcove. This meant less distraction for the Authority, but it also gave me a longer period of time to listen. I was secretly delighted when I was informed of this plan, but I was so busy for the first hour of the meal that I barely acknowledged who was there or what the conversation centered on. Now, everyone made their way through the main course, and I stood back and observed.

Assorted Guard were stationed around the room, but Julian was the only one who got the privilege of sitting, drinking, and eating at the table. I knew Nico was on duty patrolling the upper deck — he mentioned this earlier in the week during one of our escorted walks. Since our argument outside of the Elite quarters, things settled to a strange version of normal between us. Occasionally, Nico would offer up tidbits of information and insight into the Guard and the Authority.

I started to recognize members of the Authority. It was easier now that I wasn't stuck in kitchens and quarters, but my only direct interactions were with Punisher and Julian. I found them immediately, sitting across from each other, deep in conversation. Julian was sitting by the General, who was in charge of most Authority operations and the Guard — another fact given to me by Nico.

The General was a large man, with graying hair and an obnoxiously large mustache. Most of the Authority styled their hair strangely and wore interesting clothing, but the General stood out to me in particular. He was a man who took part in more excess than the rest for decades, apparently, and I immediately disliked him.

Even the Punisher, who was clearly at the top of the Authority, kept her appearance simple in another dark, fitted suit. Most of the other members here didn't care to hide their preference for the extravagance. She didn't stand out simply because of her clothing choice, though. In this scenario, women served and men stayed seated, but the Punisher was the exception.

She carried that air of sophistication and directness about her that I learned to associate with the Authority, but I didn't know if that trait was taught or if she was born into it like the Commander. Everyone in the Authority, Guard, and Elite was alluring in his or her own way — even the General.

On Island Seven, I didn't really find many people attractive. I was usually too busy to notice such trivial things, although I saw women checking out Luca and Julian from time to time. Objectively, I understood why they found them attractive, which is likely one of the reasons why Julian fit in so well aboard the ship.

It was a little desensitizing to be surrounded by such glamour at all times, but everything in my body froze the moment I laid eyes on the Commander. My mind mushed into incoherency, and my body set on fire. If I moved, I was sure I would completely combust, so I remained still, trying to find rationality. It seemed so far away.

He wasn't just attractive; he was mesmerizing — and much younger than I imagined. When his father died a few years ago and he took over, minor details such as age didn't make its way to the islands. No one mentioned his flawless, cacao-colored skin either.

My eyes raked over his crisp black suit and a high-buttoned white collared shirt, imagining what was underneath. His defined jawline, full lips, and cheekbones culled together in an alluring combination. I didn't even know I could be interested in cheekbones, but it was at the top of my list now.

Even with the affluence on the ship, most men kept their hair relatively short and manageable, but the Commander's chin-length braids were tucked back into a low ponytail. A few loose tendrils hit just above his shoulders, and every part of me wished to run across the room and tuck them behind his ears. I dug my heels into the floor.

I was drawn to him. There was no disputing that. I felt an urgency to be near him. An invisible tether pulled us together, and it took everything inside me to fight it off.

Despite my vain assessment of him, I knew those physical features weren't even his most prominent traits. I'd heard that from Emilia, but without hearing him speak, I could feel the confidence radiating off of him. His presence was overpowering. It erupted a hum in me that I'd never felt, and the sensation caused my heart to beat quickly. I wondered if my outward appearance reflected the internal havoc.

I watched him engage in conversations, waving for one of the Elite to come refill his glass and then again at a Guard to speak up — all without breaking the flow of dialogue. It was simultaneously repulsive and intriguing. He could make any thought come to fruition. Any minor whim or discomfort would be attended to with a simple command. That kind of power gave me anxiety. It was almost too much to handle along with his attractiveness.

Still, I couldn't help trying to gather details about him to sort through in my hours of loneliness. I was slightly embarrassed by my obsession, but I remembered what Emilia and the other women said earlier. He was worth talking about.

I perked up when an unexpected emotion crossed the Commander's face — boredom. Whatever the General was telling him must have been very uninteresting because his gaze began to wander.

There were a lot of details in the room itself and the people present in it that I was still uncovering, but he didn't waste any time with that. He must have been in this very spot thousands of times in his life. His eyes were roaming in a similar way that mine just did, on the people present.

I chewed on my bottom lip in anticipation. There was no reason to be busy at this moment. No one finished clearing the food on a plate or required a refill of wine, liquor, or water. I stood there, bracing myself for the moment he would see me.

He surveyed the other twenty-or-so people at the table and the Elite members actively engaging in conversation or bending down to whisper something in one of the guest's ears. The Commander covered his mouth with his hand, hiding a yawn. He looked at the kitchen through the alcove, but dessert wasn't ready yet. Seconds later, his eyes met mine.

The thread that pulled at me snapped to attention, shooting between the two of us. The room melted away, and the furniture, the people, the chatter, and the dishes disappeared. I saw a flash in the Commander's eyes and wondered if he felt it, too. I held myself completely still, not trusting my limbs to remain in line.

He was so dangerously gorgeous. I tried to emphasize the word "dangerous" in my mind, but the rest of me wasn't cooperating. It was becoming too much, and I forced myself to break eye contact. The staring wasn't helping my mission to stay unnoticed — and neither was the exhilaration I was trying to control myself under the pressure of the Commander's scrutiny.

I joined the other Elite in clearing out the growing number of empty plates, sensing his stare with every movement. I became conscious of my own body, my lines and curves, and I wondered what it looked like from his eyes. A flicker of panic lit — the Commander could just be curious about my looks. Although those in the Authority were the most exotic-looking group I'd ever seen, my coloring was still unique.

Self-doubt entered my psyche for a few short moments and then I promptly pushed it away. I had no desire for it among the other emotions circling. Instead, I focused on my current tasks. I fixated on my amazement at the amount of food that was consumed — and wasted — by the Authority.

Each course came with its own set of flavors and complexities, which was a far cry from my ration allowance. Although some fruits and nuts were native to Island Seven, it was illegal to grow or consume anything grown on there. Everything was portioned and shipped off.

It was one of many things that fed into my ever-growing fury. I wished I could garden, grow my own herbs, and gather the fruit right out of our yard. It was one of my biggest sources of anger in the Network, and I spent plenty of time complaining to Julian and Luca about it. I would have loved to pick off something from one of the trees, but they were strictly monitored.

If they were lenient with that — among other things — I might have never been wrapped up in this whole mess. Instead, I rarely got a chance to try any of the fruits that passed through Island Seven's streets on the transport trucks.

So when dessert popped up in the serving window, I was finally able to put my Commander-fueled lust haze aside. In individual, beautifully carved glass dishes sat some cold concoction topped with fresh mangos and bananas.

I could handle my distaste for the Authority and its rules. I could even endure the talk about how dreary island life must be and the varying opinions on the current Medical developments, but when it came to food, and lack thereof, these people were ignorant. And it was maddening.

I heard some chatter about the weather having a positive impact on some of the crops and agriculture, but it still shouldn't justify having a multi-course dinner followed by a strange dessert with my own fruit that I never got to try. The thought caused my anger to expand and almost overtake my level head. My hands shook as I slowly placed the glassware in front of the guests.

While serving, many Elite women lean down to capture the attention of various Authority members and engage in physical contact. Emilia's comments made me want to gag at what they were saying to these men, but serving Julian his dessert, I mimicked her behavior.

"How do you expect me to not react to this, Julian?" I hissed in his ear.

I planned on stomping off in anger, which would prob- ably have drawn the kind of attention he advised me to avoid, but he grabbed my wrist and pulled me into him, cutting off my escape.

"Not the time, Mol," he scolded.

I flinched, and his eyes stared into mine.

He loosened his grip and dropped his head. "I'm sorry." He seemed genuinely apologetic, and it cooled me down slightly — from a rolling boil to a hard simmer. Deep down, I knew this wasn't his fault. I tried to make him my scapegoat for my irritation. It was easy to. "I've been dealing with this for years, but I forget this is all new to you."

He was trying to talk me off the ledge, and it was working.

"Just be patient, please," Julian pleaded, releasing me from the awkward position on his lap.

I backed away and walked toward the kitchen. It was time to get started on the pile of dishes, but I did one last check to see if anyone else needed attending to. The Commander stared at me with a tight expression, and I swallowed. He turned and started speaking hurriedly to the Punisher, who looked over at me. Her face showed displeasure, leveling with the Commander, but her eyes twinkled with approval.

5

I KNEW it couldn't be a coincidence.

Following the big formal dinner, I was pulled away from the standard Elite duties and pushed into more of the Commander's events, which occurred almost every evening. There was always some Authority member visiting the ship or a meeting that required discussion over a meal.

Instead of serving or flipping sheets, I was subjected to hours of standing by and listening to vapid conversations. I didn't miss the laundry and dishes, but mentally, these new tasks were more draining. No one ever seemed to be making any real decisions or talking about changes to better the Network's future, but they were always grossly extravagant.

While most of the Elite made every attempt possible to stand out to the Commander and his guests, I perfected silent service. I managed to slip plates and glasses so carefully past them that a few people were shocked to discover their finished plate was replaced with the next course.

The other women flaunted themselves in front of the male guests. Leaning a little too close, hiking up the skirt another inch, brushing up against them. I watched their routine in wonderment. If there was any indicator I didn't fit in with the other Elite women, this was it. They were all experienced and outwardly sensual, and I still felt uneasy wearing a skirt.

I was out of my element, that was for sure. But Julian's presence always seemed to right me on some emotional level. He was a regular guest at the functions. He appeared to be a very valuable member of the Authority — well liked, even, which, of course, annoyed me. Almost everything did these days.

Other guests were in and out of rotation depending on the occasion. There were varying degrees of excess at these events, but I noticed a pattern of the showiest service when the General was around. The meals were always seated with the Punisher on the Commander's right side and the General on his left, a show of power.

I did my best to avoid coming in close contact with the Commander himself, who was always perched at the head of the table. I didn't dare to look at him, and it helped that most other Elite fought over who would get to serve him. Because serving the Commander his swordfish over a steamed vegetable compote gave you some sort of pedestal to stand on — or at least that's what the other Elite women seemed to think.

The extra time I was spending with the Elite at these meals didn't soften their opinions of me and vice versa. We coexisted, some silent truce formed between us, and we moved forward. Even Emilia, who loved to ridicule, eased up. I guessed I had Nico to thank for that, although I wasn't totally comfortable with the idea of him meddling in my affairs — especially since I wasn't clued into his.

Mostly, the change in duties was tolerable, and one night, during a smaller than usual but no less extravagant dinner, I finally overheard something that piqued my interest.

I made it habit of distancing from the table in favor of standing toward the serving station, but just this once, I felt the urge remain close. The last thing I needed was someone to notice my interest in anything other than my Placement, but I froze, gripping a decanter of red wine after topping off Julian's second glass.

"Commander, is this a good opportunity to fill you in on the engineering developments coming out of Island Seven?" asked Felix, a man whose name I picked up a few days ago.

"Sure," the Commander sighed, taking a large bite of the main course.

"I've just got back from one of the labs," Felix said, smoothing down the wax on his mustache. "We've endured our ups and downs. We've backtracked and moved forward. We've scratched our heads and threw up our hands, but it's all well and good now. We've learned a lot from the failures in the past few months, Commander."

I'd observed plenty of egotism. People were always nonchalantly mentioning dinners they'd shared with a "Doctor from Island Two" or the daughter of the "chief of food distribution." These people all prided themselves on perfection — or the fact that others would see them that way — so I couldn't help but be a little pleased with this man's candor. His honesty was very appealing, even if it was wrapped in a flowery presentation.

"You'd do well to focus on growing the number of successes there, Felix," the General barked out and took a hefty swig from his glass.

The Commander glanced over at the General. "We're all here to serve a purpose, after all," he quipped.

There was something strange in the way the statement

rolled off the Commander's tongue. To Felix, who was clearly trying to hide his nervousness, it seemed like an intimidating threat, but to me, he seemed to be brushing off his updates due to a lack of interest.

"Of course, Commander," Felix said, laughing nervously. "Now, General, any updates on how the military will be impacted by the latest special project?"

"No," the General said, while using his pinky to pick something out of his teeth. He snapped his fingers, which were covered in several gold rings, at Emilia, who was hovering a few steps away. "But I would love an update from this one."

She looked ecstatic to receive attention from such a prominent figure in the Authority. Emilia leaned down to him, and the General pulled her on his lap. She nuzzled his neck with her nose and mouth. He placed his hands on her back and inched them lower. I looked away, trying to hide outwardly showed my disgust.

I didn't want to puke over her interaction with the General or witness Felix's attempts at keeping a conversation going — I wanted answers on the special project, but I knew my place. I was out of the loop on everything that was happening, but then again, Luca was never forthcoming about his projects, so it was likely I would continue to be clueless.

I couldn't help but be disappointed by these distractions. Whatever was happening on Island Seven was clearly important, despite all appearances of making it seem like the least significant in the Network. I would have loved to hear more on something with an opportunity to make a big, positive impact on many people, but I was no longer amazed that no one else cared.

Surveying the table, I noticed the Commander's wine

glass was empty, and I braced myself, focusing on the pouring. I knew he was studying me, but I wasn't sure for how long or what emotions involuntarily displayed on my face. I wished my long hair was down forming a shield instead of up in one of the Elite-approved styles.

I couldn't avoid the Commander forever. After all, he was the most powerful man in the Network and could make anyone pay attention to him. I held my breath and met his gaze. He seemed pleased at this, the corners of his mouth quickly pulled up.

"Thank you," he said, low and cool, looking up into my eyes.

The room temperature went up ten degrees. Maybe fifteen or thirty, actually. I told myself repeatedly to remain calm, but my body reacted to his proximity. I had never been attracted to anyone like this, which is why it was so jarring.

His power was surely enticing to some, but to me, it seemed like a weight I didn't have the desire to lift or encourage. I'd been brought up in second-hand clothes, and he was made for this role. It was evident in every aspect of his personality, easy cockiness, and impeccable diction.

I didn't dare attempt to form words around him. Not until I stopped floating in the air, high from his presence. So I nodded in response to his graciousness and stepped back to make my way back to the serving area. The Commander placed a hand on my back, and electricity radiated. The urge to melt into his contact and feel his hands elsewhere on my body was equal to the one to pour the entire decanter of wine on him for touching me without permission.

"Stop," he said, his normal, condescending tone. He clearly wasn't feeling anything out of the ordinary, much to my dismay. "Remain here."

He gestured to the wine I was holding and without skipping a beat, he turned back to address the table. No one else seemed to notice my shock except the Punisher, who simply pursed her lips.

The other Elite were too busy bustling around and panting at Julian to notice anything out of ordinary. I smirked.

"Felix, share some of the Island Seven updates you're so keen on discussing. You're the guest of honor this evening, after all."

"Of course, Commander," Felix said, his face flushing with excitement. "You've no doubt been briefed on the latest attempts to manipulate electricity?"

"Correct," the Commander confirmed.

"Well, we've experienced a recent breakthrough — after one of the Engineers suffered a minor problem with getting electrocuted," he paused to laugh. His singsong tone covered my sharp inhale of shock, and Julian perked up. "Her wires were crossed!"

The Commander cleared his throat.

"But that's neither here nor there! Anyway, I was just about to get to, that we've been plugged in for years. You know this, obviously. We all sit here seeing each other with the help of light accompanied bellies full of prepared, cooked food. It has been instrumental in the continued development of our growing nation, but it's time for us to get our independence. We're stuck to generators here on the ship, which means we cannot establish sustainable long-term independence from our electricity-sponsored comforts."

No new information came out of his mouth, but the way he spoke held everyone's attention — even the General, who was tracing the upper thigh hem on Emilia's uniform with a few fingers, hung off of every word.

"This, oh yes, this very exciting new project will allow us to carry the power with us — right in our pockets," he burst out, clapping. "Imagine! We could be a free-floating Island Eight!"

The General hissed something very close to "over my dead body" and chuckled.

"Now, as we work through these developments, there are several projects that will be released simultaneously. I don't want to spoil it, but it's all very exciting!"

"It sounds like a truly exquisite development," the Punisher said, taking a sip of wine. "I do believe I could listen to you describe these changes all day and my attention would never waver, Felix."

"Oh, you're too kind, my dear," Felix winked. "I'm merely the messenger."

"What prompted this branch of research?" she asked.

"Our brightest Engineer discovered some spare parts in one of the storage rooms, and it spurred a many new ideas. We can hardly keep up. There's so much to do and explore!" He raised both of his hands in a mix of excitement and exasperation.

I thought of Luca, propped up on his elbows at our scratched-up table at home, forehead wrinkled in concentration, and my heart sank. We were miles across the sea from each other, and I desperately missed him. And now by some cruel course of decision-making, a strange group of fabulous, powerful people were likely talking about him right in front of me.

Julian was once the closest thing I had to another brother. He might have taught me how to defend myself from a chokehold a few years ago, but he was not the same man sitting in front of me now, pointedly avoiding me and staring at his plate.

"It has been exciting to prioritize what advancements will have the biggest splash across the water," Felix beamed. "And although we're still smoothing the kinks out on our most promising lead, I am happy to share amongst friends that it involves sharing speech across long distances."

The Commander was stoic, taking in all of Felix's comments, but this one seemed to intrigue him the most.

"You could keep in touch with those twins from Island Three, General," Felix teased then actually elbowed the General. It seemed to prompt Emilia to steal more of the General's attention, attempting to erase his past conquests with new admiration.

"When can we expect a working prototype?"

"In a few days' time, Commander."

"Shorten it," huffed the General. "I've been patient, and I'm tired of it. Speaking of which, I do believe it is time to retire for the evening."

The General stood up, tipped his hat to mumble "Commander" and escorted Emilia from the room. A tour of his private chambers was likely in order. I rolled my eyes, which, of course, did not go unnoticed by the Commander's ever-present gaze.

They were talking about technology that could change everything in the islands. It could open up trade and help families keep in touch without the help of people like Mavis, but no one seemed to appreciate it. Only me. I stood in place, close to the Commander, and tapped my foot repeatedly. The energy from the revelation desired an outlet.

"Yes, well, this has been enlightening," the Commander said, wiping his mouth and placing his cloth napkin on the table. "But I'm afraid it is time for me to retire. Julian, please see to it that Hope is escorted back to her quarters safely."

I hated the immediate jealousy that spiked — the

Commander and Julian obviously adored the Punisher, but my experience and opinion was quite different.

The Commander stood up to leave, and the others did in a sign of respect. He gave me one last glance before he left the room. Slowly, the other dinner attendees began to leave, too, which meant it was time for the full clean-up cycle to begin. Since it was a small group, it wouldn't be that lengthy of a process. I was grateful the early evening would give me plenty of time to digest the new information.

After all the guests were gone and I was left alone with my thoughts, I noticed the Commander hadn't touched his wine.

6

_____

IT WAS A CLOUDLESS DAY. The sun felt hotter than usual for the season, and I knew it was smart to move back to the shade. My skin, far lighter than all of those I went to Education with, would soon start to redden and subsequently freckle and peel. Mother would have to grind up coconut meat and put it on my skin. It would ease any discomfort that formed, but it would also cut into our rations for the week.

I couldn't bring myself to care about that, though. I was too busy basking in the sun.

I created my own sliver of paradise, laying on my back in the small yard behind our house. Everything seemed so simple from this vantage point. I could watch the breeze gently move through the trees for hours. It was entertainment with no expense.

I sighed, relaxing into the ground. I stretched my arms behind my head, feeling the spare patches of grass that survived the Authority's latest harvest. No new herbs grew, but they took some assorted plants. They left plenty of Mimosas behind — the Authority considered them to be a weed, uncontrollable and therefore useless. I loved their gumption.

The vibrant pink flowers reminded me of jellyfish, if the ones I saw stuck out their tentacles in every direction instead of washing up on the beach. The surrounding leaves were deep green, fluttering out into mini-fern-like pairs. Unlike all the other plants in the yard, and on the Island from what I knew, these suffered tangible, immediate reactions to their surroundings.

At night, the leaves close up, tucking into themselves for protection, but when the sun hits, they reopen, ready to absorb the sunshine. They move with the rhythm of the world, approaching the day with a renewed dedication. The Mimosas also reacted to touch — collapsing when disturbed. I gently raked my fingers across them over and over, appreciating their bluntness. After a few minutes, I let them have a full recovery without interference and watched them go back to normal.

I sat up and looked over at Luca, whose hair was buzzed short to combat the heat. He was a few feet away, smartly sitting under the overhang and shielded from the midday sun.

When we were younger, we were both teased relentlessly for looking so different — until Julian stepped in and defended us. We inherited our fair complexions from our mother, a blonde-haired beauty. She was well-known on Island Seven for her physical traits, but our father, six-foot-four and darker-skinned, loved her fierceness and stubbornness most of all.

They didn't share the details of their courtship, but I was aware that no one attuned to Island Seven gossip was surprised when Luca came along less than a year after they got together.

Now, more than a decade later, here he was rifling through a bag of rusty screws, trying to find the appropriate size for a square metal box that washed up on Island Seven's south beach a few weeks ago. He was always trying to change or fix something. He had a knack for finding discarded gadgets. The shelf of assorted wires and metal scraps in his tiny bedroom was a testament to it.

Our parents loved this about him. They encouraged him immensely, praising each attempt he made at bringing something back to life — in the few waking hours they were home, at least.

Father's Placement was at one of the factories on the north end of the island, fixing and testing machinery. It was dangerous and monotonous work, but I suppose it suited him. He was patient and calculated — something he passed down to Luca. Mother was on the night shift all this week in her job at the ration station. Like clockwork every week, the rations arrived on the cargo ship, and she orchestrated the pickups by sundown. I wasn't sure what else she did there, especially during the late hours.

For a long time, it seemed like a foolproof system to me. I was happy with my life; the pieces fit together for so many years, but in the past few months, things grew more confusing. I didn't understand why my parents were unhappy. They seemed to be away longer than usual, coming back to catch a few hours of sleep then heading out again. They wouldn't discuss any of it with us.

Through the crack in the window, I could hear Mother humming in the kitchen, trying to brew coffee out of the remainder of the beans. The rations weren't coming until day after next. I always assumed this was a part of the games we played as a family, but I was slowly realizing this was not the case.

"Luca?"

"What, Mol?" Luca asked, peering up for a moment from jiggling around his bag of mismatched screws.

"Have you noticed we're getting less rations?"

Surprise flooded Luca's face. He expected a question on Education or what he was working on. "I suppose so," he answered, shifting his focus back to his tools.

I swallowed, trying not to let another non-answer from someone in my family bother me. "What would happen if we ate all of our rations on day one? And there was none left for the next six?"

He scratched the top of his head. "The Authority expects us all to understand the rules, Mol," Luca muttered. "That includes effectively managing your own rations."

"Would the Authority let us starve?"

He huffed in response.

"Is that a yes?" I frowned.

Luca sighed and put down his project. "What's this really about, Mol?"

I looked up to see that Mother was lost in her own musings and likely not listening to our conversation.

"I heard Mother and Father arguing last night about the Authority again. They were trying to be quiet, but I could still hear them. It has been happening more and more over the past few weeks. Mother was upset over something that someone said to her, and Father encouraged her to put in a formal complaint and leave it to the Authority to handle."

Luca was silent, taking my words in.

"She said that it didn't matter," I continued. "Nothing would be done through the Authority, and no one cares about the people on the bigger islands. Their floating homes carry them in a 'bubble far from reality.' We're not important; we're replaceable."

His silence was validating the speculation and thoughts growing inside my head. I didn't like this truth I was growing to understand.

"Mother said that we're all stuck in this endless cycle until people are brave enough to break it." My throat felt thick, and I swallowed.

"Yeah?" Luca whispered.

"Nothing makes sense to me anymore," I answered. The slow pressure of a headache was beginning to form. I turned away, not wanting Luca to see the emotion that was building on my face.

"Maybe someday I will be brave enough to figure it all out," I said, tears pooling in my eyes. I closed the lids tightly, trying to push the little traitors back to wherever they came from.

"Mol," Luca whispered.

I ignored him, trying to push away the emotion. I refused to break down. I just needed to find the courage to do so. I dragged my hands across the Mimosa plants, channeling their energy. Luca called my name again, but I wasn't ready to answer him just yet. I took a few seconds to cave into myself before I recovered. Determination found its way from the top of my head down to my toes. I imagined the leaves covering my skin, swallowing me whole. They helped overtake the unsettling feelings.

"Mol," Luca urged. "Mol, wake up."

Only it wasn't Luca's voice anymore, and I wasn't in the backyard. I wasn't even on land — I could feel the gentle rock of the ship. The smell of the breeze disappeared, replaced by the harsh manufactured lemon and bleach scent used to clean the floors.

I sat up, wiping sleep from my eyes.

"Nico?" I asked, confusion pressing into my mind. "Am I still asleep?"

"Why? Were you dreaming about me?" he teased.

"No," I said, stretching my legs out. "That would be a nightmare."

He laughed quietly and kneeled beside the bed, fully dressed in his Guard uniform. I was, obviously, wearing my set of sleeping clothes. I couldn't recall a time when a man was this close to me while so much skin was exposed. Julian and Luca treated my small — but cozy, I'd always insisted — bedroom like it was off-limits. And I was just fine with that.

Here, on the ship, it wasn't out of the ordinary for a Guard to be in the Elite quarters. More often than not, it seemed the women chose to stay in the men's quarters. They'd arrive back in during the early hours of the morning, relaxed with their hair down. I didn't have any friends, let alone visitors or midnight jaunts.

Despite his response, Nico didn't look happy to be in the Elite quarters. His mouth was pulled into a tight smile.

"Julian sent me," he admitted, answering my question without prompting.

That got my attention.

"Okay," I said, pushing any remaining tugs of sleep away.

"As you might have guessed, our dear Commander has taken a special interest in you," Nico said, dropping the volume of his voice. "Julian is beside himself and ready to put an escape plan in action, but Hope seems to be more optimistic about this situation."

Sure, the Commander watched me, observing my reactions, but that seemed normal for him. He was typically silent and surveying his surroundings even if I wasn't nearby. Our small interactions couldn't possibly have spurred genuine interest, right? There were plenty of beautiful and more passive Elite women surrounding him. Julian was just overreacting.

"I have to go, but he told me to reiterate that you need to be careful," Nico said, looking at his watch. "And Hope asked me to tell you to keep up the good work."

After he left, I laid back and soon came to terms with the fact that I was completely awake. It was early, but at the very least, I could get a head start on getting ready for the day. The schedule wasn't even posted yet. It might be nice to spend extra time bathing in peace, my mind flashing back to the dream in the sun.

I tiptoed over to the bathroom, and the door slid open in one smooth motion. When I closed it, it shut with a loud creak. I heard the sobs and stopped. I made every effort to be quiet, but the door betrayed me. I couldn't bring myself to run and hide when my presence was obvious.

"Isabel?" Even without its typical sneer, the voice put me on edge. I made my way around spacious counter and stepped toward the showers.

"No, it's Mol," I answered, cringing at my own name.

Emilia was sitting on the floor, her knees pulled up to her chest with her arms wrapped around them. Her makeup was a black blur under her eyes, interrupted by dried tear streaks. Her red lipstick, usually so flawless that I swore it was permanently tattooed, was smeared all over her chin.

I gasped at Emilia's clothing. Some buttons were missing from the white shirt, and the ones that remained were tucked into the wrong button holes. The hem of her skirt was torn up mid-thigh, and her shoes were nowhere in sight.

"What do you want?" Emilia snapped.

A lot of things. Luca. Off this ship. Free will. No Placement. Insight into what's happening around me with all of these frighteningly good-looking and powerful people.

"A shower," I replied, straining to keep my voice level.

"Then why the fuck are you standing there staring?"

She was being defensive, caught in a vulnerable state by someone who she was not close with, someone she actually might hate.

"Look, Emilia," I said, tucking my hair behind my ears. "Can I help you? I can grab your wash items or a towel?"

"I don't need any help," she insisted. "Especially not from you."

I knelt, trying to diffuse the anger growing inside me. Maybe it would help Emilia if she talked about what happened. I didn't have much experience around women my age — or women in general, really. But I knew men like the General and the damage they could inflict.

"What happened?" I pressed. "Why did he do this to you?"

I braced myself for real emotion or more insults, but instead, I got laughter and fresh tears in her eyes.

"Oh my, this is marvelous," Emilia grinned. "You actually are concerned for me, aren't you? I thought you came here to gloat."

I couldn't even pretend to know what she was talking about, so I merely watched Emilia's emotional turmoil.

"Clearly, you've never enjoyed a night of wild sex," Emilia taunted. "I doubted there were any virgins left on the ship — let alone in the Elite. Wait until I tell the girls!"

Up until a few weeks ago, I only thought about my body while lifting weights, running, and kicking. I spent too much time worrying about surviving to be concerned with frivolous matters such as seduction. It wasn't until an unexpected fire lit in my lower abdomen in the presence of the Commander that considered it.

"We've all been wondering who you slept with to get your spot on the Elite," Emilia admitted. "Julian refuses to touch any of us, so we all assumed it was him."

She started laughing again. I was silent, taking in the ridicule. I thought about ways I could physically make Emilia stop mocking me, but I couldn't risk any more attention.

"Oh wow, I cannot believe this. You think you're so much better than all of us — and you're a prude from the Island Seven hellhole."

I could take the jabs directed at my lack of experience or appearance. I formed a hard defensive shell on that front long ago, but talking about my home, my island, prodding my homesickness, sent a direct line of adrenaline straight to my temper.

"Where I'm from, self-respect is a valued trait," I offered.

"You don't know me at all, Mol," she argued. "You don't know any of us. You don't know what we've left behind or what we do to keep our families fed and safe. You don't know a fucking thing."

Emilia stood up quickly, grimacing, and walked out.

7

IT APPEARED I no longer required an escort to my Placement duties since I turned eighteen. I was waiting for Nico to show up and walk with me to the kitchens when a new Guard informed me of the change.

Disgust gradually built in the past few hours as I processed Emilia's words. I walked to my first station of the day, and I realized how ignorant I'd been. Of course these women valued their work and did what they could to get attention — they had lives back on the islands, too. I wasn't the only one who left someone behind.

With this in mind, I vowed to make more of an effort to get to know the cooks, other Elite members, and even more of the Guard. I think, after weeks of practice, I did an okay job of talking to Nico. I respected his boundaries and valued his insight. Plus, I liked to consider us kindred spirits — not just because we both were tossed into whatever Julian was up to — but Nico also missed his family he left back on his island.

He briefly mentioned his parents one day, and I peppered him with questions. He only answered a handful of them. I also knew that in his Placement on the Guard, he normally stuck to patrols on his home, Island Five, monitoring the production of the food supply, but Nico was currently on a six-month rotation on the ship.

It was normal for the younger Guard members to be moved around, but Julian and the General spent the most time out of anyone onboard. Once I pulled some information out of him, I could ask deeper, better questions. People on the islands teetered on constant rudeness, merely using dialogue to fill a purpose or request — not to get to know each other. I was getting better at making small talk and getting more interested in finding out the trivial details of people's lives, adding them up into something bigger.

My weeks of nods and one-word answers didn't bode well when trying to start up new conversations with some people. The Elite shunned me from the beginning, but I was able to exchange a few words with someone on the prep line — admittedly, it was about the plates and utensils, but it was a start. After a failed attempt to engage one of the cooks who was chopping and stirring, I decided I would try again when everyone wasn't so busy.

Tonight's dinner was going to be the most intimate yet, which meant it required even more time to prepare for the complexity of the meal. The smaller the meal, the more intricate the dishes became. I overheard Hope telling the head cook that this would be the most important meal she could ever possibly prepare and not to take it lightly, so everyone was on edge.

Less help was required than usual on the serving side, so instead of the horde of royal blue uniforms, it was just Isabel, Emilia, and me for the evening. Emilia refused to acknowledge my existence, leaving all of the hostility to come from Isabel. The three of us were vastly overshadowed by the number of Guard members in the room, kitchens, and surrounding hallways.

The Commander, Felix, Julian, the General, and the Punisher were seated at the table in their usual spots, but they were joined by two people I didn't recognize. I picked up on the strangeness of their accents through the bits of conversation as I brought courses in and out. Their clothing differed slightly from the rest of the table's — less structure and buttons, more collar and ruffles at the sleeves. I took my my time serving and refilling, finding excuses to dawdle and pick up any additional clues about the men.

They spent a large portion of the meal discussing the state of the Authority's ships — most were undergoing repairs — and what it would take to upgrade the fleet. The older of the two men remained quiet for a few minutes, letting his counterpart ask the General and Julian questions about the current inefficiencies of the weaponry and get updates from Hope on distribution.

"Much of our attention has been dedicated to avoiding the rough waters between Island Five and Island Four," Hope said. "It has created a disruption in delivering the rations on time to the other islands."

"Can it be rerouted through Island Six?" the younger guest asked.

"Unfortunately, the facilities haven't been updated to handle the brunt of the dry goods," she answered. "I've done the calculations, and it's not worth splitting up the deliveries into multiple trips."

"We've been thinking about something that might be of interest to you, Commander," the older guest said, absent-mindedly turning his fork over in his hand. "Would you consider the idea of establishing a route through some of the uninhabited islands?"

I froze, and unfortunately, I was in the General's line of sight when it happened.

"Hold that thought," the General said, kindly as he could muster. Turning away from the table, and in my general direction he barked, "Everyone out!"

I was outside of my own body, hovering toward the kitchen with my legs barely skimming the floor. My blood was pounding in my ears. "Some of the uninhabited islands." I kept repeating those words in my head. Ignoring the questions from the kitchen staff, I made my way to the back of the room, behind shelves of pots and pans, and collapsed. So much for diplomacy. The weight of the words on my chest made it difficult to breathe. No one seemed shocked or bothered by that man's question, and it made the pressure on my lungs even heavier.

I took deep breaths.

They've trapped us all in a prison for no reason. The Authority has a hold over everyone in the Network, using people like puppets, wires controlling every movement. An unfamiliar feeling of unease sailed through my thoughts, but there was a way out, an escape option.

Among the cookware, I could let true emotions shine. I was mad. Furious, even. The rage was becoming an obsession. I imagined tearing off my stupid uniform and breaking things with my own two hands. All for the Commander, the General, the Punisher, and Julian to see.

Julian. The Punisher. Nico. Luca. The pieces came together in my mind. Was this part of the something that was going on here? Is this a small part of a big, messy, dangerous plan?

Suddenly, resolve overpowered every other emotion running through me. I credited whatever logic remained to calm my senses. After tonight, I could confront Julian. Or steal a transport boat to pick up Luca and try a life on the abandoned islands. First, I'd have to locate them, of course, but that didn't seem important now. I needed to hold my ambitions close, put a smile on, and serve dessert.

I stood up, smoothed my skirt, and waited silently with Emilia and Isabel until we were called back in the room.

My life of dressing up like a doll and aiding the people making decisions for their precious islands was coming to an end. I let my resentment fade away. Who cares if they ignored life on the islands or if their white tablecloths and extravagances kept them too far removed from the disparities? It didn't weigh me down any longer.

I smiled at my anger, finding it taxing to keep entertaining. It stirred inside me with each chore — removing Julian's plate, refilling the older guest's wine glass, plating dessert. I disconnected from it. I stood off to the side, fixing my eyes between the General and the Commander.

They were the source of it all, I was sure of it. The General had been the leader of the Guard for years, decades even, dating back to when the Commander's father was in power. And of course, the Commander, he was brought up in this. I suspected neither one of them would last a week on Island Seven — especially with the depleting rations.

The two guests were happily chatting and sipping their drinks. It seemed whatever negotiations happened over the grouper and rice went extremely well. The Commander seemed relaxed, more than usual, but still guarded. It was quite a contrast to the person in charge of the Network's safety, seated on his left. The General appeared to have gotten heavily intoxicated in a short time.

His drink of choice was some dark liquid. I smelled it while pouring some in his glass earlier. It was similar to the fuel in the distribution trucks on the island.

"Well, then," the General slurred. "Let's have a toast!"

"Hear, hear!" the Punisher said, raising her glass.

"To the future," Julian said, winking at the Punisher.

Everyone at the table raised their glasses and took a sip, except for the General, who chugged the remainder of his drink and threw the heavy glass after emptying its contents. It shattered beautifully across the floor. The two guests jumped in surprise from the noise, but it seemed the others at the table were familiar with this routine.

I tried to find peace in my tranquility, tuning out the bad, but when no one scoffed at his behavior, something snapped. The Commander didn't understand everything that went into creating that glass or what it was like to be a person who only dreamt of the opportunity to have it house uncommon liquors. The people on Island Seven were starving, and they were overindulging.

As if he could read what was about to happen, Nico caught my eye and shook his head. He was on the opposite side of the room, standing at attention. If he stood beside me, he likely would have thrown his arms around me to stop the inevitable. Instead, his eyes seemed to plead with me: "Don't do it. Please, Mol. Just don't do it."

And I almost didn't.

Everything happened in slow motion. The General alternated between laughing and taking swigs directly from a flask he pulled from his pocket. He barked at Emilia to clean up his mess. She bent down to gather the shards, carefully picking up the pieces.

The General decided either she wasn't moving fast enough or that he was too impatient for her diligent cleaning, I wasn't sure, but he yanked her by the hair closer to him. She lost her balance and fell, caught by her palms and exposed knees, right onto the glass. The pieces sliced her skin, and blood immediately dripped onto the smooth, hard wooden floor.

This enraged the General. He put his flask on the table, stood up, and threw his energy into berating Emilia. How could she be so clumsy? And stupid? Didn't she realize how useless she was? She made a mess of their dinner! And then he slapped her, hard, across the cheek with his ring-clad hand. Emilia cried out and crumpled to the floor.

Without hesitation, I lunged at the General. My instincts fueled me. I flung myself over the table. In one easy swoop, I picked up the knife from the set in front of him, grabbed him by the wrist, and twisted his arm behind his back. I held the blade to his throat, and time resumed a normal cadence in the silent room.

"Don't ever fucking touch her again," I threatened, my breathing loud and angry.

I pressed the blade deeper into the General's neck. He was bleeding, but I knew what point would cause serious damage. I wasn't there yet. I could kill him, but that action would cause irreversible consequences, leaving me no chance to escape. Not that I was setting myself up for success now.

"If you even look at her in a way I don't like again, I'll finish this," I hissed and promptly released him. I stepped back and dropped the knife. The General collapsed back into his chair.

I expected something to happen once I released him, but everyone seemed too stunned to move. Emilia and Isabel were staring at me in disbelief. Julian's face paled, and his lips were pressing into each other. The Punisher's expression was unreadable.

It wasn't until I looked at the Commander, however, that reactions surfaced. The General yelled, and the Guard swarmed me. Julian, being the most senior in the room aside from the General, slammed me against a wall. My face hit the paneling. I was sure to get more bruises. He yanked my arms behind my back and secured my hands. The General, seeing I was handled, began profusely apologizing to the guests, trying to smooth over the situation.

"This is an unprecedented event," he slurred. "I apologize that you witnessed this mess."

"Have you been teaching your Elite new tricks, General?" They chuckled and sipped their drinks.

I would have spit in the General's face if Julian's forearm wasn't pressing my skull against the white wall. He was furious with me, but I could feel him controlling his strength, revealing his anger without leaving any lasting damage.

"I'll take her to the brig," Julian forced out, and the Guard moved to get into formation. It was ironic that Julian was the one escorting me, considering he was the one who taught me everything.

"You will do no such thing," the Commander said evenly.

Objections came out promptly from the General and the Punisher, but he raised a hand to silence them.

"I have a few questions I would like to ask her before we move forward. Julian, take her to my personal quarters."

8

THE WALK from dinner was quick, with Julian gripping my arm harder the closer we grew to the Commander's level toward the top of the ship. By the end, he was dragging me along.

"This was not what I meant by keeping a low profile, Mol," Julian reminded when we arrived, then he shoved me roughly into the sitting room and locked the door.

The first few moments I was in the Commander's quarters, I stood still, taking it all in. My guess was correct — these quarters were much bigger than Julian's. Both were decorated in the same style, but for the first time in weeks, I was in a place that didn't actively remind me that I was out to sea.

The vaulted ceilings were covered in carved wood paneling, matching the dark furniture. Every surface was upgraded in some aspect. Dozens of throw pillows with tassels adorned the couches. The chairs were covered in silk. The desks and tables were finely polished. The carpet looked luxurious and soft, unlike my high-heeled shoes, which were pointed and stifling. I slipped them off and kicked them aside. Much better.

I walked over to the wall of windows. The blinds were pulled down, so I reached over to open them. There was nothing to see but the moon and the dark sea, illuminated by the lights on the upper deck. The open space made me feel oddly constricted. I didn't want to feel trapped anymore. I did find some comfort in looking outside, but I missed the sun. I was probably getting a new Placement, so maybe I'd get to see it again.

Once I found out my fate, I'd plan an escape.

For now, though, pushing my toes into the floor was incredibly satisfying. I looked up to see my reflection in the glass, momentarily reminding me of who and where I was. I was tired of the games and the costumes. Well, I could change one of those right now — the Elite clothing simply wouldn't do.

I took off the tight, cropped jacket and, going against all I learned in my Placement, tossed it onto the floor. I untucked the starched white shirt then undid the top three buttons. I quickly lost my patience and tore open the shirt at the wrists, rolling up the sleeves.

I already felt a little better altering the uniform, but I was in search of complete satisfaction. I took one of the Commander's stark white towels from the bathroom and ran it under the faucet. I spent a few careful minutes wiping off my makeup. The smear of red, black, and peach amused me. I tossed it on the floor and giggled, considering the very tangible notion that I was losing my mind.

I sat down on the cool marble floor next to the massive bathtub, which could fit a family of four without trouble. I leaned back and closed my eyes. My hair was still tucked up in the awful Elite style. I preferred my hair loose and wild —

and I was feeling a little of both. I pulled out the pins and appreciated the release of pressure. I ran my hands through my hair. I heard a sharp intake of breath and opened my eyes.

The Commander was leaning against the doorframe and peering down at me. I looked up, knowing I should have been embarrassed for being caught in my current state. I should have been afraid of being alone with the most powerful man in the Network. I should have been compliant or apologetic. But I wasn't any of those things.

That strange detached feeling from earlier in the kitchen was back, and my other emotions were standing by, waiting to be put into use. I felt that invisible thread between the two of us form once again, creating a connection. It was buzzing with anticipation at the lessened distance, but I wasn't in the mood to placate it.

I stared at the Commander, waiting to see what he would say or do. He seemed to be comfortable letting me drink him in. Then again, he seemed comfortable no matter what he was doing. His self-assurance created an impenetrable aura, an armor that I was certain guarded him whether he was wearing a full Guard uniform or nothing at all. And damn, did I want to see him wearing nothing at all. I hated myself for it.

"Join me in the sitting room," he said. It wasn't a question. It was a command.

And I immediately made the decision that I was done being pushed around. There were other options, and I wasn't going to stand for poor treatment any longer. I remained where I was, with my jaw clenched.

His brows pulled together into a scowl.

My defiance was growing. I attached myself to it, feeling courageous. It was exhilarating.

He leaned down, placing his hands on the tub, surrounding either side of my face. Two days ago, hell, two hours ago, I would have been terrified, but that version of myself died the moment I lunged at the General. I didn't mourn the loss.

"That was not a request, Mol," he reminded.

My name was liquid gold coming from his mouth, but the awkwardness of my position triumphed any other thoughts. Like so many other women, I was trapped in a situation, trying to be controlled. He was hovering over me, balancing on his hands and testing me.

I didn't move, and his eyes narrowed. I saw the muscles in his face shift, hardening. I leaned forward, and his head immediately relaxed, looking almost directly down at me.

A split-second decision to escape this position without touching him backfired, and he caught my shoulder, pinning me back. Impulse prevailed, and I threw a quick jab at his jaw, which knocked him off balance. Not by much, admittedly, but I got him to release his hands.

I gasped and brought my hands defensively to my sternum. The Commander laughed and gingerly touched his lip. I had drawn blood.

"Well then," he said, pulling a crisp, white handkerchief from his pocket to pat his mouth. "Let's try something else. May I join you?"

He stared down, eyes begging me to mock him or explode or do anything other than sit there in silence. I wondered where the Guard was, if Emilia was okay, or Julian was still seething, and most of all, I wondered what my future would be. I was sure I wouldn't get any answers if I remained mute.

"I believe when you own the world, you don't have to ask for permission."

"Ah, she speaks," he mused, slowly unbuttoning his outer jacket and gracefully sitting on the floor beside me. "But I don't own the world. I inherited it and simply keep us afloat."

I guffawed.

"You don't agree with me?"

"You have no idea what the world is like," I accused.

"Perhaps you'll enlighten me, then, of what you think I don't understand?" he said, calmly.

I thought of the market, rations, and the forbidden fruit. "Dining with those high in your ranks and getting their 'reports' doesn't paint the full picture." I figured he would interject or disagree, but he sat there, giving me his full attention, waiting expectantly.

"Have you been to any islands recently, Commander?" I asked, cautious but genuinely interested.

"Sebastian."

"What?"

"That's my name," he murmured. "Use it."

"If that is what you want, I have a condition of my own," I announced.

He stared at me, unnerving.

"I would like you to stop speaking to me like I am one of your subordinates," I said. "I do not want to be ordered around. If you want my opinion, I would like to be asked or otherwise persuaded to give it to you."

I mentally cringed, but it was too late to take back those word choices now.

"I'll remember that one," he promised, making his amusement clear. "Mol, would you please call me by first name? It would bring me great pleasure."

My skin was getting hot, so I pressed my palms against the cool floor.

"Sebastian," I swallowed. "Have you visited any of the islands recently?"

"When I was younger, my father used to take me along on his visits, but I haven't been anywhere except Island One since his death," Sebastian explained. "I do, as you have pointed out, receive updates regularly from sources in the Authority. I'm aware of some of the challenges, but I'm assured things are running smoothly on all seven."

"Who assures you?" I challenged. "Is it Felix and his creative way of glazing over details? Is it your General, who fucks Elite women in exchange for taking care of their families? Or is it your rations team, who distributes barely enough food for families to survive?"

He was purposely not reacting to what I was saying. I'd observed him enough to know that was in his rotation of action. Either no one was telling him the truth, or no one was telling him in a way that would make him listen.

"Do you think I was taking a joy ride on that boat that got me here, Commander?" I said, not bothering to hide the agitation in my voice. "Or did you think I was raised dreaming I would one day serve your meals and clean up after your crew?"

"Every person has a purpose in this Network," he said, reciting this speech for probably the hundredth time. "We all work together to create—"

"Please don't even bother trying to explain to me whatever your General and Authority convinced you is true," I pleaded. "I've lived on Island Seven my entire life. I know what it's like to have to scrape by, trying to make the rations last until the end of the week, going through Education that diminishes all hope for your future, and even resorting to selling your dead parents' stuff to survive."

After I finished ranting, we simply looked at each other.

The quiet lasted for minutes, and I could see all the emotions cross his face.

"Will you join me for dinner tomorrow night?" he asked, pressing the handkerchief against his mouth one final time. Confident it stopped bleeding, he put it back into his pocket.

I was staring at his lips, but he was waiting for my response.

"Excuse me?" I wasn't sure I heard him correctly.

"I would welcome the opportunity to dine with you tomorrow night. I am very interested to hear more about your experiences on Island Seven and your views of the Authority."

I was somewhat baffled at this offer of sick psychological punishment, making me face the General after holding a knife up to his neck while the Elite served me.

"Privately, of course," he added, sensing my hesitation. "Here in my suite or up on the deck if you'd prefer."

My eyes lit up at the opportunity to be outside. I couldn't help it. I ignored the fact that I'd be alone with the most powerful and handsome man in the Network — whom I just punched in the face. Well, I needed to eat so it could at least be under the stars speaking my mind. Maybe I'd get some insight on boats that could be stolen or a better understanding of our position at sea.

"All right," I agreed. "I will have dinner with you tomorrow night on the deck."

The Commander got to his feet and offered his hand. I shook my head in agitation and jumped to my feet, without even using my hands to help. I didn't need assistance from anyone — let alone him.

"Right," he said, dropping his hand. He walked through his bedroom and sitting room, and I followed close behind him. He turned abruptly, and I almost crashed right into him. He closed his eyes and put his fingers on the bridge of his nose.

"Mol," he said, with a tone that sounded close to anguish.

"What, Sebastian?" I asked, uneasily.

He opened his eyes. "Nevermind." He knocked three times on the door. I heard the lock click, and Nico stepped in. I didn't know what kind of security protocol encouraged locking the Commander into his own quarters. "Until tomorrow, then, Mol."

Confusion raked over me, and I looked to Nico for answers. He merely shrugged and kept moving forward.

"You don't have to walk me," I offered. "I know where I'm going."

"Yeah, you're right," he said, distantly. "I should probably go talk to Julian."

I entered the Elite quarters, and apprehension encroached. I considered turning around and hiding elsewhere. I took a deep breath and blocked it out, happy to not be spending the night in the brig. This was the latest I'd ever been out on the ship, and instead of darkness and the sounds of sleep, all the lights were on. Every single one of the Elite women happened to be awake.

I knew, judging by their immediate silence, that they were talking about me and what happened at dinner. It wasn't that big of a ship and holding a knife to the General's throat was probably big news that spread quickly for all those in Placement.

I wasn't even self-conscious with the staring. I did say a few hours ago that I should try to interact with more people, after all. Each beautiful, still-made-up face seemed to be burning with questions and a mix of admiration and bewilderment.

I nodded at a few of the women, and I made the way back to where my bed was set up, deciding sleep was more important than a shower right now. On my way, I stopped to glance at Emilia's bed. She was curled up, peacefully sleeping. Bandages covered her hands, and I assumed her knees were dressed similarly under the blanket.

It had to be excruciatingly painful to have the glass pieces plucked out from her skin, and it would likely take weeks for the skin to scab and regrow. I was accustomed to bumps and bruises, but these Elite women were sheltered from physical labor and pain.

Isabel finally noticed my arrival after a few minutes. She was sitting next to Emilia's bed, carefully watching over her. With all eyes on us, Isabel stood up and threw her arms around my shoulders, pulling me into a deep embrace.

9

WHEN SIX GUARD members entered the Elite quarters that
next morning, I figured it was the end. The General
convinced the Commander that I should be thrown into the
brig or thrown overboard or whatever the appropriate
punishment was. Reckoning time must've meant something
more than the blur of last night's interactions with the
Commander.

I thought my fears were confirmed when I didn't recognize any of the Guard members who arrived to retrieve me.
Surely Julian and Nico wouldn't volunteer to witness my
public shaming — and I was glad they didn't. One of the
Guard members told me to gather my things, which
consisted of three Elite uniforms, makeup, hair products,
and the clothing and boots I was brought to the ship in. I
clutched them lovingly.

I refused to look at any of the Elite stragglers who were
still in the quarters. The Guard escorted me, not down to
the bottom of the ship but up toward the Commander's
level. No one in my entourage would meet my eyes.

Even with practice, it was still difficult to walk up the

stairs in high heels, so I focused my concentration on putting one foot in front of the other. Someone cleared their throat, I looked up to see the General standing at the top of the landing at the Commander's level. If looks could kill, I would have been dead within the first two seconds of us passing each other. His nostrils were flared in anger, and an obnoxiously large and unnecessary bandage covered his neck.

"What a baby," I mumbled.

I swore the Guard member to my right chuckled at that statement.

We breezed by the Commander's suite and stopped a few doors down, almost at the very opposite end of the hall by the back set of stairs. I looked skeptically at the men, apparently it was necessary for the half dozen of them to be here with me.

"These are now your permanent quarters," the Guard to my right finally spoke up.

I looked down to see his name, but before my eyes reached it, he offered, "Ray."

"Mol," I said, returning the favor.

"We know," another Guard said, causing a few others to look at him in disbelief.

I sensed a rift between them all. After unwavering loyalty to their General for years, some of them probably considered ripping me to shreds, while others were envious of my actions. I didn't want to find out who was who, so I thanked them for the escort and pushed through the door.

My jaw dropped at the space — it was a similar size to Julian's, with the same carpet and furniture. There was a sitting room, secluded bedroom, and a bathroom, which was somewhat overwhelming. The bed was huge and inviting. The bathroom counter displayed dozens of scented soaps, and I hoped to find one less fragrant than the one used by the Elite. But above all else, there was a window. I dropped by belongings and jogged over to it, pressing my face against the glass.

My room on Island Seven was tiny, but I was always grateful that Luca and I had our own spaces. The Authority didn't always honor requests for siblings to have separate rooms. I tried to make it nice, turning old clothing into extra pillows and blankets. I strung up random pieces of fabric on the ceiling and hung up papers from Education. There was even a small space in the corner to do push ups and store my mismatched collection of weights. Six of my old bedrooms could probably fit into these quarters on the ship.

I was a little tentative about getting used to this space, knowing that nothing would ever truly be mine under the Authority. It would have been nice to be asked about moving, instead of having the decision made for me. I'd have to bring it up to the Commander later — after I finished enjoying seclusion.

I spent the afternoon scrubbing, relaxing, and over-analyzing. It felt wrong to pamper myself for hours while the other Elite women were doing their normal demeaning tasks and the people on the islands were struggling so much.

When the sun started to set, there was a knock at the door, disturbing me from an hour-long gaze out the window. I opened it, and a woman brushed by me. I didn't recognize her or her uniform. The Elite wore royal blue, the Guard wore their fatigues, and the kitchen staff wore all white, but this woman was in a light gray ensemble.

She dropped off a box on the table in the entryway and left, wordlessly. I immediately pounced on it, swiftly untying the bow surrounding the package. I threw the lid behind me. Parting the thin paper, I saw nothing but beading — exquisite silver beading on an incredibly soft fabric.

I pulled the garment out of the box, and the fabric extended down to the floor. It was a dazzling full-length gown. A gift, I assumed, from Sebastian to wear to dinner.

I held it up and looked at my reflection in the mirror that hung by the door. Once my eyes focused, I hastily dropped the dress back into the box it arrived in. It was the Elite shade of blue — a reminder, no doubt, of another imprisonment. I wasn't assigned any duties today, so maybe this was the Authority's way of telling me that this was my new Placement as a source of entertainment for the Commander.

I fell to the ground and put my head between my legs. I closed my eyes to focus on my breathing, attempting to control the vertigo. I couldn't very well attend dinner in my sleeping clothes, and I refused to ever put on the Elite uniform again, so I crawled over to the pile of my clothes and pulled on the ones I came to the ship in.

It felt euphoric to pull on my black pants and boots after weeks of wearing a tight skirt and heels. I found my courage again pulling on my gray henley, not even needing to pull on my jacket for the extra barrier. Plus, it felt somewhat indecent to wear if I didn't have my pocket knife to pull out at a moment's notice.

I grabbed my uniform set, makeup, and other Elite essentials and strode over to the bathroom, tossing them all in the hamper. I couldn't stand the idea of looking at them any longer and washed my hands after I discarded them. After my hands were dry, I stood in front of the large mirror.

They were somewhat rare on Island Seven, but there were at least four in these quarters alone. A few of the houses at home came with them, but they were usually broken by former residents or stolen and sold off in the market. Much like the spaciousness of the new living arrangements, I would have to get accustomed to seeing my appearance.

The Elite women were all exquisitely beautiful. It was if someone pulled all the desirable traits from the women I'd known on the island and put them into one small group. If they're going to be on a ship in the middle of the sea, I supposed these were the type of women the Authority wanted to be surrounded with.

These women were curvy and walked with a confident hip sway, but I was always gangly and thin. In recent years, I developed a strong but lean set of muscles that I loved, even if it didn't attract anyone else. I would never be dark-haired, stunning, or seductive, and after gazing at my reflection for a few minutes, I wondered if this Placement's true form of punishment was to instill insecurity.

My dark blue eyes were fairly symmetrical, and my nose and lips were thinner than every other Elite woman. I certainly didn't adhere to normal beauty standards, but I didn't think I was truly awful to look at. My hair was a little uneven at the bottom — about twice a year, I used my favorite knife to chop off a few inches when it truly got unruly, but now, it was at that perfect rib-cage length.

Growing up, I hoped I would eventually begin to look more like my mother, who was known for her beauty. Now, I merely hoped to continue to cultivate that defiance and bravery she demonstrated. I could sure use some of it now.

A knock on the main door pulled me out of my musings.

There were three Guards from earlier ready to accompany me, including Ray. I assumed we would go directly to the deck, so I headed off in that direction.

"Uh, Mol?" Ray said tentatively, gesturing to the Commander's quarters.

I told myself I agreed to this on the principle of fresh air, and my annoyance sparked immediately at the change of plans. We hadn't even started the evening yet, and I was already doubting this decision.

Without knocking, I entered the Commander's quarters. He was sitting at his table with the Punisher across from him going through a few stacks of papers. That woman loved paper, apparently.

"Just a moment, Mol, if you don't mind," Sebastian stood up and walked over. "Hope and I are wrapping up our review of some reports and then you and I will head up, as promised."

He gestured for me to get comfortable in the sitting area, but not wanting to comply for the hell of it, I followed him back to the other room and sat on the chaise near the window.

The Punisher resumed inundating the Commander with numbers — population, rations, square footage. It all went over my head, but the Commander seemed to be engrossed in the information she was providing.

"These are the numbers from last year," the Punisher cautioned. "The population growth has increased more quickly than our expansion of rice fields and fruit trees. Plus, the agricultural division is concerned about over-fishing around Island Two."

I snorted. We are surrounded by miles and miles of sea, and we have this ship and a few smaller ones — the solution seemed simple to me.

"I appreciate your diligent research on such short notice," the Commander praised. "See what else you can pull, and let's reconvene tomorrow morning."

The Punisher nodded, finally looking over at me.

"Did you not like the gown that was sent for you?" she asked. "It was selected from my personal collection."

This woman gave me a headache. Our interactions were nothing but short, confusing ones, and I wasn't sure I was up to trying to figure her out. She took my silence for an answer. "Well, this does seem to suit your more drastic tendencies," she said, gesturing to my boots and pants.

"You can't land an effective butterfly kick in sequins and fitted fabric," I said, my voice a little hollow.

At that, the Punisher collected all of her papers in record time, bid goodbye the Commander, and gave one last glare in my direction.

"Shall we head up then?" Sebastian asked, the pinnacle of politeness.

As we climbed the stairs, I couldn't hide my eagerness. Now that I wasn't restricted by pointed shoes, I made it up quickly, taking two or three steps at a time. The Commander followed close behind. Instead of his formal suit, he wore loose black denim, tucked into black Guard-style boots. His long-sleeved shirt was bright white, which could only be from mindful care and bleaching by someone on the Elite.

We made it to the top, where Julian was waiting for us. "Commander, the area has been swept, and we've pulled farther away from land, so we're all clear. But the General asked me to insist—"

"That will be all for now," the Commander said dismissively. "Please post a Guard in your place and inform him we are not to be disturbed."

Julian nodded, not bothering to acknowledge me, and swung open the heavy door.

In my time on the ship, I was limited to a few areas, but standing out on the deck, I immediately appreciated how large the vessel was. Mavis's boat was laughably small in comparison.

I walked over to the edge, taking in the gentle breeze. It was so comforting to break free from the climate-controlled areas of the ship and feel the humidity. I tried to make out where we could possibly be. In the far distance, I could see land, but it was somewhat of a blur. It would also help to have any knowledge of what any of the islands looked like from a distance.

The Commander walked over, leaned one arm on the railing, and turned to face me. "You like it?"

"That's an understatement," I breathed, turning to match his stance.

"I used to spend more time up here when I was younger," he admitted. "I was born on a different ship, but it has been in repair for years. I consider this to be my home."

"It's not bad," I offered, glancing up at the moon.

"I agree, but you've seen how my days have been spent more recently. Lots of meetings, numbers, and dinners, but I'm sure this one will be quite different."

He pointed at the lower-level of the deck. It was covered with white painted lines and a giant circle in the middle. The area was likely empty most often, but now, it was covered thick blankets, at least a dozen pillows, and ten lanterns.

"I figured this would be more appropriate, given your dislike for formal, seated dinners," Sebastian said, raising a hand to touch the healing cut on his bottom lip.

I couldn't even form a response. Under a different circumstance, my disapproval would be mounting with the wasted effort in my honor, but at this moment, I was captivated.

"Unfortunately, this deck wasn't designed for picnics, so

we'll have to climb down this ladder before we dine," Sebastian said, walking over and throwing his leg over to begin his dismount. "Although I didn't ask, I didn't think you would have an issue with it."

I gave him a small smile, and he stopped momentarily to stare. He righted himself and continued climbing down. I followed him, trying to decide if I imagined his eyes dropping to my chest and legs.

He brought a container up to his nose to check what was packed as I sat down next to him. His brows furrowed — he wasn't used to having to put this much effort into his meals.

"Let me," I offered, and I repeated his motion. "Ick, pigeon."

"Would you like some?" He held up a serving spoon and a bowl.

I shook my head. Here I was, in a gorgeous setting, with the most beautiful man, getting offered the foulest bird I could think of to eat.

"No, thank you," I answered, exaggerating my scowl. "You'd understand if you saw the pigeons we have on Island Seven."

Instead, I picked up a spoon, reached across the Commander, and dug directly into the rice and vegetable mixture he'd pulled out first. He seemed a little irked by my disregard for manners, but his irritation faded quickly when I looked up at him, clearly enjoying my first few bites. I inwardly smiled when he put down the bird and took a big helping of my preferred dish.

"So, Mol, what else is happening on Island Seven that my reports don't cover?" He tilted his head to one side, chewing slowly.

I paused, wondering if he was mocking me, and contemplated what I should say or what he would even be interested in. I took a breath then let the words spill out. I started with my childhood, the testing for Placement, and my limited time with Luca, keeping everything surface level — and leaving Julian and my dealings with the market out.

At one point, after realizing I'd been speaking for a long time without pause, I stopped. Expecting a look of indifference, I was surprised to be met with genuine interest. I continued chattering, spending a lot of time, probably too much time, talking about working out and some of the hidden spots on the island.

"I found that one recently, but I didn't get the chance to explore the cliff," I said.

"No?" He was leaning back against the pillows at this point, lazily bringing his fork to his mouth.

"I kind of got into a bit of trouble and ended up getting my Placement early," I spelled it out for him.

"Right," he said, clearing his throat. "Well, now I'm up to speed."

I stared at him in slight disbelief.

"What is it?" he asked, sitting up to move closer. I couldn't help the grin from forming on my face, and his expression changed to match it.

"You're just not what I pictured," I admitted quietly.

His tone turned light, a gentle mocking. "Not old? Or mean? Vicious?"

"Well, that's still up for debate," I answered. The sun completely set, and despite the slight breeze, I was warm in his presence. Our chemistry seemed illuminated by candles and the moonlight. "I've just grown up with rumors and speculation on the Authority and the Commander."

"Oh really?"

"It's definitely different here than on the island," I

gestured to the open sea and chose my words carefully. "Some reasons are obvious, but others aren't."

"Do you miss your home?"

"I miss the sand and the sun. I miss having breakfast with my brother and talking to him. I miss running. I don't miss the rations or the daily struggle."

His gaze chilled, and I needed that jolt.

Anyone else who saw this scene would assume we were lovers, cozying up under the stars, but in truth, I was being used for my information, for my entertainment value. I was teetering on the edge of opening up true feelings and emotion, and I tried to shut it off. He didn't play an active part in my misery — leaving most of the decision-making up to others in the Authority, but that didn't mean his conscience should be completely clear. I had to speak my mind without any reservation.

"But now, the stress has been replaced with something far worse." I pulled my legs up to my chest, protecting myself from what I was about to say.

"And that would be?" he prompted.

"Guilt," I confessed.

His eyes darkened. "I see no reason for you to feel guilty."

"You don't?"

He ignored the bite to my tone.

"Your punishment for attempting illegal trade was fulfilled in your early Placement into the Elite, which paid off quite well for the Authority until your recent altercation with the General. Although your actions were not specifically outlawed, it likely falls under the 'harming an Authority member' jurisdiction."

An emotion very close to humor rolled over his face.

"That discipline is still being arranged by Hope, but

being the Commander does give me absolute pull in overlooking events that occurred in the defense of a helpless, scared friend."

There was a beat of silence, and then I laughed.

"Sebastian, you misunderstand me."

He assumed I felt guilty for breaking the Authority's rules. The absurdity of it all was too much for me to bear without some outward emotion. Instead of patience and tenderness in his eyes, I could only see irritation and confusion.

"I don't give a shit about the Authority's rules or what is deemed an appropriate punishment," I explained.

The longer I drew this out, the bigger the wall would grow between us. The picnic crushed it to the ground, leaving only dust smatterings, but now, it began to rebuild. Brick by brick, word by word, I was distancing myself from him, allowing my anger to flood in and take control.

"And I definitely will never apologize for trying to sell my mother's necklace to get more rations or holding up the General at knifepoint. I've been stuck too long in a cycle of someone else's decisions."

My voice cracked, and I looked away.

"I feel guilty worrying about my makeup and hair while people on the islands are stitching together threads to make blankets for their children. I feel guilty about eating until I'm completely full because I've spent so much time stretching two cups of rice into three days' worth of food. I feel guilty about living in luxury when the Authority gets to dictate the drivel everyone else calls home."

I stood up to pace and yell at Sebastian until I was a few feet away from him, breathing hard and fuming. He was silent, letting me vent my frustrations. It somehow made the situation even worse.

"Most of all, I feel guilty for actually enjoying myself around you, Sebastian, because you're the cause of all of this. It's your rules, your father's legacy, your inaction that has ravaged the Network into a bunch of voiceless, compliant slaves."

I ran over to the ladder, climbed up at top speed, and sprinted past the Guard back to my new quarters. I refused to break down in front of him or anyone who would report it to him. Being in his presence challenged almost everything I believed in — I couldn't bear to reconcile my feelings for the handsome, young Commander against his suffocating leadership.

The deepest disappointment, however, came from within.

A big part of me hoped Sebastian would follow me. I imagined him showing up to my quarters, telling me that we'd figure it all out, that no feat was too great to change, and that he dreamed of spending his time with me. I was disgusted with myself as I replayed that imaginary gesture in my head on repeat. I collapsed onto the oversized bed and fell into a deep, dreamless sleep.

10

THE THICK, steel door to my quarters was at least thirty feet away from my bed. I didn't have a direct line of sight to it — the wall to the entryway obscured it slightly. At some point during the night, I burrowed myself into a fortress of pillows and pulled the covers up past my head. Even with those barriers, the muffled sounds of arguing and the tread of heavy Guard boots woke me up.

I resisted, at first. It was a strange kind of wonderful to not have to jump up and check my schedule of duties for the day. Cleaning and prepping was likely not going to be a part of my daily agenda anymore, but this new unknown wasn't exactly comforting.

I tiptoed over to the door, hoping to pick up on whatever was happening on the other side, but the words didn't translate through the hard metal. Wondering if those voices belonged to Julian, Nico, or even Ray, I opened the door an inch, just enough to peek out. The door creaked, loudly, and the two Guard members, neither of whom I recognized, snapped to attention. Their stone-faced expressions confirmed my suspicion that I wasn't supposed to know they were posted up, let alone possibly overhear any of their conversation.

I slammed the door shut and ran a hand through my hair.

Without a Placement, I didn't have a purpose — in the Authority's eyes and my own. I grew accustomed to the regimen but longed for independence almost every second. Now, I had it. I just didn't know what to do with it.

I trudged over to the bathroom, an overwhelming need to wash my face and brush my teeth surfaced, likely residual effects from the past few impeccably clean weeks in the Elite. Who knows what else I'd carry with me moving forward, how many undetectable scars and patterns I'd picked up that were now a part of me.

Once finished, I made my bed, another habit I carried up multiple floors onboard, then pulled the blinds open all the way. I wished there was a way to open the window itself. The glass looked a few inches thick, not easily breakable or repairable. I leaned my forehead against it, willing the sun rays to break through and coat my skin.

My breath fogged in little circles, and I traced my fingers through them, drawing little suns and trees. I wasn't sure when I'd get to see a tree on an island again, if ever. This glimpse of the outside teased my emotions — so did last night's picnic with the Commander. Sebastian, and his questions and perfection, and me, with all of my brashness.

I sighed and stepped back. I couldn't let myself be the girl gazing at the unattainable any longer. I considered leaving my quarters, but it would be difficult to avoid Julian, the Guard, the Elite, the Punisher, the General, and, most of all, the man at the root of it all. Essentially, I'd alienated everyone, and I wasn't sure who I could blame it on.

The prospect of long-term seclusion made my skin itch

and my muscles tighten. I anchored my feet to the thick carpet and dove to the ground, catching myself at my palms. The burn of my muscles expanded as I pushed myself through ten, twenty, then thirty, push-ups that brought a smile to my face. I let my arms recover, and I did squats, lunges, and crunches.

I missed jogging through the uneven streets of Island Seven, but the strain and release was welcome, even in my silk sleeping clothes. I funneled my frustration with the Authority, my situation, and even myself into another round of push-ups.

Each repeated movement ripped at the facade, tearing apart the promise I made to Julian, the rules I'd been adhering to, any sort of residual uneasiness over my actions in the past forty-eight hours.

My lungs expanded and contracted quickly, forcing the determination built up in my mind to spill over into the rest of my body. I jumped up on the bed, ruining the fold of the sheets. I kicked three of the pillows off, ripped down the sheer canopy fabric, and gripped my hands above my head on the sturdy wood. I alternated between pull ups and chin ups and dropped to my feet. Sweat poured down my face, along with satisfaction.

My strength prevailed. I put my hands on my hips. The discarded fabric was torn and discarded on the floor, and I howled with enthusiasm at the idea of more destruction.

I ripped off the rest of the bed coverings, punched the remaining pillows, ran over, picked them up, and repeated it again. It was too easy, so I shifted my attention to the extravagant, oversized chairs. I kicked the backs and struck the cushions with my arms. I gave special attention to every piece, making my way from the bedroom to the sitting room.

Not yet satisfied, I eyed the desk — its heaviness was

taunting me. I hated the ornate carvings and pristine finish. It was too perfect. It needed some scratches and cracks. I squatted under the writing surface overhang, leveraging my leg strength, and pushed up with my hands and shoulders, flipping the desk onto its back.

I picked up the desk chair and wavered between tossing it against the bathroom mirror and trying to break through the window. Feeling the wind won out over cracking my reflection. I raised it back, ready to strike, and the door to my quarters swung open, slamming hard against the wall.

Nico and Julian rushed in, weapons drawn. It was strange to see them both together working in unison, let alone in my private quarters. Julian halted with the scope of his gun focused on me, giving Nico a silent hand signal to stand down.

"Are you kidding me, Mol?" Julian cried, gesturing to the havoc.

I threw the chair down, causing Nico to flinch, but Julian's eyes leveled with mine. I sauntered over to him, anger pumping from my veins, into my heart, and out to my fingertips. I shoved him, hard.

"Do I look like I'm telling a joke?"

He rolled his eyes.

It wasn't Julian's fault, necessarily, that I was angry. He wasn't to blame for my circumstances, but that didn't matter now. My temper was controlling my behavior, and I let rationality sit on the sidelines. Julian didn't know how devastated Luca and I were when he disappeared for his Placement. Luca, obviously, mourned his loss in a different way, but I lost the only one who understood the fire inside me. He was the one to guide me to channel it into strength, and I was ready to throw it back at him.

"Why do you insist on making everything so difficult?"

"I don't," I answered honestly.

"Well it sure seems like it."

He stepped further in, getting more heated as he took in the damage. After putting the safety back on his gun, he placed it on one of the upright chairs and started cleaning up.

"Don't," I said, and he ignored me. "Julian, stop."

I watched him move and mumble angrily.

"Something you want to share, Julian?"

"Just seems like I'm always stuck cleaning up your messes."

"Always?" I scoffed. "You've been gone for years." I sighed, and he stopped to meet my eyes. "And part of you is gone for good," I added.

"Well, it seems like I'm making up for a lot of lost time," he said, sourly. "Can't say I'm enjoying it."

Julian stepped forward and stood straighter, using his height to try and intimidate me. I grabbed the balled up fabric from his hands and threw it. I shoved him again, and this time, he reciprocated, sending me backward a few steps.

He's strong, but I'm fast. I made up the distance quickly, catching his jaw with a jab. He blocked the cross then I dodged his hook. I backed off, keeping my hands up and ready.

"Mol, could you at least, I don't know, change clothes before you kill each other?" Nico said, averting his eyes while still trying to watch the action.

"You sure about this, Mol?" Julian taunted, shifting his weight back and forth on his legs. "Do you forget who taught you everything?"

I threw some of the last maneuvers we'd been through together on the island. The switch kick was my personal favorite, and judging by his robotic deflection, he remembered it, too.

We countered back and forth, both of us getting increasingly frustrated by the lack of progress until finally, I charged at him. I channeled the years of sadness without him as I punched him. I thought about how devastated Luca was as I kicked him. I yelled at him for disappearing on me as I chased him around the room. He tried to escape, but he was slowed down by having to leapfrog over some of the overturned furniture.

Finally, I landed a gnarly punch to his gut and stepped up, with my fist still against his abdomen. We were eye-to-eye and breathing heavily.

"Mol," his tone indicating he was on the cusp of making an apology I wasn't in the mood to hear.

"Fuck you," I breathed, inches away from his face.

The flip switched inside him, and in a quick movement, his fist hit me square in the face, unleashing a gush of blood from my nose.

Blood dripped down past my mouth, and I laughed, hitting my knuckles together to encourage him. He kicked my feet out from underneath me, grabbed my shoulders, and spun me around. His arms were around my neck in his signature chokehold. I'd never seen it in serious action, but we'd practiced it enough for me to know how to break out of it.

"Is this really necessary?" Nico asked, giving voice to inner debate on whether to pull up a chair and watch the madness or put a stop to it.

I raked my fingernails across Julian's cheek then leveraged my legs to break from his grasp. In a smooth motion, I lifted my arms and pinned his own at my sides, catching his face with my right elbow on the way down. He threw himself on top of me, and we fell to the floor in a tussle. His full weight pinned me down, and I'd have to wait for a weak spot to appear to break out of it.

"Had enough yet?" Julian smirked, and I smiled.

My shoulders and arms were pinned, no doubt he'd been trying to focus on what I'd been using to inflict the most damage. He chuckled, and I headbutted him hard enough to momentarily distract him. I thrashed my legs and kneed him in the crotch. He fell back, wincing, and I jumped on top of him, landing a series of punches. He caught my wrist and held them to his chest.

"Well isn't this a nice little family reunion?" Hope tutted, walking in through the wide-open door. She brought a large package with her, which she casually dropped on the floor beside us.

"Nico, be a dear and get the door, will you?"

She turned a chair upright and sat down. Julian and I were entwined, a mix of limbs and agitation. I assessed his damage — a few bruises and scratch marks were forming on his face. I could feel the blood caking onto my skin from my nose, but other than that, I felt fine. We'd both have headaches, rug burns, and sore muscles tomorrow.

"Julian, I expected more from you at least," Hope said, and we were both offended by that statement for different reasons. "I thought you had Mol moved up here to protect her — not fight with her."

I looked at Julian, surprised that his best intentions had been behind my relocation. The look he gave Hope indicated he hadn't wanted me to find out, and I didn't completely understand why. His eyes, filled to the brim with emotion, met mine, and I wrapped my arms around his neck. He enveloped me in a hug, pushing us both upright without unlocking from each other.

"There we go," Hope clapped. "Let's have a nice chat while we're all in one place for a few moments before anyone discovers both of you missing. It's going to be difficult to explain why you two look like you got into a fight."

"Well, I mean, we did," I offered, looking over at Julian, expecting a smile. Instead, he bit his lip, and I crossed my arms across my chest. I had him back, my version of him, so briefly, but it only took a few seconds for him to harden back into a Guard, standing at attention.

"What if we just told them the truth?" Nico suggested, and we all gave him varying looks of confusion. I didn't realize everyone was clued into mine and Julian's past.

"Mol and Julian both realized their love for me and were in the process of fighting until the death when you interrupted?"

Julian smirked, and the Punisher chuckled. Apparently humor was only okay when it came from one of their own.

I looked down at my knuckles, the broken skin red and puckered. The post-exercise high was coming down rapidly, and I was exhausted. "While I appreciate you all making the trek to my quarters, could you all get the hell out of here?"

Julian's eyes flashed. "That's no way to address someone in the Authority, Mol."

"Could you all please get the hell out of here?" I asked, adding a coat of sugar to my tone.

"Ma'am," Julian prompted.

"Oh, no need for such formality, Julian, 'Mol,' is fine with me," I said dismissively.

He clenched his fists by his side.

"Mol, I think it's time we talked seriously," Hope said, leaning over to pat Julian's arm. He immediately relaxed, and I chewed on the inside of my cheek. "What's happening here is bigger than all of your petty rage, although some of is justified, but I think you'll be interested in—"

"I'm not."

"You haven't even heard what I'm offering."

"I know."

"Mol, stop being so stubborn," Julian hissed.

Her eyes flashed between us. I hated this dynamic — I was tired of being angry, of being powerless. I accepted I would never be in control on the ship and that I was at the mercy of these people.

"I don't want to hear what you have to say. I don't want anything to do with the Authority, games, or the dinners, or the lies, or the deceit. I don't want a part of it."

"So tell, me Mol," Hope deadpanned. "What do you want?"

I wanted to leave this place and forget my time here. I wanted to move to one of the abandoned islands and live in peace, without deciphering the codes and norms of the Authority. I wanted to live without the Authority. I rubbed my eyes and ran my hands through my hair, tugging through the knots. "I want to talk to Luca."

"Not happening," Julian chided.

I ignored him and moved closer to her. "A letter. That's all I'm asking. Can you do that? An exchange for whatever help I've accidentally already provided?"

He was my one soft spot that I was ready to break free from, to mold myself into a completely hard shell and move on, enough to swallow down the disgust when I added, "Please?"

Hope smiled sadly and stood up. For a nanosecond I thought she was going to walk out, but she grabbed a pad of paper and a pencil from one of the drawers in the upturned desk.

"Write something quickly," she said, handing them over to me. "I'll see what we can do."

It took me a mere three minutes to scribble on the pristine parchment. I wrote about how sorry I was that I got captured and caused him to worry. I told him how much I loved him and missed him and that I was okay and I hoped he was, too. A pressure lifted off my chest — even if the letter never made it to him, I still felt relieved to put those emotions somewhere outside my body.

"All right, men, it's time to clear out," Hope said. "I can't make you any promises on this, Mol."

She patted the letter, which was now tucked in the pocket of her suit jacket, and followed Nico and Julian to the door.

"The Commander asked if you'd join us for breakfast tomorrow morning in the main dining room," she added. "He told me to make sure I emphasized that he was asking, not telling, you to join us."

The door clicked shut. I let out a loud breath. Eating in the same room where I served in my Placement seemed like an awful idea — but I wasn't sure if I was in the place to deny the Commander's request. Even if he did ask, which suggested I did have the option to decline.

I groaned and turned to the bathroom in search of a long, hot soak in the tub. I tripped and caught myself, cursing for forgetting about the package Hope brought in. The box was a similar style to the one the dress came in, and I opened it with hesitation. Instead of a blue gown, I found clothing that looked eerily familiar. I dug through the folded garments and found pairs of black pants, gray long- and short-sleeved shirts, black socks, and black boots.

My breath hitched at the familiarity. It was like my clothing back on Island Seven, but the fabric was lovely.

Even by merely holding it up, I knew these clothes would fit better than anything else I'd ever own.

Remorse settled at the front of my mind. I shouldn't have been so snippy with Hope, but she's too tangled up in all the unknowns for me to have understood her intention. This was obviously some sort of reach for middle ground. Like so many other things in my life, I'd dismissed the opportunity before I even understood it.

11

THE ELITE DON'T SIT down for meals. They eat bites of whatever extra food the cooks made at dinner or devour a sandwich in the laundry room between shifting towels from the washer to the dryer. So, apart from Sebastian's picnic, breakfast would be my first time sitting down and dining with others while on the ship.

My appetite, which all but disappeared in the time I wore the royal blue uniform, was back. The growling of my stomach echoed off the walls. I made my way down to the main dining room. The dread for this experience didn't even exist — I was too ravenous to focus on much anything else.

Instead of an elaborate, multi-course affair, breakfast seemed relaxed. The table was covered in platters of mangoes, sliced bananas, and many other fruits I'd never seen or tried. There were at least four different types of sliced bread paired with a dozen assorted bowls of jams and jellies accompanying them. I smelled coffee, and my mouth watered instantaneously.

Hope was resting her elbows on the table and taking small bites of a golden apple while reading over one of her ever-present reports. This was our first time being alone together since she dished out my assignment to the Elite, and despite my budding bravery, I still felt little uneasy around her. Hope wasn't exactly a warm motherly figure, but she also wasn't the least friendly to me. I considered apologizing for my abruptness yesterday, but I had yet to receive an apology for anything that had happened to me in my life, so I dismissed that idea.

Instead, after deviously thinking of taking Sebastian's seat at the head of the table, I sat next to her and quickly discovered the font on her documents was a little bit too small for reading from my angle.

"Are you going to eat or just sit there and stare at me?" Hope asked, nonchalantly.

"Probably a little of both," I replied, popping a round purple fruit into my mouth.

I scooped a heaping platter of food onto the plate in front of me, some of it slipping right off and rolling on the table cloth. Someone in the Elite would have to scrub the yellow mango stain out due to my carelessness, and I frowned.

Hope finally glanced over to show her annoyance at my lack of grace but turned to amused as she took in my black eye. Adrenaline shielded me from noticing that injury for a few hours yesterday, and I audibly gasped when I saw my reflection when I stepped out of the tub. I spent the rest of the day sitting by the window with a cold, damp washcloth covering the side of my face.

I played with the sleeve of my shirt while she studied me. I spent hours of serving dinners taking in her habits and appearance, but she didn't know much about me other than what was in her precious files. Still, she managed to provide some level of comfort for me, and I was grateful.

"I wanted to say thank you," I blurted out in between bites.

"Oh? What graciousness have I offered to warrant your gratitude?"

"These, of course," I said, gesturing to the black pants and gray long-sleeved shirt. "You've noticed I'm not a ball gown type of girl, and these are perfect."

Hope's expression was indecipherable.

"You should have your seamstress sell these in the market on Island Seven," I continued. "I'm sure she'd pick up an overwhelming amount of pigeon meat and illegally grown herbs in exchange."

Hope laughed. Truly laughed.

"Ah, I think she'd prefer the accommodations here, but who knows what the future holds now," she said, waving her hand.

If I could rely on nothing else, Hope would always manage to confuse me with her choice of words and questionable insinuations. I stood my ground with her less than twenty-four hours ago and now we were chatting while eating.

"But unfortunately, as lovely as it is to hear you doing something other than arguing and yelling, I cannot take credit for your wardrobe," she said, with a note of cheeriness. "It was the Commander who insisted."

I stopped, my fork en route to my mouth.

"Our young Commander is quite smitten with you, Mol, although I'm sure you already know that," she acknowledged. "However, what you do not know, and it seems like you're much more agreeable to hear today rather than yesterday, is that much like his father, women have always been seen as disposable objects."

Great, she'd be happy to fill me in on how I'm just

another woman to toss away, a brief distraction in a life of monotony. She was so happy to inform me of this, and I wondered if masochism was a requirement to be in the Authority or if it was a trait everyone possessed. I now understood Julian's caution, why he warned me to stay under the radar. I assumed it was because some sort of hidden agenda — not because Sebastian could be interested in someone like me.

"A few years ago, he went through quite a reckless stage."

Emilia. The General. The Guard of strong, gorgeous men. The Elite of frail, beautiful women. The smugness and sex talk. I shuddered. Hope took a long sip of coffee, and I noticed my fork was still in the air. I dropped it then pushed my plate away, my hunger disappearing.

"It wasn't until his father fell ill that Sebastian retreated into himself, managing to straighten himself out in the process," she explained. "The sicker his father got, the stricter Sebastian became, pushing away everyone but his advisors, listening and barking out orders."

I hung on her every word, taken aback by her honesty, and part of me wondered out of all the time I'd been under her thumb, why was she being so straightforward now.

"Sebastian's father always hoped Sebastian would follow in his footsteps. I suspect, with time running out, Sebastian tried to help his father's dream come to fruition. When he died, though, Sebastian no longer felt the need to put on an act, and he delegated his responsibilities to others in the Authority, including myself. It seemed he was determined to atone for his behavior, settling into the man we know now."

"Ironic, considering he has the Network and everyone in it at his fingertips," I seethed.

"Mol, don't you see what's happening here?"

Of course Hope would want to glorify Sebastian, even with his despicable behavior.

"Yeah, the Commander is a bored, sad man. A pathetic excuse for a leader, making ill-advised decisions with no regard for the consequence. He is—"

"Changing," Hope cut in. "For the better. And it's because of you."

That shut me up — and sent my brain into overdrive.

Sebastian's interest in me could have been a fluke. My coloring stood out in the Elite, enough to attract some level of attention, but if I kept my silence and faded into the background, like Julian urged for, I would have been soon forgotten. I could have been switched into other assignments within the Elite that didn't involve serving or seeing anyone in the Authority.

When I picked up the knife, I slashed away the chance to have that future. If embracing my true defiance and strength would lead to my downfall, I couldn't think of a better cause. There was no turning back — of this, I was more confident than anything else in my life.

But my feelings for Sebastian triggered waves of confusion. He was the basis of everything I'd hated for my life, but in his presence, it all melted away. I tried to force myself to be distant, to allow my disgust to set precedent, to not allow infatuation to sway my ambition, but if I accepted Hope's version of the truth, it could change everything.

I couldn't allow myself to fall for a Commander of a destructive, suffocating Authority, but I could get to know a man, Sebastian, who grew up under the thumb of his father, with no one teaching him what's right or what the world is like, with no one telling him no.

"Why are you doing this?" I whispered.

"That is a story for another time," Hope said, waving me

off. She turned back to her report, and the door to the dining room opened.

"Sir, I think this could be a game-changer for the strategy we discussed earlier," Julian said, slowly strutting in.

I noted, smugly, that he was walking with a slight limp.

"Not even just the Guard — the Authority and throughout all the islands," he continued, wringing his hands. "Felix agrees with me, and yes, Commander, I know that's not your favorite source of information, but it's true."

Sebastian ignored Julian and stared at me. I smiled over one of the blue jams, and when he didn't return it, a warning went off in my head.

Did Hope lie about him wanting me here? I'd just come to terms with what she said, but Sebastian might have a completely different viewpoint of me and whatever was between us. I didn't see or hear from him after I stormed off, ruining what otherwise would have been a beautiful evening together out among the stars and salty air. He was so curious about my opinions and my life on Island Seven. I'd indulged his questioning for hours, but I now supposed that could have just been a Commander questioning one of his subordinates.

I took a breath and reassured myself if that were true, he wouldn't need a picnic or delegation of my own private quarters — he could merely use Hope to dole out another sentencing. He, and he alone, pulled me out of the normal process, shielding me from any Guard or General treatment. He tried to understand me. To get to know me. To be with me. I wanted to reciprocate, which I realized at the same time that I noticed Sebastian hadn't even been staring at my eyes — but at my bruised face and scrapes.

"You think this is bad?" I asked, attempting to channel

Nico's humor and lighten the mood. "You should see the other guy."

I gestured at Julian, whose face was far more bruised than my own. He was also supporting several scratch marks across his cheeks down to his jawline. Sebastian's head snapped to Julian's. He moved toward me, sidestepping the table to get a closer look at my eye. Armed with the knowledge Hope shared, I didn't cower at the fire flaring inside me. Instead, I let it fuel me and met his eyes.

"Julian," Sebastian snapped. "While I am now privy to the scope of your relationship here, I do not appreciate half-truths to questions I ask."

"Yes, Commander," Julian said, meekly. "Won't happen again, sir."

"I'm sure he didn't want to cop to getting his ass kicked by an Elite," I suggested.

"Yes, I also recommend you avoid doing that for the foreseeable future," Sebastian said.

He raised his hand up to my cheek. I released a warm exhale, and he took his spot at the head of the table. I immediately missed his touch. The three of them continued the discussion on the project Julian was updating Sebastian on when they arrived.

Julian, always rigid, seemed a fraction softer than usual. Perhaps it was due to the General's absence or the fact that Sebastian's leg was casually slung over the side of his own chair, setting a relaxed precedent. They were chatting like old friends excited to sneak out after curfew — not a Commander and his Guard plotting the implementation of life-changing technology. Hope was a balance in the trio, backing up statements with facts and numbers.

The three of them were so absorbed in their conversation that I was the only one to notice the General's arrival.

"What is going on here?" he bellowed, putting a hand up to the slightly less overbearing, but still unnecessary, bandage at his throat.

"Breakfast, General." Sebastian said. "Sit and eat. Julian was just filling me in on some updates."

"And what exactly is her role here?" he asked, his finger wagging in my direction.

"She is my guest," Sebastian answered.

"Do you forget that this is the same woman who held a knife at your General's throat?" he said, attempting to keep his voice even.

"You question your Commander?" His response was so simple and cold that I shivered.

"No, sir."

The General strode over to the table and paused, waiting for Julian to move out of his usual seat, but he and Sebastian already resumed their conversation. He huffed and took the only vacant seat, right across from me. The next few minutes were silent, from him at least. He stabbed his knife at one of the yellow jellies.

I prepared to watch the rest of the meal play out, quietly amused. I wondered if this would become a routine for them, like the one Luca and I established. Instead of old coffee grounds, quiet contemplation, and stale bread, there was an abundance of food and casual banter.

I imagined Hope warming up to me, explaining how she got her position in the Authority while Julian and Sebastian became true friends, and they all bettered the Network. I envisioned Sebastian stealing glances at me while in deep conversation with others. And most satisfyingly of all, I pictured the General never showing up to a meal again.

In the middle of my thoughts, the doors swung open again, and Felix ran in. His usual caked on, waxed appearance was cracked. His hair wasn't gelled into a hard helmet and his shirt was untucked. I'd never seen him look this frazzled, and I wasn't alarmed by it at first. I didn't know if this type of behavior was normal for this time of day, but when Felix shot a pained expression in my direction, a shrug of apology, and I felt ill.

"Your delivery, General," Felix whimpered and rushed off to press himself against the far wall, where I stood dozens of times in the Elite.

I stood up, bracing myself. Four of the Guard marched in. They were each holding an end of a massive chain, forcibly dragging whatever was attached along. It wasn't happening quickly enough for the Guard bringing up the rear of the line, and he vented his frustration by winding back and landing a kick. A prisoner — no, a person — received the full force of it.

He fell forward, revealing torn clothing. His body was covered in a sickening mixture of blood and dirt, so blended that I couldn't tell what was what. His arms and legs were shackled on the receiving ends of those chains the Guards were whipping around. I could tell that his left shoulder was dislocated, and his left wrist was likely broken. I was no stranger to bumps and bruises, but this man clearly had been tortured — or at the very least, heavily abused.

The man looked up, and my vision tunneled. I pushed away the blackness by bracing myself on the tabletop.

Glassware tumbled to the ground, but I didn't even hear it crash. I wasn't in the dining room anymore. I wasn't aboard a ship or even in the same dimension. I was floating in a mixture of absolute horror and panic, watching the scene from above, until I forced myself back, feet rooted into the floor, and a very familiar pair of blue eyes looked up.

"Luca," I whimpered.

All of the frustration in my life, multiplied by ten, did not prepare me for the anger that overtook me. It took one heartbeat for me to fling myself at Luca, not caring what destruction I left in my wake. The General, sensing this, jumped back to avoid my path, but I didn't pay attention to him — that would come later.

The four Guard members hadn't been expecting anything but praise at their arrival, so when I approached the closest Guard, who was pulling at Luca's injured left side, there was no defensive move when I pounced. I landed a powerful kick between the Guard's legs, causing him to drop the chain. I sent an uppercut to his nose and landed another punch straight on. Luckily for him, he passed out.

The second Guard dropped the chain and reached for his baton. He swung it, but I swerved, grabbing onto his vest, and I kneed him in his stomach. He collapsed, and I turned to face the other two Guards.

Liquid fury was pumping through my body. My muscles ached for more violence. I stepped toward the men holding the chains at Luca's right side, but strong arms pulled me back. The General stood up and ordered the Guard to remove their fallen colleagues and disappeared with them.

Julian unfroze and darted to Luca, examining his wounds and pressing his palm to his forehead while yelling at Hope to help. Anger wracked my nervous system, and I continued to fight. I slammed my weight against my captor's foot, earning a slight release. Sensing the opportunity, I spun around and threw my forearm at his neck, slamming him against the wall.

It wasn't a Guard, though. They all left with the General. Felix was slumped in a chair, shaking. It wasn't anyone else in the Authority — Hope and Julian were tending to Luca.

The haze cleared in my eyes, and I stood inches away from Sebastian.

Even with his air supply cut off, he was relaxed. He was waiting for me to realize what was in front of me. The irony wasn't lost. I released him immediately and ran to Luca. A teary-eyed Julian whispered that Luca was in and out, and he seemed be in a lot of pain.

"Go get a Medic," Sebastian ordered, and Felix scurried out out of the room.

I sat silently, grasping onto Luca's uninjured hand and waiting for help to arrive. My lips pushed into a hard, painful line, as the Medic popped his shoulder back in place. The pain caused him to wake up and cry out, so he was given shots through a needle.

"For the pain," the Medic explained to no one in particular, then turned his attention to wrapping up Luca's wrist and tending to his surface wounds.

I didn't say a word when the General came back, but the yelling didn't process in my brain right way, even though we were in the same room. Slowly, the shouting match began to make sense.

"You requested I bring you the inventor of your new technology, Commander," the General challenged. "We sped up the process, and when this one wouldn't go willingly, we took certain measures."

I guessed this special treatment was decided when my connection to Luca was uncovered — really, it would take one glance at one of Hope's many files. I imagined the General gleeful, getting to exact his revenge on me where it would hurt the most. Then, he could feign innocence.

The Medic gently removed Luca's hand from mine, and a few of people, all clad in white, strapped him to a board and carried him off. I was paralyzed on the floor.

"You are so blinded, Commander."

"On the contrary, I've never seen things more clearly."

"They're manipulating you. They are all trying to turn you away from your father's legacy. He would be disgusted at your behavior, Sebastian."

"I'm very familiar with my father's legacy, Hugo, I don't need a reminder from anyone — especially not you."

The shackles clanged together. Ray, Nico, and a few Guard members circled the General. Julian, standing beside Sebastian, was venomous.

"I think it's time you've gotten a full understanding of your preferred method of imprisonment," Sebastian growled. "General, can I have your assistance?"

Only he wasn't talking to the fat, overconfident man standing in front of him. Sebastian's head was turned, looking directly at Julian.

"Take him to the brig," Julian said, raising his chin. "No need to be gentle."

They complied without question.

Julian stepped forward to confer with the Commander, and I was suddenly too tired to sit upright. I slumped all the way to the floor, in the spot Luca just vacated, soaking up all the spirit of him I could. I closed my eyes, forcing the conversations around me to exist in a quiet murmur, and unintentionally let it accompany me to sleep.

I felt strong arms surround and lift me, but I didn't open my eyes. I sighed with pleasure and curled into Sebastian chest, breathing him in. He touched his fingers to my temple, a tender send-off into nothingness.

12

I woke up sometime later, still too drained to be anything but numb. I passed out only a few hours after waking up, but it appeared I slept through the day and a good chunk of the night. I was on Sebastian's bed, facing the window, witnessing the early signs of sunrise.

The yellows and oranges were vibrant, meshing magnificently with a long, red line. I wished I could bottle up the sight. My mother always loved the sunrise, which is why she never minded the late shift in her Placement.

I used to wonder if she minded being on opposite schedule than my father, but there seemed to be an unbreakable bond between the two, no matter how much disappointment mounted or little time they spent together. It was also something I didn't have a desire to experience firsthand until recently. Now, I appreciated how beautiful it was to wake up beside someone, even under the current circumstances.

Sebastian was silent and still, but I felt his presence. I wasn't ready to speak yet, and I didn't know if that was okay. I rubbed my eyes and rolled over. Sebastian was awake, looking me over. He was still wearing his clothes from yesterday, just like me, and we were laying on top of the once-perfectly made bed. There were creases in the duvet from our gentle movements, which were illuminated with rays from the rising sun.

He raised a hand, tentatively, and I nodded.

"Luca is okay," he whispered. "Resting with the help of some Medication."

He brushed fallen pieces of hair away from my face. His long fingers gently stroked the bruise under my eye. He touched my neck, collarbone then my arms. His hands traveled over me, and my skin was sensitive under his touch. I was getting addicted to the sensation.

His mouth, his full lips, were parted slightly. His hands moved to my side, touching my hips, and gripping my upper thigh. Finally, in our seclusion, he seemed as charged as I had been all along. I almost burst, releasing the energy I'd been suppressing for far too long. He grabbed my hand, and I winced. He scowled and brought my hand up to his lips, gently placing his lips on my bruised knuckles.

My blood was pulsating, and I was certain that his lips could cure anything.

After studying me for a moment, he dropped my hand, gracefully, on an errant pillow. Sebastian leaned back and grabbed a mug. Sensing his objective, I sat up, and he brought it up to my lips. I gulped the warm liquid and coughed.

"You don't like it?"

"What is it?"

"Ginger tea with peppermint leaves," he explained. "You're not familiar?"

He took a sip and placed the mug back on the bedside table.

"Oh, I am. My mother used to try and get me to drink that stuff when I was younger, but I refused."

He smiled. "Mine did, too, oddly enough."

"I've never been a ginger tea person, though." I admitted.

"What kind of person are you?"

"Coffee," I answered, chewing on my bottom lip. "Black. Two day old grounds are the best, but after three or four, you have to toss them."

My intention was lightheartedness, but it came out slightly accusatory. I hated the silent mix of pity and anguish in his expression as he mulled it over. I was desperate to say the right thing, but I just didn't know what it was. I craved his warmth, his touch, again, not the hardship.

"What kind of person are you?" I whispered.

"I don't know anymore," he admitted after a moment of silence, digging deeper into my question.

My heart ached. I was cognizant of my limited experience with men in general, but I didn't truly appreciate my inexperience until now — while completely alone with a very attractive man, who also happened to be the most powerful and handsome person in the Network. I was clueless.

"You don't have to," I answered honestly.

He chuckled, and he reached down to place his right hand in my left, the non-bruised one. "You can't really believe that?"

"I do," I insisted. "Sebastian, you've had almost every decision made for you your entire life. Where you'll live, what you'll eat, who you'll talk to, how you'll lead. You've never gotten a chance to find out what you want or experience anything just because you thought it was right."

"That's mostly accurate," he agreed. "But I'm not innocent. I may have been naive to some of the consequences of my decisions, but I actively went along with what I'd been surrounded with, never questioning anything."

"But it's not like you knew there was anything to question," I prodded. "Right?"

"You could say that my skepticism has been gradually building up and recent events have alerted me to all of the cracks I'd been turning a blind eye to since my father died."

"And now?"

"Onward," he vowed, bringing our hands up to his chest.

We flittered in and out of consciousness while holding onto each other until I heard movements in other parts of the ship. I didn't want to wait around and get discovered by one of the Guard — I didn't need that getting back to Julian — so I slipped out, carefully, from Sebastian's hold.

"The medical bay is two floors down, to the right of the landing," Sebastian said, eyes still closed, looking beautiful and stoic.

"Thank you, Sebastian. For everything."

I made my way back to my quarters to shower and gather up the courage to face Luca. This situation was pretty much my fault — not just my insistence on selling off our parents' items so we could live comfortably — but everything with the General.

Selfishly, I hated the thought of seeing Luca knowing I played a part in his physical pain. Julian and I were accustomed to altercations, but Luca always sat on the sidelines, lost in his own thoughts. This wasn't fair to him.

I passed a few of the Guard on the steps down where Sebastian instructed, getting a nod from Ray, who was on patrol. The medical bay looked as I expected — a few cots and privacy curtains, various tools, and endless rolls of gauze. Julian sat on the end of Luca's bed when I arrived, and they were chatting happily.

"I see you got my letter," I said, gesturing to the note sitting on Luca's lap.

It was more wrinkled than when it was in my possession. Luca looked relatively unscathed compared to yesterday. A sponge bath, bandages, healing herbs, and a bit of rest could do wonders, apparently.

"Hand delivered by yours truly," Julian chirped.

"Yeah," I acknowledged. "Just not under the circumstances I hoped."

The lightness in the room evaporated, and I cringed.

"Well, I guess I'll get back to patrol," Julian sighed. He stood up and kissed Luca on the forehead.

"Don't expect me to call you 'General,'" I warned.

"Wouldn't dream of it."

I sat down in Julian's vacant spot, getting an up-close look at Luca's injuries. The cuts were stitched and clean, deep and abundant across his cheeks. In guilt, I dropped my eyes to my shaking hands.

"Mol," Luca cleared his throat. "Look at me. Come on, look at me."

I didn't want to. I could feel the emotion building up, and I didn't want it to spill out.

"Look at me," he pleaded, and I obliged. "I'm fine."

I smiled, trying to hide my sadness.

"Julian has been filling me in on what's been happening around here," Luca explained. "I know this isn't what either of us imagined happening or even predicted you would have received as your Placement, but at least I know you're safe here — especially with Julian around to keep an eye on you."

He gave a pointed look to my black eye. "Or at least he tries to," he added, chuckling.

He looked so close to death yesterday, and now, he was telling jokes. Luca never told jokes. The Medic must have been a little generous with his dosages.

We all healed in our own ways, and I felt a bit fortunate that we were in a place where Luca could be mended. It gave me hope that in the coming weeks, I could feel whole, like everything wouldn't be a fight anymore. I took a shallow breath in and considered that in a few weeks, I could breathe deeply, and it was exhilarating.

"Luca, do you think it's possible to change, really change, in a short period of time?"

The words tumbled out of my mouth. I really wanted to talk to someone about how I felt. Luca had at least somewhat of an idea about my defiance and anti-Authority thoughts, but only Julian understood the eagerness I suppressed in being my truest self. But I didn't understand, with my contentedness and happiness pushing to the surface, why Luca's face darkened a fraction.

"Look, Mol, I know that you have been somewhat secluded from hormone-driven interaction in your life thus far, but there is a lot more happening here than you understand."

"What?" I asked. "What do my hormones have to do with anything?"

"Julian told me all about the Commander's interest in you," he added, sensing my confusion.

I rolled my eyes. "Sebastian has nothing to do with this, Luca."

"Are you sure about that, Mol?" he offered, in a frustratingly calm way, like our parents used to do when we were young and disagreeing over something silly. "Look at you —

special quarters, new clothing, no Placement. You're getting a taste of freedom, and the Commander is going to use it against you."

"Luca, I don't even know what you are trying to say," I confessed.

"You might think the Commander is changing under your influence, but I think it's the other way around."

"Because I'm some sort of lovesick, naive girl fawning all over the Commander?" I snorted.

"That's not what I meant, Mol, and you know it."

"That's not what I meant, Luca," I huffed. "You haven't been here. You have no idea what I've been through or experienced or fought for. And I would have thought you could muster up the decency to ask me for my side of these past few weeks instead of lapping up everything Julian says."

Indignation was my preferred emotion these days, and I thought I was moving away from that. In fact, that was what I specifically hoped to talk to him about. Now, my words were acid, and I couldn't stop the burn.

"I'm glad you two finally enjoyed a little reunion — which, by the way, thanks for not telling me you've been in contact with him," I roared. "If anything, you're the smitten one, Luca. You've been keeping secrets from me. All for what? For what, Luca?"

He gritted his teeth. "I guess you're right, Mol, people can really change in such a short period of time. I don't even recognize the person right here in front of me."

I could tell he immediately regretted saying that, but I didn't placate him. He exhaled and looked at me with wide eyes.

"I'm worried about you," he admitted. "That's where this is coming from, Mol."

I swallowed down a weird prickly sensation.

"Do you remember learning in Education about Stockholm Syndrome?" he asked cautiously.

It took me a minute, but I remembered. "When a victim grows affection for his or her captor," I whispered, feeling about two inches tall.

"All I'm asking is that you test the boundaries of that trust you think you have and see where it gets you. Can you do that, Mol? For me? For Julian?"

I looked at him, finding those words eerily similar to the ones Julian used against me weeks ago. This time, however, it came from Luca, my brother, my blood, not someone who disappeared for years and then swooped in making demands and promises. Still, I couldn't let go of the feeling of Sebastian's hand in mine, and I wasn't sure I wanted to.

"I suppose so," I agreed, not loving how happy my words made him.

Who knows what would happen to us in the coming months. I supposed I could appreciate the little smiles and positive emotions however they came about. After all, they were somewhat of a rarity these days, and I wasn't sure how long I'd get to spend with him.

"Luca, how long will you be here?" I asked, tentatively. "Do you have time onboard to recover before you are sent back to Island Seven?"

His smile grew bigger, erasing years of stress and frowns from his face. I couldn't remember the last time he seemed this young or cheerful — and it was less than twenty-four hours after he'd been beaten by Guard members.

"I'm getting relocated in my same Placement," he said, with a sparkle in his eyes. "Right here on the ship."

13

THE PAPER-THIN CURTAINS in the bedroom weren't wide enough to cover the window pane. I'd learned long ago to sleep through the sunlight, but lately, I'd been waking up at dawn, twisted up in my sheets.

The muffled sound of my parents arguing broke through the wall separating our rooms almost every day now. I missed the days of uninterrupted sleep, but I also didn't want to miss out on the details of their conversation. A better daughter, a more respectful one, would have closed her eyes and burrowed under a pillow to drown out the sounds. Curiosity triumphed, though. I didn't think it was necessarily a bad thing.

I rolled closer to the wall, the entire length of my body pressed up against the white plaster, and I used my hand to help press more of my ear against the surface. Sometimes they would just talk. About their days, about me, about Luca, about the rations, but it usually escalated into some level of disagreement by the time Father finished getting ready for his Placement.

It was impressive how much energy Mother brought

home after the twelve-hour night shift. Her Placement merely built up the intensity of her opinions. The more she said, the harder Father closed the drawers of their dresser.

"Aman, will you just sit down and listen to what I'm saying?"

The bottom drawer squeaked open and then closed.

"He is getting sick, and he's not going to be able to hide it anymore," Mother said, emphasizing almost every word with an extra syllable. "His inner-circle knows the truth, but soon it will be leaked to the rest of the Authority."

Once again, Father did not respond. His footsteps were heavy, echoing as he paced around the room. Under normal circumstances, he was stoic. He believed every movement should have a purpose, while my mother darted around, usually dancing or humming.

"You know what this could mean for us, for our children, for everyone on the islands," Mother said. She was excited, no doubt, but there was ferocity, too. "Change could happen, real positive change with a new Commander."

I gasped aloud, and all movement in their bedroom stopped. I closed my eyes and tried to make my body's position appear natural for when they came into reprimand me for being awake or for eavesdropping.

"I don't think so, Eva," he murmured. The bedsprings creaked to support his weight on their bed, and I breathed a sigh of relief. "You know just like I do that the boy has been brought up for this. He has been trained to be just like his father, cruel and ruthless."

"No," Mother gasped. I was on the receiving end of being told no by her many times in my life, and her power made you immediately close your mouth. "The Commander has been complacent for forty years. He is immune to our suffering, but surely the boy will seek to understand the world around him."

"Why would he? He has been raised without want. The Elite, the extravagance, the power, the snap of a finger that can make any whim a reality. The boy has been at his father's side for his entire adolescence, bred to step in at a moment's notice. Even his looks are close to his father's."

"Do not chastise me, Aman."

"You haven't seen what I've seen, Eva," he answered, simply.

"Yes, I haven't been aboard the ship, and no, I don't get the firsthand knowledge you do at your Placement, but I've seen and picked up enough. Do you forget who you speak to? What I've been through? Who I know?"

"Of course not, my love," he said, with unabashed tenderness. "And I admire your hopefulness, but I don't share it. We will have to continue on with the plan and hope for the best."

I could sense her despair, and for the first time ever, the energy drain from her. Father's words were direct but not cold, and she gave in to them. They found their bliss in the middle ground between two very different opinions and resumed talking in low tones until I could no longer follow their dialogue. Eventually, I drifted back to sleep.

The heat on my back comforted me in slumber, but the intensity was too great when my eyes opened. I extended my arm out to pull on the shades, blocking out some of the light from the window. I buried the growing disappointment in myself — no girl from Island Seven should ever shun the rays, but where I grew up could no longer define my whole existence. The sooner I accepted it, the faster I could dedicate my time and energy into something more important than inner crises.

By the looks of the outside, it was around 0700. I stretched out and let my muscles melt into the mattress.

The dream, clear as the crystal in the dining room, settled. I remembered those mornings now but dispelled them from my mind long ago. I couldn't bear to think of anything but happy interactions between my parents after they died. There weren't a lot of them left now. That morning blended into so many others, and there was no reason to bring it out of suppression until now — the memory resurfaced out of relevancy. I probably kept thousands of them, tucked away, waiting for some event in my life to trigger it, writhing its way free from my collection. Hidden until the timing was right.

A few days ago, I wasn't interested in or ready to understand what was happening with Julian and Hope's plotting. I never had an inkling that anything would come full circle. Life on the island seemed so different, so disconnected from what I experienced in the Authority. The realization that everyone — even my parents from their graves — were part of something without me made the room spin.

They, in full consciousness, left me out. I was not a part of what they were planning for a big, beautiful future. Maybe I was too young or reactive or incompetent in their eyes or, worst of all, they did it to protect me.

I pulled my legs up to my chest, trying to combat the sweaty sickening feeling that threatened my mental state. I didn't want or need someone to look out for me. They'd pushed me out of the circle of secrecy. It didn't help my situation. In fact, it might have made it far worse. I was never afforded the luxury to choose my own path, something I expected with the Authority but not with my family. I clutched a pillow to my chest.

The only person who could understand me was my

complete opposite. Sebastian, my antithesis, was my kindred spirit. I'd been suffocated by indecision and a lack of opportunity, and him, luxury and complacency. He was completely honest with me. He answered any question I asked, and he seemed to value my insight. He was a stranger in some respects, but I felt a connection to him.

I was embarrassed by my misplaced resentment. I'd been the ignorant one, allowing everyone else's words to shape my judgment. I'd let prejudices guide my decisions, and now, I was full of regret.

I'd been an outcast my whole life, I'd known that, but I would have never pictured it among those I trusted and loved. Well-intended or not, they'd all shielded me, and it hurt. I didn't know who I could trust anymore. What was Hope's motive for helping me? Which side of Julian's split personality would I meet today? How could Luca, of all people, withhold?

Insecurity circled my psyche, and I wondered if Sebastian felt a sliver of it in his own self-reflection. I, alone, could hypothesize for hours, but he held up the weight of being the Commander. There were rules and regulations tying him to meetings. He was responsible for thousands of livelihoods, whether he truly accepted that or not. If he were to leave, the system would fall apart. There would be chaos, starvation, and violence. Even a failing system was better than the alternative at this point.

My heart broke for him, and I felt a twinge of urgency. My dwindling sanity and I craved his presence, a pull I couldn't credit to his attraction or power, just to him.

I found more pencils and paper in the desk, the same drawer Hope pulled the materials from after I begged. The furniture was upright now, but there were nicks and chips across the surface. I traced my finger over a few of them then tried my best penmanship.

Sebastian,

Picnics might not be my thing, but you, sunshine, and the sea air are. Roof deck at 1000?

Mol

P.S. Although I imagine you're delighted to hear from just me, wouldn't it be nice to receive notes from other people in the Network?

I folded the note in half a few times, tiptoed out, and slid it under his door. After a quick workout and a long bath, I made my way up to the top of the ship and found Nico waiting at the door.

"Hi," I offered, not completely sure of where I stood with him. "I'm surprised to see you — isn't your shift at the bottom half of the ship?"

"Not anymore," he said, his face masked with indifference. "I've been promoted to the Commander's special detail."

"Oh. Is that a good or a bad thing?"

"I haven't decided yet," he admitted. "Seems like there are a lot of changes happening these days. You wouldn't happen to know anything about that, would you?"

I returned his half smile. "Nope, definitely not."

When I stepped out, Sebastian was leaning against the same railing from our first night together. His braids, loose at his shoulders, moved gently in the wind. He was wearing the Guard-style boots with loose black pants tucked in, but instead of a form-fitting button up, a plain black shirt with the sleeves pushed up at his forearms.

He was so stunning that it was borderline paralyzing. I needed a minute to pull myself together — sixty seconds of pure, gratuitous appreciation for him. I slowly counted down and attempted to push away all traces of lust. This wasn't the time or place for that.

I joined him, and my damn knees weakened slightly when he smiled. I didn't notice the two tall, glass mugs he was holding until he offered one to me. I eyed him quizzically.

"Unfortunately, we only had fresh grounds this morning. The cooks were confused when I showed up to the kitchens asking if we had two-day old ones."

I took the cup of coffee, hot and black, and took a sip. It was rich, the richest I'd ever tasted, with cacao undertones. An involuntary sigh of happiness escaped me.

"Thank you, Sebastian," I said, tracing my finger along the line of the rim. It was all I could muster with the emotion threatening to spill out of my mouth.

He took a sip of his own drink, which was some fruit and mint tea concoction. "So, I got your letter."

"I figured that out," I admitted.

He put his hand on mine, and I pulled away gently, not missing the confusion in his eyes. I wouldn't be able to focus on anything other than touching him.

"Want to take a walk?" I asked, and he nodded.

"I've been mulling over what you wrote this morning," Sebastian said, keeping a slow pace for both sets of our long legs. "And I think you're right."

"About the letters?" I clarified.

"Yes, but it is the opening to a bigger conversation we all need to have," he explained. "We need to review our current laws and decide what works, what doesn't, what the people in the Network want and need."

Speechless didn't cut it. I dove head first into mute territory and struggled to resurface. His revelation, so easily said, blindsided me. This was everything I hoped for, what it seems like my parents dreamed of in the new command, and I accidentally helped push it forward.

His face fell, mistaking my silence for disapproval.

"No!" I blurted out. "I mean yes. No, I don't not approve." We both smiled. "I think it's a great idea," I clarified.

"I was hoping you'd say that."

"What are you going to do first?" I asked.

Sebastian drummed his lips. "I'm trying to sort that out. I was making some headway this morning when a note slid under my door from a beautiful girl asking me to meet."

My heart skipped, and I took a sip of coffee. "Sebastian, I've actually been thinking a lot about this."

"Which part?"

"Well, I was thinking about how different life is here on the ship than it is on the islands — at least Island Seven," I let out a breath. "I think that you might not even realize the luxuries you have been afforded and how it impacts the rest of the Network."

"Very fair," he agreed.

"So I want you to see the world from my point of view."

"I don't think I'd look good in an Elite uniform. Plus, your new quarters are smaller than mine."

He was trying to keep the conversation light, flirty even, but I just mustered up the nerve to ask him a question that could change everything. I didn't want to let it distract me.

"I think it would be beneficial for you, and others in the Authority if they are interested, to see Island Seven," I blurted out. "Can we go?"

"I don't see why not," he said after a few steps. "It would

be good to see where these inventions your brother has been updating me on came to fruition."

Luca conveniently got in the middle of everything it seemed, but at least I was keeping with my promise of testing out the trust with Sebastian.

"Plus, you can see the Education halls, the rationing station, and if we have time, the house where I grew up," I said, eagerly.

"Let me talk to Julian and the Captain about the logistics, but I'm sure we can wrap up a few things and head out by the end of the week."

It was hard to stop myself from smiling enough to take another long sip of coffee, which dropped the moment Julian opened the door to the deck. He must have sensed my good mood and found an excuse to ruin it.

"You're needed, Commander." His eyes were daggers in my direction.

"I'll meet you downstairs, Julian," he said. I loved how his voice shifted from conversational to a Commander role when he spoke to Julian. I appreciated the big, flashing boundary around us.

Julian didn't move, still taking in the scene of Sebastian and I, enjoying each time with each other, standing closer than I'd realized.

"General, do you need me to repeat myself?" Sebastian asked, all politeness evaporated, and Julian excused himself. "I'll have Nico or one of the other Guards stop by your quarters when the plans have been laid out, if you'd like to be included?"

"Yes, of course," I nodded. "I would appreciate it."

"In the meantime, you should explore the ship," Sebastian encouraged, his tone teetering aggressively on an order.

"Agh, Commander," I coughed.

"Sorry, sorry," he apologized, acknowledging the line we'd drawn. "You're able to do whatever you please, but just so you know, your brother's lab is located next to the medical bay."

"Okay. Thank you for the update, Sebastian. And for the coffee."

I placed my hand on his chest, as if it were the most natural response. He moved even closer, and I breathed him in. He lowered down, his mouth moving past the side of my face and settling on my ear.

A chill shot through my body. There's no way he missed that. He lowered his hand to my jawline. His rigid exterior was no reflection of how gentle and calm his movements were.

"Anything for you," he whispered.

And then he was gone.

14

"MISSING YOUR OLD UNIFORM?"

Nico arched a brow, and I toyed with the hem of my shirt.

Since Sebastian encouraged me to wander the ship a few days ago, I tried talking myself into the idea that a visit to the Elite quarters was a good one. It felt like years of experience and burden built up quickly when I was escorted out by the Guard, and I was reverting into a simpler, shier version of myself at the mere thought of returning.

I'd caught glimpses of perfectly done up hair and royal blue jackets, but I hadn't spoken to anyone since my relocation. While I never particularly enjoyed the company of Emilia, Isabel, or anyone else in my Placement, I occasionally wondered how they were doing, and if Emilia's physical scars were healing any faster than my mental ones.

My life knocked off course at my own volition, but everyone else's likely remained the same — just with some added gossip. Or animosity.

"Have you gotten an update on Emilia lately?" I asked.

He looked at me with disapproval, clearly hoping I'd stick with light chatter.

"Depends on what kind of update you're looking for," he said through gritted teeth.

"Definitely not in the market for any makeup tips," I huffed. "Remember that one time the General threw her into a pile of glass, and I retaliated by threatening his life?"

"Doesn't ring a bell."

"Nico," I whined.

"She's fine, Mol," he said, crossing his arms over his chest. "Lighten up, and go ahead in. Fingers crossed you'll survive wandering around the shared quarters."

I opened the door tentatively. "Can't say I miss the risk of you showing up at night."

"Oh, good, you haven't noticed me sharing your bathroom, then."

I playfully shoved him, and the door closed between us.

The quarters were the same as I'd left them, mostly empty since it was midday. I meant to come earlier, or later, but my intentions were thrown by my nerves. Two girls sat in the dressing room, happily chatting about their duties. I'd seen them around but never spoke to either. No doubt they were present for my grand escort out of the quarters, judging by the abrupt stop in the conversation when I stepped over.

"Is Emilia around?" I asked, and they both stared at me.

"The ship's not that big," the woman on my left sneered then resumed painting her toenails, her stockings and shoes discarded close to where I stood. "You could find her if you put a little effort into it — or get the Commander to do your bidding and have someone track her down," she added, feigning innocence.

"I think she's in the washroom today," the other offered,

gesturing to the tacked-up schedule, which earned a glare from her companion.

"Right," I muttered. "Okay, well if you see her, can you please tell her I'm looking for her?"

One woman nodded, and the other sighed in displeasure. I took it as my cue to leave.

Indecision on my next move halted my movement. Yesterday around this time I'd studied the Guard patrol on the deck. They rotated between training and staring at the horizon for hours, but I talked with Ray for a few minutes until he was summoned back to his duty. The other men gawked at me, and not wanting to find out if they were loyal to the new General or the previous one, I went back inside.

My legs led the way, and after a few minutes, I ended up walking toward Luca's lab. Even though I'd thought of nothing for weeks but getting in communication with him, I had yet to visit. I left the regimented Elite schedule behind, free to move around the ship, but Luca probably didn't have the same opportunity. In fact, I'd be willing to bet all the fresh coffee beans on the ship that Luca's hours only increased since boarding.

In my visits to his Placement on Island Seven, I always felt like I was interrupting a big breakthrough for him, but I was glad I did it. Now, I could reminisce about the time we spent together, just the two of us. Maybe I could establish something similar here.

I was still uncomfortable with the idea that he wasn't being completely honest with me, but I couldn't help the growing excitement. I wound my way through the hallways. I passed the medical bay, where two people dressed in all white were trying to organize the chaos of supplies. I half expected Luca to re-organize everything while he was on lockdown in recovery, but his brain was probably already focusing on other tasks.

It was a good thing, though, that he could pick up his Placement onboard. No doubt Sebastian immediately approved his transfer, but I suspected Hope and Julian were involved, too. The Authority seemed to be favoring me — and after years of struggle, I wasn't going to complain. That didn't mean it was easy.

I made my way down the hall, toward the large room at the end I assumed turned into Luca's laboratory. So much changed in the past few weeks, but somehow, finding familiarity put me at ease.

When I stopped in the doorway, a surge of unanticipated jealousy swung, and I caught it in my chest. I expected to bounce in, hop down next to Luca and bombard him with questions, as I'd done many times on Island Seven. Instead I stumbled upon Luca, with a small screwdriver in hand and a scrap of metal in the other, joined by Julian, who was affectionately touching Luca's back. I swallowed a large mouthful of air. They were happy, and I was envious. I'd never seen them in this type of environment, happy and carefree, and it crushed me.

Maybe this is what they discussed in their secret communications — planning the future without any preventions, only accounting for their own wants. I'd been picturing a life with the three of us, but this was the first time it occurred to me that they probably saw it differently. After all, who would choose a life with your sister tagging along over any other alternative?

I turned and ran, choking on my embarrassment.

Self-pity formed somewhere in the back of my skull, and I suppressed it. They found their own little perfect version of bliss, while I stumbled into situations. Whenever I felt inches away from steadiness, something inevitably disturbed my foothold. I craved understanding but instead, I uncovered nothing but my own vulnerability.

I hurried past the medical bay and ran down the stairs. Each landing held a reminder of some mistake or brash decision I made — the level with the dining halls, the multiple levels of quarters, the laundry and kitchen facilities. Recognition blurred. I willed my legs to go faster.

It was difficult to get away on a cramped ship. I refused to let my determination falter. I felt the temperature drop the lower I went. I debated on venturing to the floor with a "HEAVY MACHINERY: DO NOT ENTER UNLESS AUTHORIZED" sign but made a quick decision to breeze past it.

Finally, I reached the bottom of the ship and pushed open the heavy door. The huge room seemed crowded, packed with hundreds of large, wooden crates. Many of them were stacked four or five high, with some labeled "AMMUNITION" or "NON-PERISHABLE" or other words I didn't recognize. They were all nailed shut, and I didn't feel the overwhelming need to open any.

Peace was cramped and musty, and I didn't mind. I climbed up, trying to find the perfect place to perch.

"She is so uncooperative," a husky voice broke through the silence, interrupting my meditative state.

I was up high enough and tucked away at an angle that it would be difficult to spot me outright, but I still silently scooted backward.

"Pity not anger, Ray," a female voice chastised, and I knew without even looking that voice belonged to a certain red-haired woman.

He huffed in response, and if he formed words, I couldn't make it out.

"She simply doesn't fully understand her place here or the consequences of her actions," the Punisher explained.

"Anyone with a pulse should be able to understand if they don't belong," he fired back.

My body swayed, and I bit down hard on my lip to stop the motion. When I tasted blood, I let go and wrapped my arms around my legs.

Everyone was subject to their own opinions, sure, but it hurt to hear it spelled out like this. I preferred direct confrontation. I could react in the moment and get it all out, but here, I took it in slowly — and that was painful.

"Mavis is unaware of how badly she could have complicated things for us," she said cooly. "Luckily, everything seems to have fallen in place without much interference."

I released the air from my lungs, and all my feelings of unease went with it. The rest of their conversation tapered off as they walked toward the exit. Hope's heels clicked in a steady rhythm to count down until the moment I'd be alone again. When the door slammed shut, I jumped from my hideout. My brain was moving hundreds of miles per hour, but my body was sluggish. I stepped back to where Ray and Hope came from.

Mavis was from Island Seven, a legend in the market, a known rule breaker, and best of all, she knew my parents. I palmed crates I passed, using them to combat the growing darkness of the room. The lights were increasingly sparse the further I went, and I could just make out the bars of the cells from the far-away glow.

I gulped down my intimidation and stalked forward.

After what felt like an eternity, I was close enough to see the outline of Mavis. A single, bare light hung from the ceiling at the end of the row, revealing her sleeping figure against the floor-to-ceiling bars of the cell door. The shadows illuminated the sunken skin on her bones — from a lack of sunlight or nutrition, I wasn't sure. On the island, she was high up in the illegal food chain, and she rarely went without. Her plumpness made her seem so intimidating, and now, seeing how much weight had fallen from her body, my fists clenched.

"Mavis," I cried involuntarily and immediately regretted it.

Movement in at least one of the other cells paralyzed me. I stood completely still, breathing quietly, for what could have been hours, until my muscles ached.

I stared at the U-shape of the cells, willing Mavis, in my direct sightline, to look up and see me. The thick metal bars were cemented in five feet of plaster around each enclosure, which I could use to my advantage. If I crawled silently all the way down the narrow row, I wouldn't have to face whatever occupants were locked up. At least, until I made my escape. Then I'd run for it.

Holding in a sigh of pleasure when I lowered my stiff limbs to the floor, I moved forward, not loving how my knees clashed with the cold floor. I paused sporadically, making sure my presence went undetected. I craned my neck, swearing that Mavis stirred, pushing me to move faster. My heart pounded in anticipation of the answers I'd get from her about my parents, about the Authority, about these beautiful and mysterious people on the ship.

A force grabbed me by my hair, slamming my head against the door to my immediate left. The force of the impact didn't make a sound, but it ricocheted in my head.

"Not so bold are you, now?" The former General purred the question into my ear, sending a combination of dizziness and nausea to my senses. "Not without utensils at your disposal down here to threaten me with."

He pulled my hair at the roots with one hand and moved his other around my neck, tracing my collarbone lightly. I shuddered in disgust.

"You can't even begin to understand how insignificant you are," he breathed, his mouth pressed up against my neck. "I have more power than you could ever imagine, more loyal followers that you could ever know, more of everything that you could ever hope to have."

His chin rested on my shoulder, and I craned my neck the other direction, earning a yank on my scalp. He murmured promises of destruction and a long and painful life for me, as repayment for the inconvenience I caused him. I focused on the putrid smell of liquor, ignoring my curiosity at who gave it to him, and reminded myself that I had the upper hand even though he currently controlled my air supply.

"I will come for you, and I will hurt you," he promised.

I sank into his grip, then broke out of his hold without much fight. It would have been far more satisfying if he was hurt in the process, but instead, I merely turned around to face him.

Stripped of his uniform, he looked like a sad, old man clothed in simple gray fabrics that seemed scratchy and too thin for the drafts this far down. I'd felt his stubble on his face, cringing at how close in proximity he was seconds prior. His hair was loose and stringy around his eyes. When I moved closer and smiled at him, his anger radiated.

In a flash, my fist connected with his oversized nose through the bars, and he cursed loudly. I shook out my hand, enjoying his pain and allowing the adrenaline to block out my own.

The door at the entrance to the floor swung open with a loud clang.

"I look forward it," I admitted to him, casting a longing glance at Mavis, who stared at me in surprise, then I disappeared from view.

Although Sebastian suggested I explore other areas of the ship, and I wasn't in the mood for another confrontation with Hope or Julian. I slipped past the Guard by weaving between the crates and headed straight to my quarters. I needed to put my fists through some furniture.

15

I PLANNED my path for more destruction and had it finalized by the time I reached my door, but I groaned when I saw it was open. Stepping through the threshold, not in a mental state to have someone else in my private space, I sighed.

Emilia sat on the armchair by the window and traced the outline of the bandages on her knees.

"Uh, Emilia?" I coughed.

The dark-haired beauty stood up and glided over to me. "Sorry for breaking in," Emilia apologized. "Isabel heard you were looking for me, and I'm a little ashamed I didn't come find you earlier. You know, to say thank you and everything."

"Not necessary," I waved her off. "I lost my temper, and you happened to be there to witness it."

I aimed to end this conversation even before it started.

"No, Mol," she objected. "You don't realize what you did for me — for every woman on the ship. Maybe even every woman in the Network."

I narrowed my eyes and hers filled with tears. "For as long as I've been in the Elite, hell, for as long as I've been alive, I've been an object to these men. It started on the islands, and it only got worse when I received my Placement on the Elite. Soon, I took advantage of it to help my family, but eventually, I got taken advantage of."

Her voice cracked, and my demeanor softened. "The General, he was the worst of them all, and I've been subjected to him the longest. I don't know how much longer I could have lasted, Mol. You changed everything for me. Even if nothing has changed with the Authority yet, it has changed for all of us."

Emilia wrapped her arms around my neck. I returned the embrace, and we held each other in comfortable silence.

"I'm so sorry I was horrible to you," Emilia said, softly.

I drew back, ready to dismiss her apology, but she leaned forward to place a slow, soft kiss on my lips. My body stilled, and she drew back.

"Thank you, Mol," she said, breathlessly. I opened my mouth to speak, and she pressed her perfectly manicured pointer finger against my lips, stopping me. "Promise me you'll be careful.

I nodded, and she moved the door.

"I know how the Authority functions, probably more than anyone on the ship," she pressed. "Don't let your Guard down around the Commander, no matter what he promises you. I've watched him for many years." She brought her hands up to her mouth to collect herself.

"He's bored, Mol, and you're the complete opposite of boring."

Groaning loudly after the door closed, I made my way to soak a long, hot bath to ease my growing tension headache.

I needed time to digest everything and the information everyone — Emilia, Luca, Hope, Julian, and even Sebastian — presented. So for the next few days, I kept to myself, ignoring knocks at the door and sneaking out for meals during off-hours. I tried to make sense of my longing for Sebastian, for the protectiveness when I thought of Emilia, for the disappointment in Luca, the sadness for Mavis, and the urge to fight with Julian.

One of the days, I found a training room for the Guard. There were weights marked with numbers that were all different shapes and sizes and mats perfect for push ups and crunches. I used the bar attached to two beams of the ship to do pull ups. I passed Nico a few times, along with a few other Guard. They were usually coming into the room for training when I was finishing up, and I'd nod politely in greeting. There were too many things swirling in my head to try and fit in anything else.

On Friday morning, while I was laying in bed and looking out the window, a series of forceful knocks pounded against the door. I attempted to ignore them, but they were more persistent than usual, so I begrudgingly jumped out of bed.

Nico and Ray stood, decked out in their Guard uniform with their rifles strapped to their backs. I rolled my eyes at their professionalism — it seemed unnecessary. What could they possibly need automatic rifles for in my doorway?

"The Commander requests your presence," Ray announced, the corners of his lips forming into a small smile, eyeing my appearance. I crossed my arms across my chest.

"Oh, does he now?" I asked, nonchalantly, trying to hide my self-consciousness at answering the door in my sleeping clothes.

"Immediately," he pressed, his expression still showing some form of entertainment, like he was baiting me into doing a trick. I chewed at my nails and looked over at Nico.

"Shut up, Ray," Nico barked. I was surprised by his aggression, but Ray didn't seem phased. "Mol, we're finalizing the plans for the Island Seven visit at breakfast and then departing. The Commander sent us up here to ask if you would please join him at breakfast this morning to give your input."

I could work with that. "I'll be down shortly," I answered. Neither of them moved.

"There's no need to wait for me," I said. "I don't think the dining room has changed locations in the past three days."

"You'll be there?" Nico asked, waiting for me to spell it out for him.

"I said 'I'll see you there in a few,' didn't I?" I scoffed and slammed the door.

Their guarded reactions confused me, and I wondered how many people picked up on my self-induced isolation these past few days. I bathed quickly then made my way. Sebastian, Julian, and Hope were all in their usual spots at the table, but I was happy to see Luca, Nico, Ray, and a few others.

"Ah, Mol," Hope said, a little too sweetly. "I'm so glad you could join us."

Goosebumps rose on my arms when everyone in the room stopped mid-conversation to watch me walk over to take my seat next to Hope. The attention I'd previously grown accustomed to hit me in the chest. I slathered a dark red jam on a piece of toast, only looking up once they resumed talking.

"Let's review the logistics again," Sebastian said sharply. "So we're all on the same page."

I met his stare and immediately felt guilty. I hadn't made much headway in deciphering my feelings. I merely managed to justify every emotion I felt at different points and eventually made a promise to myself to just be cautious. Admittedly, I could have let Sebastian in on it.

"Yes, sir," Nico spoke. "At approximately 1100, we will be twenty-five miles from Island Seven. Far enough away that no one will detect the ship but close enough that our largest aqua boat can get you, Mol, Ray, Luis, Paul, and I there quickly—"

"Julian, you aren't coming?" I asked, my genuine curiosity coming across somewhat accusatory.

"Had you been here earlier, you would have known that Luca and I, you know, being from Island Seven, would cause a stir if we both returned," he said, patronizing me.

"No one cares about you, Julian," I answered honestly. "And Luca hasn't been gone long enough for anyone to ask questions."

"You're being flippant about precedent here," Luca chided.

"It's risky enough that you're going back, Mol," Julian jumped in. "Or is that thought too difficult for your brain to process through your selfish, stubborn skull?"

The Guard members who I wasn't familiar with were looking back and forth between us with wide eyes. Everyone else chose to ignore our bickering, which was quickly growing to full-on yelling until Sebastian's voice cut through.

"Nico, can you please resume the rundown?"

That shut Julian up immediately, and by default, me. I sat back.

"Yes, Commander. When we reach the west end of the Island, Luis and I will step on shore first and give a signal back that it is clear for you and Mol to leave."

"What about Mavis?" No one glanced in my direction except Sebastian, who was dressed to blend into Island

Seven — even with the looser clothing he looked gorgeous.

"What about her?" Julian challenged, annoyed at my interruption.

"Really, Julian, if you can't answer a simple question without barking, how do you expect to be in charge of a full Guard with ammunition?"

He sighed.

"What about Mavis, Mol?" Luca asked.

"She's here, Luca," I answered. "In the brig and slowly starving."

"How do you know that?" Luca asked, skeptically.

"Guess we know who was trespassing the other day," Nico muttered.

Luca turned to Julian for an explanation.

"Minor oversight," Hope said, dismissively. "With Mol's pardon—"

"My what?"

"With Mol's pardon causing some backlash within the Authority, the Commander has now decided to look at the entire process of punishment and retribution," she declared, rolling right over my question. "By default, Mavis is in some-what of a gray area."

"And that means she has to rot next to the General?"

"It means we need to hold her until we figure out how to move forward," she said, irritated, which was slightly better than her ignoring me.

"That's bullshit," I exclaimed.

"What would you suggest we do, Mol?" Sebastian asked.

I chewed on my bottom lip for a minute, considering. "Take her back to Island Seven with us. Her time in the brig surely served as penance for her crime, but you'll still have a chance to figure out how to handle things moving forward without holding her here."

Everyone seemed to be mulling over my response. "Even though that law is archaic and unnecessary," I added, low enough to be nonchalant but loud enough for everyone to hear.

"I agree," Sebastian stated. "Nico, please plan accordingly. Mavis will be leaving the ship with us today. Hope, please notify the Authority and add Mol to our regular Authority meetings — of course, Mol, if you'd like to join?"

I gave him a small smile and nod. In between taking bites of toast and sips of coffee, the realization that I'd soon be home sunk in. I thought about the beach, the smell of the coffee plantations, the hot sun.

"Mol, can you hang back for a minute?" Luca asked, interrupting my thoughts. I was surprised to see everyone clearing out when I looked up. Either I'd been staring off into nothingness for quite a while or the plans weren't as complicated as implied.

Luca paced nervously around the room until we were alone. I sat back into the chair. He closed the door then grabbed the chair beside me.

"I know things are a bit strange right now, Mol," Luca admitted.

"Oh really?" I snorted. "I hadn't noticed."

"I'm happy to see you, though, even if it's brief," he said, pointedly ignoring my sarcasm.

I looked at him, really looked at him. He wasn't saying these words for me — it was for himself.

Lines of guilt circled his eyes, rings around a pained expression. He waited for more hostility, but I wouldn't let that happen. I was stronger than him, stronger than almost everyone. I tried to build a fortress around myself to protect from their alienation, but now, I had to play the role of supportive sister. I could sense Luca's self-loathing and regret.

I smiled at him, trying to be reassuring. He needed it, and he pulled me into a hard hug. He held me for a few moments. My forced expression turned genuine. I could feel the burden of responsibility lifting off of him each second I returned his embrace.

He pulled away and smoothed my hair down, just like Mother used to. "I also have to ask you a favor," he admitted.

My spine stiffened, wondering if I'd been conned into thinking this entire rouse was authentic. "What is it, Luca?" I asked, cautiously.

"Could you grab the stack of journals and notes from my bedroom?"

I bit my lip, remembering the state he'd arrived to this very room in. The General's Guard probably grabbed Luca so abruptly that his work sat untouched. Pages of valuable information next to a half-finished cup of coffee while they dragged him outside to beat him.

"Of course, Luca," I shrugged. "No big deal."

I was so amicable, so trusting in Sebastian who everyone warned me about, yet I was so eager to resent Luca and Julian at a moment's notice. But Luca put his hand on my arm, and the look of pleading crossed his face, I felt justification in my emotional up and down.

"There's something else, Mol," he said, hesitating over the words. "I know you're not going to like this, but it's important."

I offered him a blank look and braced for the impact.

"You'll have to go into Mother and Father's room," he cringed.

I avoided that room for years, not wanting to disturb

how they'd left it — bed unmade, drawers half open. Every day was a struggle in their absence, and somehow, if the door was shut, it helped me form a mental block, making it slightly easier. It took weeks to gather the nerve to enter their room, gathering the courage to seize our valuables to sell them. Their scent of sun and coconuts still lingered in the room. The memory made me feel queasy, even now.

"Mol, please push everything else aside and focus," Luca pleaded, grabbing my hands. "Go into their room and move the nightstand on Mother's side. Underneath it, you'll see the floorboards are loose. Pull them up and grab the box. Bring it back here, and make sure no one knows about it."

I rubbed my eyes and sighed. "What's in the box, Luca?" I asked, and he dropped my hands.

Julian knocked on the door while opening it. His eyes flickered between Luca and I, waiting for one of us to say something, but I only glared in his direction.

"It's time to go, Mol," Julian announced.

He gestured for me to leave the room. I passed him and drove my shoulder into his, hoping it hurt.

16

ONE OF THESE DAYS, I'd show up early to something — or at least on time — and it would play to my advantage. Mavis was already in the boat when I arrived, and she seemed determined to distance herself from the ship and everyone on it.

I brushed past Nico's extended hand and jumped, landing softly on both feet. The boat swayed slightly, but Mavis didn't turn. She was basking in the sun, soaking up the light. The beams only highlighted her frailty, but she seemed at peace. The hard-worn lines carved in her face seemed to be slowly melting away each passing second she faced the mid-morning rays.

I wanted to talk to her, but it felt wrong to disturb her state of euphoria. She'd spent weeks in that small cell in the gut of the ship. Bombarding her would be cruel.

Instead, I sat down on the opposite side and leaned back. Maybe I could pull Mavis aside when we escorted her back to her house on the island. It'd be a short walk — I was fairly certain she lived in one of the shared complexes on the west side of the island, but I could talk fast.

I wondered what her conversations with Hope were like when we were first brought on the ship, what happened to those men who were aboard with us, how she interacted with my parents, if they were vocal about their feelings on the Authority.

"I hope you don't mind, but I had Nico grab this for you," Sebastian said, quietly, causing me to jump.

He handed me my jacket, the one I'd arrived to the ship wearing. I was at a loss for words at his gesture, but he seemed to expect my annoyance at doing something without asking. I shrugged my arms into the familiar material and zipped it up. I was shivering.

Sebastian sat next to me, and the boat shot to life. Within seconds, we were out in the open air. The small crowd that gathered to see us depart dispersed, but I turned back in time to see Luca wrap his arms around Julian.

I snapped my head back forward, trying to appreciate the vastness ahead. I breathed in the air and tasted the salt on my tongue. The stress became smaller and smaller the farther the boat moved from the main ship. I leaned my head back, wanting to expose my face to the rays. I extended my arms out behind me, and the boat hit a small wave. A small splash of warm water sprayed over me.

I smiled at the whipping wind, causing my braids to beat against my neck. I started to take my hair out of the confinement. Sebastian watched me, entranced by the light strands waving in their release, and he moved closer to me until our hips touched. The feelings between us heightened my inhibition. Each interaction between us was building up to something big, and I wondered if he felt it too.

I watched a grin spread slowly, the same one he'd given me on the roof deck over coffee. I'd thought of his smile hundreds of times since then, but I hadn't built up any sort of immunity. His teeth were a stark white contrast against his dark skin. I wagered I was one of the few fortunate who saw his smile recently — or ever. His braids were tied back, giving me a full view of his thick, glorious neck, which connected to broad shoulders and a hard chest.

It both was a shame and a privilege to witness his presence here in the beautiful open sea.

Lust pulsated through my veins. Combined with the weightlessness of zooming across the water, I felt brave. I leaned into him, knowing close proximity was the only way he'd hear me. I inhaled deeply, pressed my lips against his ear. "You know, you're pretty handsome," I pointed out.

His laugh, low and deep, cut through the wind. I'd never been more certain of anything than the idea that I could listen to nothing but that sound for the rest of my life. I willed him to understand how I was feeling. He put one arm on the rail behind my back.

"I've missed you," he admitted, tangling his fingers into my hair.

I melted into him. He pressed his palm against the outside of my knees, I curled both of my legs into his lap. We sat like that, appreciating the closeness, and watched Island Seven grow from a blip to an expanse on the water.

Our breathing paced evenly, and our limbs moved even closer when the boat turned. The closer we got to land, the harsher the current. After the fifth hard wave, I untangled myself from him, just to reassure myself I could hold steady on my own, without some part of him touching me.

His eyes were curious, searching my face for an understanding of my abruptness. I brought one of his hands up to my mouth, and I placed a soft kiss on fingertips.

"Commander!" Nico yelled in our direction. "We're about five minutes out."

I forgot all about the other people on the boat, and suddenly, I was very aware of our audience. The four Guard members, including Nico, were watching us, all with varying expressions of confusion. Sebastian squeezed my hand, and as I turned back to him, I caught Mavis's eye. Whatever emotion she felt was guarded. I opened my mouth, unsure of what to say, but she immediately averted her eyes.

A pang of disappointment tugged, but I was quickly distracted with executing the plans the Guard and Sebastian made over breakfast. It was so methodical and precise that I managed a chuckle. This wasn't a war. This was Island Seven, a place where everyone was too hungry and poor to pay attention to anything that was going on. In fact, we probably were drawing more attention to ourselves flanked by Guard in their full riot gear than if we just made a quiet entrance in Island Seven garb.

When the boat touched sand, Mavis scurried off, and I opened my mouth to call after her.

"Okay, Mol," Sebastian said, refocusing my attention. "Now what?"

I asked for this voyage, but I hadn't given any thought to what we'd do when we actually arrived. A part of me pushed the task away, not wanting to jinx my chances at returning home, which I now realized how incredibly stupid that was. I spent most of my time at the market, a secluded beach or two, the Education Hall, home, and visiting Luca. Those would all be good starting points. I mustered up all the positivity I could manage.

"We walk," I decided, hoping my feigned confidence made its way through.

"Works for me."

"We need to ditch the guns," I said, gesturing over my shoulder.

Nico stepped up. "Not happening, Mol. Julian would kill me." There was a little grumble in his voice, so he cleared his throat. "Commander, I do not think it is in your best interest to be without escort here."

I scoffed, and Sebastian looked between the two of us.

"Okay, let's find some middle ground here," he offered. "Nico, you and the others should maintain a hundred-foot perimeter around us, so you'll be there if we need you."

"Which we won't," I assured him.

Nico and the other Guard glanced around the beach and eyed the road ahead, unsure whether to believe me. "Yes, Commander," Nico said finally, then wordlessly communicated with hand signals to his counterparts.

"Ready?" I asked, extending my hand for Sebastian, and we spent the next few hours wandering.

At some point, I could have drawn every inch of Island Seven on a piece of paper, but with Sebastian, I was a stranger seeing some of the aspects for the first time. Living here and scraping by each day numbed me. After living in luxury, I had to digest the poor conditions.

The roads were in shambles. I stumbled a few times, and Sebastian gripped my waist to steady me. That was a bonus, but it didn't quell the uneasiness — two months ago I could have walked through here barefoot and blindfolded with no trouble. I'd lost the ability to easily navigate over the unevenness. I doubted that was even an issue on Island One and Island Two.

Sebastian remained almost completely silent, simply taking in his surroundings and nodding in understanding at my explanations. Most of the buildings on Island Seven grew worn down over the years and were haphazardly repaired. Few people had windows, although all of the homes had doors — that was a recent initiative to keep stray dogs out.

I showed him the large, cement rooms where children went for Education. There were a few books and papers scattered on the floor but otherwise empty. It looked quite ominous, but I remembered going home for lunch almost every day. I pointed out other areas of interest to Sebastian — where I once got into a fight with a kid twice my size, where I climbed a tree to find a great view of my favorite beach, where I once found a ream of cloth, almost completely undamaged.

When we circled further south, I finished my deliberation on whether to take him to the market. I decided it was wise to show him what a poor rationing and rule system can drive people to do, which outweighed any possible resentment for the fear of punishment in bringing a member of the Authority to the area.

The market ran in an area of abandoned, boarded-up buildings with little-to-no sunlight, but the darkness didn't hide mine and Sebastian's presence. A handful of people did a double take at the handsome stranger, but otherwise, we were left alone.

The corridor was narrow, but it was more crowded than I'd ever seen it. People, with evident desperation, carried around small bags and spoke in quiet tones. The makeshift tables were littered with items washed up on the beaches. Pigeon carcasses hung from pieces of driftwood, and I pulled Sebastian's attention away from a child attempting to pickpocket him to point them out.

"Told you they were foul," I bragged, and he either didn't hear me or chose not to respond.

I passed yet another woman selling bags of rations then

stopped abruptly. A man, short, dirty, and unrecognizable to me, turned an old wood barrel into a makeshift jewelry show-case. Assorted trinkets littered the top, and I dug through them. I never did find out what happened to Mother's necklace when I was captured, and I looked for it eagerly. It was too valuable to sell here, and I had nothing to trade for it back, but that didn't stop the disappointment from flooding in when I didn't find it.

"You okay?" Sebastian asked, finally breaking hours of silence.

"Just looking for something," I said, moving my eyes over all of the items one last time. "Didn't find it."

"You've spent a lot of time here?"

"Unfortunately," I answered. "The Authority doesn't give out enough rations for the people of Island Seven to survive, and since we're forbidden to eat from the trees in our own backyard, we've resorted to creating this. Over the past few years, I've sold off all of my parents' possessions. Well, all except one — I intended to sell one final piece on Island Six, but I was picked up by your Guard."

It wasn't lost on me that the man responsible for all that hardship was walking by my side.

"Luca never approved, but he couldn't stop me — we were desperate." I swallowed. "After we were notified that our parents died, we did what we could."

We reached the end of the market and were standing back in the sun. The last few moments felt like a trial, a final test to show myself how much I'd changed. I wasn't sure if I passed or failed my own assessment.

I smiled up at Sebastian, but I knew it didn't meet my eyes.

"Well, I believe you're all caught up on all the rules I've broken," I teased.

He assessed my false happiness and put his hands on his hips. "Oh yes?"

"Fighting the Guard, holding the General at knifepoint, fleeing my Placement, selling off goods, writing illegal letters," I listed off on my fingers. "I might be the most dangerous person on the island."

He pressed his lips together, a failed attempt at hiding his amusement, and stepped closer. "Maybe I should have the Guard hold a closer radius."

"Maybe — but there's one thing I think we should do first," I said as my heart pounded in my chest.

"What's that, Mol?"

In theory, it would be so easy to slide in even closer and press our bodies against each other, to escape this miserable place for a few minutes of euphoria with him. I bit the inside of my cheek.

"Do you trust me?" He nodded before I even finished saying the words, and I lost my resolve.

I caught flashes of the Guard following us, and the urge to ditch them overtook everything else. I grabbed Sebastian's hand gleefully, letting a giggle escape.

"Run!" I yelled, and we took off.

We weaved together in and out of trees, following the hidden paths I'd uncovered long ago. We checked over our shoulders to see if Nico and the other Guard kept up, and after twenty minutes of making our way deep into a bank of coconut trees, I brought us to a stop. We both tried to catch our breath.

"You're fast," he praised.

"You kept up easily enough."

He tilted his head. "Is that what you wanted to do? Escape from the Guard? Albeit successfully this time?"

I laughed at my own nerves and threw my head back. I

froze when I saw what was above me. Without a word to Sebastian, I made my way over to the nearest tree and began climbing.

"Mol, I don't think I can follow you up there," Sebastian called up to me.

I ignored him and continued upward. My arms were wrapped around the sturdy trunk, my feet positioned to push me up in a jumping motion. I was already about twenty feet up when I looked down at Sebastian. His arms were crossed, and he was leaning against another tree, watching me.

My pace quickened, and I made it to the top after a few more pulls. I wrapped my legs around the trunk to hold myself in place. I grabbed one of the fruits — a coconut, something I hadn't seen in years — and twisted it out of place.

"Watch your head, Sebastian," I shouted, then let it drop to the ground. I repeated the pull and drop motion a few more times, until Sebastian gathered a small pile at the bottom of the tree. I watched his smooth muscles move, appreciating his patience for this little momentary reprieve I led us to.

"He's here!"

"Commander?"

Nico and the other Guard members approached, all panting from the exertion with their heavy gear.

"We're fine, Nico," the Commander held up his hand, quelling his panic.

"Where's Mol, sir? I'm going to—ouch! What the hell?"

I threw a coconut in his direction, not necessarily intending to hit him, but my aim was better than I thought. I scurried down the tree and jumped to the ground to apologize.

"Damnit, Mol! If you wanted coconut, we could have just jetted over to Island Two," he said. "Would have saved a lot of running and pain."

"Where's the fun in that, Nico?" I asked, innocently.

His expression hardened. "Julian is—"

"Not here," I answered and turned to one of the other Guard. "Can I have your machete, please?"

"Sorry, what?"

"Your machete," I said, gesturing to the knife encased at his waist. "Can I borrow it?"

The Guard looked at Nico then Sebastian for some sort of approval, and one of them gave it to him. He handed it to me, and I made a show of slashing it through the air. The blade came down hard, stripping the hard, green husk of the fruit until it met the cream-colored nut, the inner shell. I dug the tip of the blade down, creating a sizable hole, and handed the coconut to Guard whose knife I borrowed.

"Thanks for letting me use your blade."

He took it, tentatively, not sure how to proceed.

"Ever had fresh coconut?"

He shook his head.

"You can drink the water," I explained. "And then scoop out the white stuff, the meat, and you can eat it raw. It's all very sweet."

I didn't wait for his response and got started on the second one. In about ten minutes, we all sat, leaning against the trees, hydrating and making small talk. It all felt very strange and normal at the same time.

"Where to next?" Sebastian asked, reaching for my hand.

"Home."

17

My entire house could fit in Sebastian's quarters on the ship. After all, it was only one story with three small bedrooms, a tiny kitchen, and a small room off of the front door that connected all the others. We mostly left everything our parents set up. Although, once Luca converted our kitchen table into one of his many workspaces, we moved the couch closer to the wall. We were lucky — not every family secured a couch.

I usually kept to my bedroom, and compared to my quarters on the ship, it was juvenile. The bed, just big enough for me alone, took up most of the room. The rest of the floor was littered with assorted objects I used in training, all various weight.

As I stood in the connecting room with Sebastian, the contentedness among the trees and coconuts in the jungle faded, leaving only embarrassment and sadness. I had nothing to be ashamed of, but even as I reminded myself of that fact, I couldn't shake it. I felt the need to apologize to him for the chipped mug I poured tea into, the cracked walls, the uneven floors, the mismatched items.

Sebastian was silent. He took a sip of peppermint tea — the only kind I could find — and set it down on the table. He liked to have the facts before he formed an opinion, I knew this, which is why he mostly kept to himself, weighing all options prior to making decisions.

But I was too vulnerable here to tolerate that.

The lock was broken when we arrived, and my emotions were raw when I crossed the threshold.

"Remain outside, with the Guard, Nico," Sebastian ordered, stepping in behind me. Heading off Nico's argument, he added, "Not up for discussion."

I was so grateful for him in that moment, but I couldn't put voice to it. My throat felt scratchy and thick.

"Tea?" I asked, coughing out the one syllable.

"Sure," he answered, looking around.

I studied him now, sitting next to me on the couch, unsure of what to say but knowing I didn't want to stay quiet — the lack of conversation created a vacuum of pity I wasn't ready to face.

"My apologies, Sebastian, I didn't offer you the grand tour," I said.

I pointed out the kitchen, Luca's room, the small bathroom, my parents' room, and finally, mine.

"So that's it," I finished. "This is it."

"I see."

"I know it's not much," I offered.

"No," he paused. "It's just not what I expected."

"I bet none of this was covered in Hope's files," I muttered.

He seemed startled by my response. It pulled him out of whatever deep, dark soul-searching he was doing and cleared his throat.

"I can't believe how bad this is," he admitted.

Instinctively, I pulled away from him.

"No, wait, Mol, sorry," he apologized. "I'm not saying this right."

He stood up and paced around the small room. He lifted his arms above his head, resting his palms on the top of his skull. His shirt pulled tight against his back, and I averted my eyes.

"I was born to be the Commander," he explained. "I thought there was no choice but to go along with what my father, my mother, the Authority, the Network expected of me, and obviously, I sought no need to question it."

For once, his eyes weren't on me. They were fixed into nothing, lost in memories.

"Why would I?" he asked rhetorically. "I had everything at my disposal. Food, clothing, alcohol, women."

I winced.

"I've probably been to a few thousand of those awful dinner meetings. In my younger years, I treated them as a joke, and no one encouraged me to do otherwise. After all, I was somewhat untouchable.

"It wasn't until my father got sick that I understood the full scope of responsibility, and I poured everything I had into becoming what he wanted me to be. I was ruthless. I was efficient. I gave no second thought to what impacted thousands of lives. Essentially, I became a mirror image of my father, and once he died, I gave up. I was bound to carry out duty, and I was too comfortable to consider any alternative.

"Over time, I began to heal, and I started to notice the holes. Some of the reports weren't adding up. The General seemed to spare no expense for the Authority, but he was extremely diligent about what went on in the islands. And of course, you're familiar with Hope's preferred method of guidance."

He turned to look at me, and I nodded for him to continue.

"In the past few months, I've started to dig further. Secretly, of course. I couldn't trust anyone. I couldn't be sure of anyone's true motives, and I didn't know what I would uncover.

"I began to put pieces together but, again, I was trying to figure out how to proceed and what — and who — people were loyal to. It wasn't until the night that you jumped the former General that everything was revealed to me. Julian, obviously, was mortified at the General's behavior. Even Hope's ironclad facade dropped a bit when that Elite woman fell into the glass. And of course, the guests there were friends of Felix. Although I want to believe he has the best intentions, his delivery is a little off sometimes.

"I've been working with Julian and Hope to get a full picture of the Authority's control and damage to put a plan of action together to move forward. Unfortunately, we don't know exactly who favors Hugo's moral compass over one more like yours and mine, Mol."

"I don't know if I'm the best metric of morality, here, Sebastian," I admitted. "Haven't you seen how much pain and trouble I've caused in the past few weeks?"

His eyes lit up at the joke I didn't understand. "I seemed to have downplayed a key part in this story."

"What's that?" I asked.

"You."

I blinked.

"You came in, ready to fight, eager to stand on your own beliefs, despite all consequence," he explained. "And now, seeing how you were raised, and the conditions you were raised in, makes me even more in awe of you. How could such ferocity and beauty come out of such a horrible, desperate place?

"You sparked a new wave of action. There's rarely an hour that I don't think about how lucky the Authority, the entire Network even, is to have you."

I gulped, feeling suffocated by his words.

"Sebastian," I said, evenly. "What if this isn't what I wanted?"

His demeanor shifted, scrambling to pull himself back together after he'd cracked open his ribs and exposed his heart.

"I suppose we could find you a Placement elsewhere," he answered, somewhat distantly.

"What if I don't want a Placement?" I pressed. "What if Placements aren't right for people? What if I don't want someone else deciding what's best for me?"

He mulled this over, and I interrupted his thoughts. "I don't fit in at the Elite. I can't be an Engineer, and I probably don't want to be a Medic or a Foreman. I don't know how to cook, and I'm a mediocre seamstress. I'd actually probably be most suited on the Guard."

"Is that what you want?" he asked, a hollow humor in his tone.

"I don't know what I want, Sebastian," I admitted. "And that's the point. I don't know where I belong anymore."

"Well, it's certainly not here because no one belongs here," he said, dismissively. "People are starving. The facilities are in terrible shape. The homes are held haphazardly together. There's not enough room or rations here to survive, let alone live."

His anger built with every sentence that came out, and

in a weird reversal of roles, I collected all of the sparks ready to erupt from my mouth and swallowed them down.

"I know," I soothed. "I'm one of those people, Sebastian. Or, at least, I used to be. So where does that leave them — and me?"

"Mol, I don't have all the answers yet," he confessed. "I'm not sure I ever will or that you really want me to. I don't know where you belong or anyone else."

In two quick strides, he was in front of me, kneeling and placing his hands on my knees.

"But I do know that with whatever authority I have within me, I will make this life worthy of you," he promised.

Chills ran down my arms, contradicting the burn in my throat. After months of lies and deceit from everyone I'd been surrounded with, I finally had confirmation — Sebastian was true. He was the real deal. His words were the most honest thing I'd ever heard, and I accepted them. I wanted to respond, to tell him how much that meant to me, how our short time together has meant everything, changed me in so many ways I have yet to completely understand, how much faith I have in him, and most of all, that I believed him.

Instead, I kissed him.

I leaned forward, and in one smooth motion, our lips met. We moved together, gently, at first but then my unspoken words and suppressed emotions surged, and I parted his lips with my tongue. My heart swelled, and with it, an urge to touch every inch of his skin. Soon, our hands were everywhere. My hair. His neck. My waist. His abdomen. I couldn't get enough.

I relied on instinct, feeding off his sighs of pleasure and tightening grip. My tongue glided over his bottom lip, and when he ran his hands over my chest, and, the pleasure was so intense I trembled. I felt the hardness between his legs, pressing against the apex of my thighs, and I wrapped my legs around his waist. All I could think of was that I was desperate for more. More Sebastian. More movement. More touching. Less clothing.

I pushed him off, forcing him to lay on his back, and his eyes widened in surprise. I straddled him and deepened our kiss. An involuntary moan escaped my mouth at the friction, and he gripped my hips, hard. There was too much fabric between us, stifling the rhythm between our bodies.

We moved to my bedroom wordlessly, barely breaking apart. The hems of our shirts lifted over our heads. I dragged my fingers over his chest and abdominal muscles. His hands, then his mouth, explored my lines and curves.

The tempo changed to an excruciatingly slow, but necessary, adoration. I loved how the veins of his arms stuck out from his muscles, creating a pathway all the way up to his hard shoulders. He coaxed me to fall back onto the bed with a few nips on my neck, and his body was heavy on mine.

His lips moved along my jawline, down to my neck, then back up to my ear. "Does this mean you'll stay, Mol?" he whispered. "With me?"

I traced my finger lightly over his lips. "I'll stay."

Something snapped within him, a renewed desperation, and we moved together in a frenzy of friction. I could have sobbed from the intensity.

"Commander?" Nico called, stepping in, and I froze.

We stared at each other, shocked to speechlessness, for the longest beat of my life. His eyes met Sebastian's, whose gaze I refused to meet, and Nico shook his head, quickly turning his back to the room.

"Sorry, sir," he said, hurriedly. "It looks like rain is approaching from the east. We should make our exit now."

And then he ran out.

"Thank you, Nico," Sebastian called out after him. "We'll be out momentarily."

I jumped to my feet, gathering random articles of clothing and throwing them on. Sebastian rolled over onto his back, crossing his arms behind his head. I tossed his shirt onto his chest and sat down on the edge of the bed.

The temptation to replay my mortification on repeat crept up. Nico saw me half naked and in a compromising position with his Commander. I considered asking him not to tell Julian, but I also was willing to bet Nico hoped to never think or speak of this again.

"I definitely prefer my bed on the ship," he said, letting his immunity to any type of embarrassment shine.

"It is much bigger," I agreed.

He kissed me quickly. I closed my eyes, and my throat constricted against his chest. His arms snaked me in a protective hold. My vocal cords were lost somewhere with my common sense. This was probably not what Luca meant when he advised me to "test out the trust," but I wasn't that surprised to discover I didn't really care. I made my choice. I would return with Sebastian and help him navigate the uncertain waters of the future aboard the ship, indefinitely.

"Sebastian, can I have a minute alone? I don't know if I'll ever be back here again and—" My voice faltered.

"I'll wait outside," he said, tugging on his shirt on.

He headed to the front yard, closing the door behind him. I laid back on the bed. Within twenty-four hours, I went from the undesirable girl from Island Seven to kissing two people. I brought my fingers to my lips and pressed my hands against my waist and chest, trying to hold onto the thought of his touch for just a little longer.

Sighing, I grabbed a spare sheet from underneath my bed and tied it up into a pouch. There was nothing here in my room, where I spent my life, worth keeping. I had plenty of clothes on the ship, and I didn't need much else, but Luca did. I shoved the papers and journals from his room in my makeshift bag, and then crossed over to my parents' room. I was in and out within a minute, and I held my breath the entire time.

After a turning around to silent goodbye to the memories of the house, I glanced out the back door, where Luca and I spent hours in sweet ignorance, and a Mimosa plant caught my eye. I took a deep breath, appreciating its determination to grow and thrive while maintaining a careful defense.

Without a second thought, I grabbed my spare pocket knife from my bedroom.

18

I HAD no patience for Luca's eagerness when we returned to the ship.

The trek across the choppy water wasn't an adventure — it was nauseating. I was ready for a long, hot bath followed by many hours of uninterrupted sleep. But my brother stopped me after I stepped up out of the transport boat.

"Commander, good evening," he said, quickly, acknowledging Sebastian in a sign of respect.

The Guard members, including Nico, were dismissed for the evening. Luca eyed their exit until it was the three of us, and I tapped my foot impatiently. "It will be a better evening once you get out of my way, Luca," I grumbled.

"Did you get my notebooks?"

"Yes," I answered.

"All of them?"

I shoved the bag into his arms. "It's all in there, Luca. Now if you'll—"

"Wait," he said, sharply. "Just a moment, please."

I sighed, and Sebastian draped his arm across my shoulders. We watched Luca dig through the bag. His hands moved frantically when he found then flipped through the notebook with the well-worn black cover.

"As much as I love standing here and watching you read, Luca, I want to get back to my quarters," I said, ready to succumb to exhaustion.

"Actually, I think you both should to come with me," Luca argued, holding up a page of scribbles. "Or at least, I think you'll want to."

"Lead the way, Luca," Sebastian offered.

We followed him up to the lab in silence. Sebastian placed a reassuring hand on my back, and I reached for it, holding it proudly. An unfamiliar sense of attachment settled over me with Sebastian, hidden behind an oblivious and happy Luca. He muttered to himself and sped through the empty halls.

The lab had evolved to a replica of the one on Island Seven, catching me by surprise when we entered. There were scraps of metal and random notes sprawled across a few tables, but instead of the rundown rooms at his other Placement, they were surrounded by pristine white decor.

"Did she get it?" Julian asked hopefully, ignoring the fact that he could have asked that question to me directly.

Regardless, Julian breathed an audible sigh of relief when he nodded then hopped up on one of the stools. Luca picked up a few tools to start making adjustments, his head snapping rapidly between the pages of the propped-up notebook and his hands. Not only did he have the most spare parts I'd ever seen him collect in one place, there were also huge boards with buttons and a few large boxes at his feet.

"What are those?" I asked Julian, pointing to the mess of wires and metal pieces.

"Circuit boards, parts of a radar system, a navtex receiver."

I blinked. "What do they do?"

"Well, I'm not exactly sure," he admitted. "But Luca has been tearing apart pretty much every piece of the ship with defunct electronics on it. That big piece over there came from the bridge — apparently it hasn't worked for decades. Most of this stuff hasn't."

"Oh," I nodded. "Isn't that what those ministers were discussing a few weeks ago, Sebastian?"

He raised an eyebrow. "No one has spoken with either minister, to my knowledge, since that evening. They are primarily overseeing the repair and upkeep of some of our bigger ships that have been out of commission since my father became the Commander."

"Why aren't they focusing on this ship?" I asked. "I mean, it looks fine to me, but this one has some pretty precious cargo."

He beamed down at me, a smile tugging at the corner of his mouth, and I brushed away the jolt of attraction that shot through my body.

"The thought process was to focus on getting us out of this 'cramped' space and onto a bigger ship," he explained. "We'd be able to cover a greater distance in a shorter time and carry more supplies with a bigger vessel."

I mulled that over, knowing he saw the humor that these quarters could be considered small.

"I'm sure we can find some furniture for you to destroy once we relocate."

Our smiles folded in, and we became enthralled in watching Luca for at least thirty tedious minutes. The faster his hands moved, the faster Julian's leg shook with anticipation. I seriously considered stabbing him in the thigh. I moved closer to Sebastian. His eyes remained fixed on Luca's work, but he wrapped his arms around my waist, pulling me into him. I hummed at the gesture, and Julian's leg immediately stopped moving. His head snapped so quickly I was surprised his neck didn't break.

"General, could you please go and collect Hope?" Sebastian asked. "Perhaps Nico and another Guard you trust to stand outside the door?"

"Yes, Commander, of course," he said, through clenched teeth.

Sebastian had a way of diffusing tension without directly calling attention to it. His ability to observe and calculate a practical solution is what made him a great leader — or rather, will make him a great leader. There was just a lot he needed to sort through.

"I wouldn't have been too hard on him," I whispered.

"Your definition and mine probably differ dramatically," he argued. "I doubt Luca would take kindly to the two of you doling out more black eyes while he was trying to work."

Julian and I didn't seem to agree on anything these days, except that we were angry at each other. Sebastian sensed my acceptance of his statement, and I watched his lips form a smirk.

When Hope arrived with Julian a few minutes later, I fought against my knee-jerk reaction to spring away from Sebastian. I didn't need anyone's approval, but that still didn't stop me from noticing Hope's praising eyes. Nico and Ray popped in the room to greet Julian before taking their places outside the door, ensuring we wouldn't be disturbed.

Luca chewed on the end of his pencil.

"Did you get everything, Luca?" Hope asked.

After a few beats of silence, Luca nodded and held up

his pointer finger. He sat up and flipped to another page of his notebook then began the frenzy of movement once again. We all took this as an indicator that he would be ready to share and leaned in toward him. Everyone was expectant, but I was completely in the dark. I was the only one who wasn't in the loop on his project, but I refused to ask what was going on in front of Julian, imagining his condescending look, so I squinted and tried to piece it together myself.

Luca was holding some sort of rectangular electronic piece with a metal stick poking out at the top. Metal buttons were scattered on the side, and two circle mesh pieces took up the front of the contraption. There were ten similar pieces lined up to his right, each with a little different configuration. Almost simultaneously, he used a screwdriver to tweak a much larger green box. It had a few knobs on it and a large dial with numbers from one to eighty-eight.

I sorted through my memories of General and Felix — people who mentioned Luca's projects. Could this be the radio technology they were discussing? The ones that could allow people to talk to each other over long distances? Such a shame the General couldn't use it now to keep up with women...

Luca jumped up and thrust one of the devices into Sebastian's hands, ignoring all the typical formalities of interacting with the Commander. His eyes were wide, bloodshot, reflecting the rest of his disheveled state.

"If you'll do me the honor, Commander?" Luca said. "Okay, so, just turn it on using the switch at the top..."

When Sebastian and Luca flipped the switches, on the handheld and large green device in tandem, a green round light appeared.

"Well, that is a good sign," Sebastian praised.

"Now, if can move dial to the number seven... yep, like that, we should be able to start communicating."

Luca picked up a black device, which was attached to the box with a cord, and stood proudly, waiting for the Commander to use his own device.

"And I'm supposed to do what exactly?"

"Right, my apologies, Commander," Luca said, sheepishly. "Hold up the device to your mouth, press the button on the top, and begin speaking."

He mimicked the movement while explaining it. Sebastian raised the mesh to his beautiful, full lips and pressed the button at the top. A garbled buzzing sound came from Luca's device that hurt my ears. Everyone else seemed encouraged by it.

"Well done, Luca," Sebastian said in person, and his voice came out a little lower than usual through the green box Luca attended to. Everyone in the room cheered, including Ray and Nico, who turned to watch us instead of the hall.

"We'll have to test for distance and clarity next."

"How fast can you get the others up and running?"

"Do we have more pieces we can use?"

"Who do you think we should test this out with?"

"This is incredible!"

"Luca, you're a genius."

My head swirled with the dialogue and questions, trying to reconcile how much was about to change, and I noticed the grin falter from Sebastian's face.

"What is it?" I asked, reaching up to tuck a fallen braid behind his ear. "You aren't happy?"

He stepped to the middle of the room and let out sigh.

"I'm afraid these walkies and the radio development are going to push plans further along more quickly than I hoped. Because while I trust everyone in this room, and I'll admit it has taken me some time to, I do not trust others in the Authority with this type of technology or the other ideas Luca has put forth."

Sebastian sat down heavily on the stool Luca previously occupied, gingerly placing the walkie on the tabletop.

"In the next few days, I will reveal plans to disband the Authority's chokehold on the islands and seek other means of growing and maintaining the Network." My jaw dropped open along with Luca's, Ray's, and Nico's. Hope and Julian didn't seem phased by this announcement, and I wasn't entirely comfortable with that realization.

"We'll begin by lifting the curfew and all bans on communication via letters, trade, and inter-island travel," Hope jumped in, a slight brag to her tone. "There is still so much to go through — the ration details, Placements, et cetera."

Sebastian promised hours earlier that we'd figure it out the future together, and something felt off about this declaration. It wasn't just my jealousy — I was self-aware enough to know that.

"We feel this will be a good start into kicking off a new era of prosperity and trust with the Authority," Hope said, cheerfully.

There it was. The "we."

I couldn't pin the blame on the Authority any longer. I was surrounded by the people who were looking to make changes, now making me an accomplice in any changes that were rolled out. I refused to be an enabler.

"And how do you plan to make these decisions moving forward?" I challenged, failing to keep mistrust out of my question.

"By data and research, of course," Hope said

dismissively.

I scoffed. "Because that's been going so well for the past few decades?"

Silence fell between us. It wasn't the calm, tentative quiet that prevailed while we were watching Luca.

"And I suppose you have the solution?" Hope frowned.

"I can only speak for myself and through my own experience," I admitted.

"Obviously," Hope injected.

I paused to look at her, surprised by how quickly she turned from approving to angry. At this point, I guess I couldn't expect anything otherwise. I was way past the point of growing my list of friends. Ignoring Hope, I turned to speak directly to Sebastian.

"You've sat aboard this ship for almost all of your life, and until today, you had no understanding of what life was really like on the islands. And shouldn't that be a key part in making changes?"

"Point taken," Hope snapped. "Perhaps you'd like to explain this idea to the Authority directly?"

I gulped. Although today, among the coconut trees and even briefly in this room, I felt a sense of security, but I wasn't totally comfortable with the idea of meeting more Authority members — let alone speak in front of them.

"Thank you for the suggestion, Hope," Sebastian cut in. "I think that's an excellent idea."

I groaned internally, but outwardly, I nodded.

"I disagree, Commander," Hope said, eyes narrowing. "Respectfully, of course."

"How do you expect to make real change if you shut down other viewpoints and ideas?" I fired at her, not oblivious to the back and forth motions of all the heads watching this conversation unfold. "Respectfully, of course."

She ignored my jab. "We're in favor of transparency, obviously," she explained. "That's where the reports and numbers come in."

"That only tells part of the story," I argued. "I grew up on the most feeble island in the Network, and when I offer up my experience, you dismiss it?"

I was slowly walking toward Hope, clenching my fists. Julian stepped in between us, facing me, his eyes tight. I straightened my posture, attempting to grow four inches in a matter of seconds.

"I think we've had a lot to take in today, wouldn't you agree, Commander?"

"Don't patronize me, Julian," I spouted, pushing my anger onto him. "It's not like I was going to pin her down until she agreed with me. We're not arguing over attention, here — we're making important decisions that could save or destroy everything!"

"Oh, we are, are we?" Julian scoffed.

"Enough," Sebastian declared, standing up. "It's time for us all to retire for the evening."

The Commander stood next to me, putting on a show for diplomacy's sake. I was too irritated to concede. Every part of me refused the inclination to look at him.

"I would encourage you all to think about what our opportunities are, and I will do the same," he said, moving toward the exit. "And thank you, Luca, for sharing this with all of us. I look forward to hearing the results of your further testing."

"Yes, Commander," Luca said, moving back to his desk and picking up a few half-finished devices.

I looked at Hope and Julian, then the quiet duo of Nico and Ray before I finally met Sebastian's gaze. Then I stormed out.

19

THE PULL away from sleep was strong, and I fought it. I'd been struggling to catch even a few hours of rest these last few nights because of Mother and Father's arguing. It was happening more frequently, and they were less stealth about it.

Still, I could only pick up bits of their jabs back and forth. The desire to listen in faltered days ago. I closed my eyes and distanced myself from the wall. I positioned my pillow to cover both of my ears and thought of crashing waves in front of me and hot sand underneath my feet in an attempt to lull myself back to another world.

"It's now or never!" Mother hissed, the pitch cutting through the cotton pressed against my ears. Something smashed against our shared walls, and I sat up. It was silly to remain optimistic about keeping my eyes closed now.

"Eva, please," Father pleaded. "Calm down. You'll wake the children."

She laughed. "We need to wake them! What don't you understand? This is our chance."

"There will be another opportunity," he promised. I imagined my mother shaking her head at this, knowing that she wouldn't be pushing so hard if that was the case.

"No, there won't," she said. Her tone was emotional, the kind that resulted from anger not sadness.

I pulled a pillow up to my face. The desire to scream into the fabric was growing, but when I opened my mouth, nothing came out. My lungs were empty, uncooperative caverns.

I felt lightheaded, unable to keep up with my parents' arguing in low tones. My throat felt too small. I sucked in air, each intake painful and exceedingly difficult. Blackness encroached my consciousness, but it wasn't sleep. I wasn't entering a tranquil state or calmly sinking away. I was panicking.

My parents were such strong, steady figures in this life, and listening to their relationship falter made the world crumble around me. There were cues building up for weeks — months, now that I was paying attention — but I hadn't pulled them together until now.

Something happened, and something would happen. I couldn't make out the details, but Mother's experience was so vile it seemed like it physically pained her to discuss with Father. This urgency, though, was new. Rash decisions were never a part of the dialogue, and I didn't know what to make of it.

A deep, powerful cry from Mother froze my entire body. My skin chilled completely, and my toes went numb. My lungs were raw, gasping in air.

"It's okay. It's okay. It's all going to be okay." My father promised, and the sobs became muffled. "We'll go."

The effort to understand was too great. Pressure

mounted on my lungs so heavily that the anxiety overtook all my other senses. The worry was suffocating me. Every whimper and sniffle was torture, and I willed it to stop.

My eyes opened.

I was no longer victim to the repercussions of my parents' mistakes, not under their roof, in my bedroom, or even on Island Seven. It wasn't even the emotion causing my distress. It was the General.

His body was on top of mine. His weight pushed down onto my upper body, restricting my movement and airflow. His hands were so tight around my throat that there was no chance at screaming for help. I wondered if I'd ever breathe normally again.

I wrapped my hands around his forearms awkwardly and dug my fingernails into the sensitive flesh of his wrists. He wasn't much stronger than me, and I silently thanked his years of pathetic, overindulging behavior for benefitting me just this once. He was bigger, though, and he was determined to inflict serious pain.

I thrashed my arms, attempting to throw him off balance. My legs, freed briefly, aimed to kick the sensitive spot between his. My knee made contact, and he groaned, releasing my neck slightly and readjusting his hold. My shoulders were now pinned into the mattress by one arm and the other covered my mouth. I breathed in greedily through the space in his fingers and wondered if my bite was strong enough to tear one off.

"I don't want to kill you yet," he slurred, sending spit all over my face and onto the pillows. "I just want to cause you pain."

I shifted my head from side to side, trying to force him off, but it wasn't effective. I looked up at his red-lined, beady eyes, and noticed my knife — the one that was confiscated when I first arrived on the ship — in his front pocket. He could easily jab the blade into the soft skin of my stomach or chest.

I pushed aside all traces of panic. Panic shouldn't be anyone's first instinct. It's an important emotion, but it's useless most of the time. To break out of his hold, I needed to relax. I would have to do it. Struggling would only tire me out. I willed my muscles to unwind, focusing on the General's odor, a mix of sweat and liquor, instead of his grip. If I had any control over my body at this moment, I would surely vomit.

My muscles shook with fear, but I traded it for determination. If I acted quickly, without him realizing what was happening, he wouldn't get the chance to hurt me.

Again, I moved my legs, but he had the leverage in this situation, even as he mumbled incoherently. I'd have to stoop to his level of insane vengeance to survive without lasting damage. I forced my limbs to go slack. It was a ridiculous idea, but I laid under him, acting lifeless.

His instant confusion was what I'd been hoping to invoke, and I threw my arms up to break out of his hold. I rolled out of bed and stood up. My hands grasped my throat, not that it could ease the pain and help air move through it. The General fell into a confused, drunken heap on my bed but was in the process of righting himself.

I stepped forward to grab my knife, looking up just in time to see his fist flash in front of my face. It made contact. The nerve endings all exploded at once, and I collapsed.

The beating of my crumpled body didn't stop on the floor. Punches would require him to lean over and exert extra effort, but kicking was equally effective. It was probably even better for what his goal was. I defended my head at first, not wanting to add to the throbbing pain, then moved my hands to my midsection. His boots connected with my back, thighs, and ribs. I slid inches across the floor with each blow.

He kneeled down and leaned over me, taunting more promises that I could barely hear above the ringing in my ears.

"It's time, General," someone yelled. The voice sounded familiar. Maybe it was closer than I thought. I couldn't be sure. I tried to open my eyes, but the lids were too heavy.

The trembling of my muscles and insides kept me awake. Once adrenaline faded, the numbness passed quickly. Sharp pain erupted up and down. My cheek throbbed more than anything, followed by my sore neck. I inhaled and rolled over toward the window, taking a few minutes to appreciate that I'd made it to see the early dawn sun.

Me aside, it looked like a normal morning in my quarters. The sheets were tangled from my earlier sleep, and everything else was fairly neat and organized. Whoever let the General out of his cell carried a key to my quarters because the door was still in tact. Whether it was carefully planned or spur-of-the-moment decision upon his escape, he sought me out to leave a message. For whom, I wasn't sure — me, Julian, Sebastian — because anyone who turned against him was fair game.

Alarm bells hadn't sounded in the ship, meaning no one knew the General escaped or paid me a visit. By now, he was likely long gone, taking up residence in one of the abandoned islands or shielded by Authority loyalists. I stood up, wincing at vertebra attempting to righten.

I decided if I could get to the kitchens, I could do anything. The supply cupboard was stocked with pain salves and bandages. I could get ice from the freezer. The thought of putting a freezing pack across my burning hot skin drove me forward. I made it down the back staircase to the kitchens in record time — for someone who just got the shit kicked out of them, at least.

I brought up a hand to my eyes, shielding my pupils as they adjusted to the bright kitchen light. My head was pounding from the exertion. I beelined to the walk-in freezer. Emilia was just exiting it, closing the large steel door behind her. She yelped in surprise then rushed to guide me to a chair. It was metal and cool, and I sighed in relief. It irritated my throat. I gingerly touched where the General's hands were.

"Ice," I choked out, not recognizing the sound of my voice. "Please?"

The General should have forced me to swallow broken glass — it would have been less painful.

Emilia grabbed a towel from the fresh stack on the counter, wasting no time running back into the room she just left to get a massive handful of ice. She kneeled in front of me and gently placed the pack to my neck. I relaxed into her care, listening to her mutter about how bad the bruises would be.

"Who did this to you?" Emilia asked, bringing her ear close to my mouth.

I huffed out air, finding that I couldn't make the man's name roll across my lips. I pointed to her knees where the flesh was still pink and recovering. Her eyes widened in surprise, and she transferred the pack of ice to my own hand and sprinted out.

I grabbed a few ice cubes from the pack and sucked

them down, hoping to calm my swollen insides. After a few large, deep exhales and inhales, I was no longer alone, and I didn't even have to look up to know Sebastian entered the room, closely followed by Julian. I was, however, genuinely surprised to find Hope silently hovering by the door when I finally raised my head.

Julian and Hope stared at me in disbelief, but Sebastian's expression was composed. His eyes raked over my slumped figure in the chair. I noticed his hands were clenched so tightly together, they shook. Julian paced around the kitchen, spewing profanity. I could see the anger radiating from him, and I appreciated it. He was the embodiment of how I was feeling, but I couldn't react on it. I slid another ice cube into my mouth and glanced at Hope.

"You're not the only casualty tonight," Hope sighed.

Her words were another kick to my stomach. Blinking lights of terror shot on in my brain imagining Luca or anyone else aboard getting attacked. I swallowed, with great difficulty.

"Luca?" I croaked out.

"He's fine," Sebastian added quickly. "But his lab isn't."

Hope raised my blood pressure in a matter of seconds, but Sebastian's words brought instant relief. Even with the scarcity of electronics and tools, those could be reworked; however, Luca was irreplaceable.

"It appears whoever orchestrated our former General's escape also managed to raid the engineering department," Hope explained. "All of the walkie prototypes were stolen, and there's a lot of damage. Luca is seeing what is salvage-able right now."

"Nico is up there with him," Sebastian said, assuaging me.

He knelt to examine my injuries. His fingers grazed the

side of my face then drummed against my midsection. I gripped his hand, somehow expecting he'd hold me together.

"I know you're tough, Mol," Sebastian said, low and breathy. "But I don't know how much more I can take of seeing you like this."

His words warmed my fragile insides, and I visualized them healing at expedited rates. His lips grazed across my cheek. I brought my hands up to his shoulders. A banging caused us both to jump in surprise. Julian swept his arms across the counters, sending metal serving utensils crashing to the floor. He was releasing all of his rage toward the General and our situation, but above all, I could see the disappointment in himself for such a horrific turn of events on his watch.

His destruction was familiar. I mentally swapped kitchen tools for bedroom furniture and watched him wreck the area. After a few minutes, he was breathing heavy. I could see the anger dissipate, and his face turned apologetic.

"I know I haven't been there for you or even very good to you recently," Julian confessed, his voice threatening to break. "But I will track the General down and make him pay for what he has done to you and Luca and the rest of us."

From anyone else, I could appreciate the valor. He pledged to avenge the harm inflicted, but I was not in the mood for a tender moment.

"So dramatic," I said, hoarsely.

The words crawled out of my throat and sliced the all the way up. My vocal cords were raw, but if I didn't show my strength now, I was afraid I'd be sidelined. And I was ready to fight.

"Put me in Guard training," I demanded barely above a whisper.

Julian looked at me as if I'd grown a beak in a matter of seconds. I slowly and painfully stood up. Sebastian grasped my outstretched hand.

"And show me how to use a gun."

20

"THEY'RE HERE," Sebastian announced.

Luca didn't even notice his Commander's presence as I coaxed him into nibbling on bites of food he claimed he was too busy to eat. Starting from scratch on another set of walkies taxed him to a new level in the past few weeks. It'd been difficult for him, but it wasn't much easier for me to watch his deterioration.

Aside from coordinating the transport boats to bring in the scraps from Island Seven, Julian wasn't much help. He was too much of an enabler. He also disappeared from the lab for long stretches of time to put the Guard, the ones left, anyway, on an even more rigorous training program, which I joined along with some others on board. Emilia and a few other Elite approached Nico and I one day asking for rudimentary training of their own. I spent afternoons with her and the others, always surprised by their ferocity and strength, and I healed.

I didn't notice it at first, but after a few days of constantly being surrounded by people, I realized Sebastian and Julian set it up so I'd never be alone on the ship. I understood their concern, but any residual mental complications from the General's attack morphed into a calculated desire for revenge I swore to myself I'd get to enact. Still, I didn't press the issue with either of them. We were all too busy, and secretly, I loved the attention.

For the first time in my outcast existence, I'd formed friendships, and I'd been missing it without even being able to fully understand it. Albeit, most of these people were ordered to be by my side, but they weren't forced to be nice to me or get to know me, so I overlooked it. Even under the strained circumstances, I found contentment and a purpose that I paved for myself.

Nothing quite met the satisfaction I felt up on the deck, though, when Julian and I learned I was a better shot than him. That discovery, with the weight of the metal in my hand, was more gratifying than punches I landed on him during training. He was full of trepidation at first, hovering over my stance and aim, but after I fired a few rounds at the targets, hitting almost all of them in the bullseye, he backed off.

It quickly turned into a round of "I bet you can't hit that," and he scrambled to move the target around the deck and placed it at odd angles. He refused to acknowledge my skills and chalked it up to beginner's luck. Eventually, he grew so annoyed at my accuracy that I was dismissed for the day.

I beamed at Nico, who had been secretly working with me on handling and aiming a weapon since the night of the attack.

There was plenty to do other than sharpen my aim, too. Once the missing crew members were accounted for the day after the General escaped, the Placements reshuffled and the rations and artillery needed inventoried to assess the damage.

The ship should have seemed empty with fewer people on it, but it felt more full. There was idle chatter in the hallways with people hurrying to their next shift of inventory. Sit-down meals were no longer heavily regulated and only available for a few of us — the dining room became an open, welcome place for everyone to gather. I slipped in on occasion, grabbing a spot next to Emilia and suffering through her grilling me for details on Sebastian, Luca, and Julian. We laughed over fruit and coffee when I told her about the mortifying time I walked in on Julian and Luca in his bedroom, and she filled me in on some stories on her family and the other islands.

I'd gotten to know most of the Guard, too, but I was pretty shaken to learn that Ray was one of the departed. It was likely he who tipped off the General about the walkies and grabbed the key to my quarters. I moved my hand up to protect my throat.

"Mol?" Sebastian asked, gently, pulling me out of my thoughts. "Did you hear me?"

"Yes, sorry," I apologized. "All of them? Is everyone from the Authority here?"

He shook his head. "Not yet. Everyone is arriving in waves due to our shortage of transport boats."

Sebastian was a vision in a fitted, light gray suit, but instead of his usual high, tight collar, he left several buttons undone, revealing his hard chest. He playfully tugged on the ends of my hair, shifting his attention to Luca for a progress update. I'd gotten one myself by simply watching him. He'd made miraculous progress in such a short time, getting major headway on replicating the walkies, and version two seemed to be slimmer in weight and size than the first.

Sebastian patted Luca on the back, praising his production rate.

"Mol, can I have a word with you?" Hope called out, walking down the hallway.

"Just one," I said under my breath.

I followed Hope to the stairs, taking them two at a time. She led me to a room I'd never been in. The mahogany desk took up most of the space, flanked by rows and rows of files — a dead giveaway that this was where she conducted much of her work.

I stared at her expectantly, waiting for whatever reprimand or advice she was going to offer up.

"I know in the past you've expressed a certain distaste for a style of clothing different than your own," Hope acknowledged. "I'd like to ask you to reconsider for the evening."

"Oh?" I asked, curiosity overpowering indignation. "Why's that?"

Hope sighed and walked over to the oversized cabinet, pulling out a set of Elite-issued beauty products and a large garment bag.

"Although I do appreciate some of the statements you've made in front of a few Authority members, tonight is all about damage control and setting a new precedent," she explained, handing the items over. "We don't need any additional distractions or deterrents from our goal."

"What are you implying?" I inquired.

She straightened up and looked at me directly. "I do not know what to expect in that room tonight, and while I know our Commander respects your opinion, others will not."

"I'm not going to mess this up," I snapped.

She squinted at me. "Your temper will stay in check? No outbursts? No anger? No attitude?"

I saw her point, but I would never admit it. Sebastian planned to announce some major changes that will cause enough trouble without a girl from Island Seven clad in fighting gear ready to stab anyone who makes a foul statement.

My boots and the floor suddenly became very interesting to me.

"You follow my line of thought here?"

"I know what is at stake," I admitted, still not totally conceding her point.

"As I've heard it said, it's probably not best to rock the boat in already choppy waters," Hope said, an unusual sparkle in her eye. "Now, let me help you. The two of us moving quickly should help this process."

The next few minutes sailed by in a whirlwind of hairpins, lipstick, zippers, and snaps. I helped Hope dress in her gray gown, her signature color. Her neckline was somewhat high, and her sleeves were long.

"Uh, Hope, are you sure this is okay?" I asked timidly.

"Of course it's okay, the Commander insisted you attend."

"No, I mean this," I swallowed and gestured to my exposed skin.

She laughed and pointed at my reflection in the glass outside the dining room. I didn't recognize the person staring back at me.

My long blonde locks, normally thrown back or in a messy braid, were tamed. The makeup covered any residual bruising I'd sported from training or the General's attack, and it highlighted the features of my face nicely. The dress was sleeveless and gold, touching all the way down to the floor with beading flattering my nonexistent curves. The neckline fell right below my collarbones. From the front, it looked at least somewhat conservative, but down the back, there was a deep slit along the spine. It started at the shoulder blades and ended just above my hips.

I preferred pants and boots, but this look didn't seem to be completely terrible.

"Oh good, you're here," Emilia said, breathing a sigh of relief to Hope. "Introductions just started, but I'm still waiting for — oh wow, Mol, I didn't even recognize you."

Insecurity flared up when Nico and Julian appraised my appearance. My legs shook in nervousness, and I shifted my weight between my feet, which were laced up in high heels.

"You look amazing!" Emilia exclaimed. "Wait until the Commander sees you. Doesn't she look great, Nico?"

He looked at me again but kept his mouth shut. We resumed normal interactions under the guise of training or guiding others, but we still were recovering from him seeing a little more of me than we'd both like to admit.

Julian, eager to move on, pushed me into the room, and I looped my arm in his.

"You're beautiful, Mol," he said quietly, meeting the eyes of those who were staring at us.

I waved him off. "It's all an illusion, Julian," I promised. "You know this isn't the real me. I feel more Elite than Island Seven right now."

"I'll admit the dress helps accentuate things, sure," he admitted, pulling us to a stop so he could turn to face me. "But you've always been the most beautiful woman in the Network to me. I mean it."

"Even when I'm completely red-faced and determined to show you up?"

"Especially so."

I smiled to cover up my speechlessness and grabbed his arm a little tighter. Letting the awkwardness settle between the two of us, I glanced around the crowded dining room, seeing some familiar faces from other meetings — and a woman by each Authority member. I'd expected a formal dinner laid out, but instead, the table was adorned with paper and pencils.

"My dear, you're looking exceptional this evening," Felix bellowed from across the room, eliciting a few head turns in my direction, causing Julian to sigh. "Oh, I must introduce you to everyone!"

I released Julian, and Felix spent the next few minutes spinning me around the room, gushing about me and the person he was introducing me to. I usually only managed to politely smile and nod before he whisked me away again. His eccentricities made me feel at ease, oddly enough. Instead of straining under the pressure of meeting so many new people, all of whom examined me thoroughly with their gazes, I felt light.

He introduced me to a gentleman from Island Three, whose name and Placement I didn't catch, when Sebastian entered the room. Everyone turned to face him respectfully, and he waved, encouraging everyone to continue. He started speaking to a group of people close to the door, but his eyes wandered.

The man Felix introduced me to asked about my history, whether I was from Island Two, and if my father was an Authority member. Felix answered on my behalf. I wasn't good at multitasking like Sebastian, and he already knew every member of the Authority quite well — he was raised to attend these functions, after all.

It wasn't until he got Julian's attention and started speaking hurriedly that I knew he was looking for me — he just hadn't recognized me. There were a number of other women in the room, but it wasn't like I blended in.

Hope tapped a water pitcher with one of the rings on her hand, the airy sound of clinking glass cut through. "Ladies and gentlemen, shall we begin?"

As if it were choreographed, everyone made their way to sit. Dresses twirled, contrasting the lines of all the men's suits. I stood still, uncertain of my place, until Hope appeared and guided me.

Like most meals, Julian sat at Sebastian's left and Hope at his right, with a space for me next to her. I took my time walking behind Hope, wanting some sort of attention from Sebastian. We were in a room full of people, some of them more dangerous than others, and I craved a signal, some recognition from him that we were in this together.

He stood at the head of the table, and I walked slowly, finally catching his eyes. A sense of pride swelled when his eyes traveled all over my body and he exhaled. Holding his gaze, I made a show of walking around my chair, so he could appreciate the show of skin on my back. I sat down, and he cleared his throat.

"Members of the Authority, I thank you for your schedule adjustments in making this meeting possible," he said, graciously. "As you know, there have been quite a few changes in the Network over these past few weeks with the General's departure and some exciting new technological developments."

There were several nods of approvals, but a few others mumbled their grievances. I tried to memorize who the others were, suspecting they'd give us the biggest trouble. Hope waved her hand dismissively under the table when I reached for a pencil. She inclined her head toward Nico, who was doing exactly what I was attempting. He, however, blended in on the side, and when I glanced back to the table, I noticed a few men were watching me. I turned up the corners of my mouth at the ones I met and folded my hands on my lap.

"What you may not know is the changes that happened with your Commander during the same time."

All residual whispers cut off immediately. I bit my lip nervously and flipped my gaze between the Authority members around the table and Sebastian.

"You have watched me grow up and into this position, becoming your Commander, and I have not questioned a single task I've been asked to oversee or decision you all have made," he said, pausing for emphasis. "That stops now."

The room was at attention, that was for sure. Even the Elite, who were supposed to be attending to the Authority and filling glasses, were still.

"Over the past few months, I have been looking into the Authority's reign — the rations, the Placements, even visiting the conditions on Island Seven. Needless to say, I am appalled."

One person scoffed out loud, earning a glare from Hope.

"While you have all been enjoying luxury and having every whim fulfilled, there are people in our Network facing starvation and illness for no reason other than your poor decision-making and abuse of privilege." He gritted his teeth. "As of tonight, the Authority will be disbanded and new leadership will be rolled out under my direct advisement."

That's when the yelling started.

It wasn't even directed at Sebastian, necessarily, the one who was making the change — but at each other. It was as if they were finally caught doing something bad by a parent, and they were trying to blame it on their siblings. They all created their current reality, and they were acting like misbehaving children.

Sebastian let this carry on for a few moments, even leaning over to say something to Julian that made him smile, and he called out, "Silence."

The room immediately stopped buzzing.

"My hope is that we will build a future that far exceeds what we've built in the past," Sebastian continued. "Have you ever stopped to ask yourself why there is no inter-island trade? Or any freedom of choice in Placement decisions? Or why we ration so strictly? And why people cannot even eat the fruit off of the trees that grow in their own backyard?"

My breath hitched in my throat. Julian's eyes caught mine, and I beamed with pride. Sebastian, this beautiful, graceful, intelligent man with such swagger about him, so much power, was talking about the fruit trees that were so important to me. He was good. He would be good, do good. He would establish prosperity and happiness for the Network.

I couldn't see why people didn't appreciate it.

The doors to the room opened quietly. I could make out Luca's figure in the doorway, and I immediately tensed. He whispered something to Nico, who gave a nonverbal cue to Julian, then disappeared. Sebastian opened his mouth to speak again but closed it when he caught Julian's expression. Julian stood up to deliver the message to his Commander, who nodded and waved him to leave. He turned, once again, to address the room.

"If you've never considered a new reality, I encourage you to," he said, offering a small smile. "If you are eager to usher in a new way of life alongside me, I'd be excited to include you."

Sebastian stepped to the side of his chair, closer to Hope,

and every eye in the room followed him as he moved toward me. Every muscle in my body held still, mesmerized by his movement.

"If not, you can show yourselves out or go running back to the former General. Either way, you are no longer welcome here unless you want to adopt this brand of ideals and leadership. Now if you'll all excuse me, I have to go clean up the mess you've made."

He offered his hand to me, and I took it, standing up to be by his side.

21

"WELL COMMANDER, if I may say so, you and this lovely lady caused quite a stir this evening," Felix proclaimed.

Julian, Nico, Hope, Sebastian, and I were huddled around Luca, who managed to configure a new, extra large technological box into "picking up" the walkie waves — whatever that meant. Unfortunately, there were dozens of different frequencies that he was currently switching between. The tension was palpable. We'd all been brought up here on the promise of a breakthrough, but Luca was still struggling.

"We don't have time for your games, Felix," Luca spoke up, not breaking his concentration on locating the right channel.

"Oh, Luca, my—"

"Are you in or out?" Luca cut him off.

My tolerance for Felix was high, but Luca, after spending years under his thumb at his Placement, clearly didn't share my sentiment. I didn't know the details of whether Luca reported to him regularly or what part Felix owned in the development of projects, but out of all the

Authority, Felix seemed to be the only — if not one of the few — who ventured outside of comfort to understand what was happening around the islands. I gave him credit for that at least.

"Luca, I have to admit that I am a little perturbed that you do not already know the answer to that," Felix sputtered out.

Finally, Luca glanced up to him, his expression expectant. His eyes dropped to Felix's fingers, which were smoothing down his mustache.

"Let's take down the bastards and start fresh."

I laughed, and the tightness loosened a few notches between all of us in the room.

"Can we expect others to join us?" Julian asked. His forceful tone surprised Felix, but he righted himself.

"I daresay once they stop arguing with each other over nonsense, a large portion of the Authority — or former Authority, shall I say? — will be stepping up," Felix mused. "Of course, they will want to retain their wealth and luxuries, but I believe eventually they will be okay with the idea of sharing."

Hope nodded. "We can work with that."

A low, humming sound emitted from the box Luca toyed with. The noise started out small, but every millimeter he turned the dial, the larger it grew.

"What is that?" I asked, fascinated by the rumbling sound in my ears.

"Static," Luca explained, letting his excitement spill out in measured breaths. "It means I'm narrowing in on their signal."

The static dropped in and out in a few torturous minutes. The sound tapered out, and so did my enthusiasm, only to be reinvigorated each time it roared back to life.

When a screech erupted from the box, the loudest yet, Hope's hands shot to her ears.

"Sorry," Luca muttered, wiping off the beads of sweat I'd watched accumulate across his forehead. He snapped two pieces together then adjusted his grip on a screwdriver and resumed his slow, steady movements.

"Okay, I think I've got it back," he said.

The static held steady. Our bodies all moved together, closing any remaining space in the semicircle around Luca's desk. I stole a glance at Sebastian, who remained quiet. His eyes were narrow in anticipation, but he didn't give away anything else on his face. I looked down to take his hand and noticed my gold heels were still dangling from it. He wrapped the other around my waist, much to my satisfaction.

"On my left…"

"Move that … they … he …"

Luca's attention moved to another one of the many knobs, and he turned it, twisting his screwdriver in the opposite direction.

"We need to take another inventory … you … no …"

The dialogue was muffled, but it was there. I leaned into Sebastian, unable to hold the anticipation on my own two feet any longer. I could feel the apprehension radiate from those around me, but no one was affected more than Luca. Each word seemed to shock him, jolting his core, causing him to tweak his position ever so slightly.

"I've counted at least fifteen … down here."

"Will that … enough for…?"

"Yes, that ship only has … which won't be enough to withstand our attack."

Their words ricocheted over the walls, bounced off the floor, and collided with realization in my mind. They were planning an attack. I didn't think we were prepared for it. We'd been practicing hand-to-hand combat for weeks, yes, but most of the ship's firearm training was lacking. We'd need more time to prepare for a full-blown battle. Days could be spent studying defensive maneuvers and analyzing tactics.

I swallowed mouthfuls of air, and Sebastian tightened his hold on me. I drew from his resolve, haphazardly attempting to remain calm. These people so loyal to such an evil man, were arrogant enough to spill out their plans over a technology that they didn't understand. Surely this was an indicator that they wouldn't pose that much of a problem.

"We can reach... in a half day's time from our current position."

"How do you know they haven't... since we left?"

"They've been bringing Authority members to the ship all day. They're... giving away their position and bringing some of our side onboard."

Luca made one final adjustment then dropped his hands in finality.

"The General wants us to drift more west. Alert the Captain."

"Isn't that farther away from the target?"

"Yes, but we want to catch them off-Guard. It'd be stupid to try and attack tonight, when they are already riled up. We expect whoever remained to need at least three days to formulate retaliation, so we want a quick movement in and out."

They couldn't possibly expect those they left behind to stand idly by in the wake of their destruction. I almost yelled at the box, demanding these men tell me what they thought this would accomplish and why they thought this was in their best interest.

"We'll be long gone by then."

I inhaled sharply at the sound of that voice. Sebastian, Julian, and Luca all exchanged a look of annoyance, and after Sebastian's nod of approval, Luca handed Julian the wired-in walkie.

"Ray, it's delightful to hear your voice again," Julian said, bitterly, after he pushed the button down to halt their sounds.

I half expected Ray to jump back on and offer a snide comment, but there was only silence. The feed was strong, confirmed by the low static. I smugly imagined the escaped Guard staring at each other with their jaws dropped open in panic.

"Put the former General on the walkie immediately," Julian demanded. "He and the Commander should chat."

Seconds ticked by. We all stared silently at the black box, wondering what uncharted territory we moved into. They probably all received Education on negotiation or managing high-pressure situations, but all I could do at this moment was bite my nails and look on.

I quickly became painfully aware of how much about the Authority, Sebastian himself even, that I still didn't know. But now was not the time to ask.

The static halted, and a deep, definitive throat clear came through. I shook off the repulsion, knowing that sound came from the mouth of a man I despised, who climbed on top of me, put his hands on me, and kicked me until I passed out from the pain. Sebastian kissed my shoulder, and Julian handed over the receiver.

"Sebastian," the General broke through, his voice was gruff and dripping with disdain.

I brought my hands together against my stomach, pressing against all budding nausea and outrage inside me.

"Hugo," Sebastian replied, coolly. "How are you doing this evening?"

I'd hoped he'd fire back at the General with equal fervor. He was, after all, the man responsible for so much unnecessary torment. The Sebastian I knew, however, refused to let his anger overtake his decision-making. He was too level-headed, and I wished he would borrow some of my careless agitation.

The General paused, and it stretched for miles.

"What do you want, child?" he barked. "Notice anything missing from your ship? Called to thank me for the gift I left behind?"

His eyes flickered to me, and I watched something very close to rage maneuver over his features.

"Actually, Hugo, I was just mulling over your plans for attacking us and wondered if we should expect you in the morning or if you'll need more time to collect your intel from some of the people who are making their way back to Island One?"

The General didn't release his finger off the button before he started shouting. A smile pulled at the corners of Sebastian's mouth. He glanced around at us, appreciating the opportunity to unbalance the General.

"If you're done, Hugo," Sebastian bragged, "we have plenty of other things to discuss."

"We have nothing to discuss," he barked back.

"There's no need to resort to violence—"

"I do not need your opinion," the General snapped. "I, unlike you and your gang of misfits, have decades of experience, and I will carry out my plans."

"What do you really want, Hugo?" Sebastian kept his voice even, but I could see the struggle when laughter erupted from the speaker.

"Well, my boy, at first, I just wanted an endless supply of women and booze, which I enjoyed happily for many years until that stupid bitch came along," the General barked. "Then, I wanted to see you in pain and take all of your power. Now, I will see to it that all of your ideals will be destroyed — and trust me, I know what they are after that little stunt you pulled tonight."

As the General spoke, the sound became slightly muffled and more venomous, his lips closing in on the speaker. The effect was grating on my confidence.

"There are still many loyal to me in your midst," he explained in a sing-song tone. "I will love nothing more than to watch you see everything fall apart."

Sebastian swallowed his words and turned to Felix and Julian. "Get a firm grasp of our ammunition and range of attack," he demanded. "Vet all of the remaining Guard and see how many volunteers we can gather from the rest of the crew."

He pressed the button again while watching both men run out under his order.

"Surely we can work something out that satisfies you without bloodshed?" Sebastian asked, innocently.

Again, the General's only response was laughter.

"Fine, Hugo, I tried to be diplomatic," Sebastian continued. "I'll be at Fernandina at 1100 and ready for protocol. I'll see you there."

He stepped back and handed the receiver to Luca. "No more correspondence from us until then. Monitor all of their dialogue — they might think we cannot track a switch of channel. Keep me informed."

"Yes, sir," Luca nodded. Instead of picking up his tools, he placed two large circles around his ears that were held together by a strap at the top of his skull. A line at the end of the left ear connected to a cord that he slid into the black box.

I looked at Sebastian for an explanation.

"Lucky find from Island Seven," he shrugged at me and turned to Hope. "The Captain should be familiar with the coordinates for Fernandina, although it has been a few years since we've made our way to the island."

He looked at his watch. "And he'll have to hurry to get us there."

"What orders do you have for the others, Commander?" Hope asked, straightening up her posture. She was readying herself for her place in this battle.

"Get the intel and then some rest," Sebastian answered. "Meet back here at 0600 to finalize strategy."

Sebastian reached out for my hand. "Shall we go prepare ourselves?" I inclined my head and followed him.

With our fingers entwined, we walked upstairs in comfortable silence, digesting everything that happened in the past few hours. All fragments of panic that circulated in my bloodstream molted into eagerness quickly.

Once we were both inside his quarters and very alone, he dropped my shoes.

He stepped around me, and I forced my mind to erase the tension, worry, and confusion that overtook most of my brain. I should ask Sebastian more about Fernandina, his experience there, or even where it was. We could strategize a plan once we reached the island. There were a million other things I could have done or asked, but I kept my mouth shut.

His fingers moved excruciatingly slow, tracing the deep V line down my back. I shuddered noticeably, and his body reacted similarly. His hand paused over the zipper of my dress.

"May I?"

I nodded. He placed one hand on my hip and carefully pulled the zipper down. I appreciated his care, his proximity, the new and wonderful sensation of being undressed by someone else. The gold fabric slid down with his help, replaced by a trail of kisses. His lips burned against my skin. The intensity between us was heightened by his movements.

He monitored my body's reaction to his touch, and seeming satisfied, he let the dress slip to the floor. I was completely bare underneath it. His eyes grew wide with anticipation, the same ones I'd seen earlier in the dining room. He opened his mouth to say something, but I dragged my pointer finger over his lips and shook my head. We'd have time to talk later, to remember who we were and what was up ahead.

My shyness was recently been replaced by hard-earned self assurance, and confidence overshadowed any doubt. I didn't feel the ship's coldness over my body any longer, only in my chest, which ached. Judging by the way Sebastian was staring, he'd never get the thermostat turned up again.

I reached up my hands to unpin my hair, letting the loose ends tumble down. He remained still and observed every tendril. I dragged my fingers through my hair, down my neck, and across my chest slowly, delighting in his paralysis.

He edged back against the door, raised a knuckle up to his mouth, and bit down. We were about to put everything and everyone at risk, and I simply needed him and I to be together, sharing this intimacy before we gave ourselves over to everyone else.

I leaned in closer to him, dying to feel him against me again, and he moved to take control of the momentum. I grabbed his wrists and slammed them against the door-frame over our heads. I smirked at his stunned expression. I nipped his lips and let his hands fall.

I unbuttoned his jacket, taking care to run my hands over his abdomen and shoulders. I didn't mirror his gracefulness as I removed the fastenings on his shirt and at his wrists. I undid his belt and let his pants drop to the floor. My hands shook slightly, but I distracted him by nibbling on his chest. I stepped back, allowing him to remove his socks and shoes, and suddenly, we were both completely naked and staring at each other. No fabric, rules, or inhibition separating us any longer. We were equal.

In a flash, his arms were around me, and he was kissing my lips, my chin, my temple. I soaked it in, pressing my face against his chest and shoulder when he cupped the back of my neck, pressing our skin together.

He whispered sweet, calming words into my ear, and gripped the back of my thighs. Effortlessly, he lifted me, and I wrapped my legs around his waist. By the time we made it across the room, both of us were gasping, panting, and crushing our limbs together, and then we fell back onto the bed and into each other.

22

"WHICH ISLAND IS THAT, SEBASTIAN?"

His eyes followed the line of my finger, which was pointed straight ahead off the roof deck, perpendicular to the front of the ship.

"Isla Fernandina," Sebastian said quietly, a hint of a smile tugging at his lips. "If you turn around and squint hard enough, you'll be able to see your home, Island Seven."

The confusion settled over me. I tried to find my bearings, but it was impossible out in the open sea. I glanced back at Sebastian whose silhouette contrasting slightly against the early morning rays.

I folded my arms across my chest. The sun hadn't started to beat down quite yet, so the breeze still felt a little chilly. I appreciated the cold; it kept me on edge against the lull of the water's calm movement. Under different circumstances, the water hundreds of feet under me could be smoothing, but now, the constant rhythm of the waves paired with the apprehension on the deck reminded me of a clock counting down.

Everyone stood on the deck, confirming plans for the hundredth time in whispers. Julian and Nico briefed the Guard and volunteers hours earlier, and now, we waited for the inevitable, which would be in about twenty minutes, according to Luca's walkie sleuthing.

"We're all set with our stations, Commander," Julian announced as he and Hope joined the two of us.

Sebastian nodded in confirmation, but his gaze remained fixed outward. I fidgeted beside him.

"Perhaps you could check in with the volunteers?" Sebastian suggested.

Julian turned to look at the non-Guard members, a mismatched crew of people standing awkwardly in their designated spots. "Yes, that is an excellent idea, sir," Julian agreed, and he wrapped his arm around Nico's shoulder, speaking hurriedly before sending him off.

"One can never be too prepared," Hope said, wringing her hands in anticipation. "Especially when it comes to the future of thousands of lives."

I choked out a laugh, finding humor in her nonchalant attitude.

"Are you sure you're ready for this, Mol?" Hope asked.

"Oh please," I brushed her off. "Fighting might be the only thing I'm actually good at."

"Fair point," she admitted, signs of amusement spilling over her expression. "I'd say that along with 'causing a general disturbance.'"

"She cleans up okay, though," Julian teased.

"Not that it's doing us any good right now," Hope huffed.

We all watched the sun slowly climb its way higher into the sky. I felt a little jealous of its definite, unwavering confidence in its movement, but I was grateful the light gave me a better view of Island Seven. I'd found plenty of other things to hold a grudge about in my life. I felt fine about letting this one go.

Luca burst through the roof deck door, letting it slam against the ship's exterior. Felix, very out of breath, followed him. Luca looked outward between Fernandina and Island Seven. Between pants, Felix was in a fit of nervous energy. His eyes darted at all of us, our weapons, and whatever Luca and Sebastian were focusing on.

"They should be approaching any moment," Luca said, his voice shaking slightly. "From their dialogue, I confirmed that they will arrive from the north."

"The transport boat is ready for you, Commander," Felix said eagerly.

"Thank you," Sebastian offered to both of them: "I'll wait for their arrival before departing."

I'd run through all the details of the plan in my head so many times that I could probably recite it backward. Sebastian, Julian, and a few of the Guard would ride in the transport and attempt to negotiate terms of a treaty with the General and his men. Apparently, it was customary for the two leaders to meet in the middle prior to a battle. From everything I knew, we'd never had a fight or anything close to this in the Network, but they all seemed very familiar with the practice.

Wishful thinking and many hours were spent speculating what would satisfy both sides. Hope and her endless files were crucial to preparing the document that seemed to satisfy everyone. That was the easy part. Readying the rest of the ship for the backup operation was nerve-wracking. No matter how much confidence Sebastian instilled in the group, I could see the jitters right alongside the piles of weapons.

I had to show strength. For the volunteers, for Sebastian,

for the people at home, for the memory of my parents. It would be easy to fall into a spiral of uneasiness, but we'd come too far. There was so much opportunity ahead of us. We could establish true change for everyone in the Network. If this was one small roadblock to making that happen, so be it. I could withstand anything for that.

"What is that?" The cry rang out from the lower deck, but it carried. The man could have shouted that in my ears, and it would have provoked the same gut-wrenching induction of panic. He was standing on the exact spot where Sebastian and I shared our picnic, but instead of throw pillows and dinner, an assortment of guns littered the ground. I clenched my fists, my brain somehow knowing this was a sign of what was to come.

A blip appeared on the horizon to the north, which Luca predicted, and we watched stoically. The dot drew closer, and the details became clearer. In a matter of minutes, the tiny, toy-sized ship grew into a ginormous, thundering piece of machinery. Our ship was sizable by my standards. Its round, bloated body served its purpose. It navigated waters steadily, large enough not to be too noticeably swayed until this moment. But I immediately understood why it was small in everyone else's mind — it seemed like a joke compared to what approached.

The vessel the General commanded was monstrous. It was oddly triangular and incredibly sleek, with rows of windows and stacks of weapons protruding out, directly at where we stood. It was intimidating, to say the least.

"I'll check on the transport boat," Felix stuttered and took off, almost sprinting back through the door.

Many shared his concern, I was sure of that, but I was too determined to back down or judge anyone else for being terrified. I was happy to give all I could for this cause, and I was surrounded by enough people who were, too.

A pang ripped across the open air, closely followed by another. The sound continued, steady, and echoing. The first shot landed in the ocean, about fifty feet away. The frightened yells and screams from our own ship drowned out some of the firing.

"Cover now!" Julian yelled, and everyone ran for protection. A cloud of bullets cascaded overhead, seconds away from scattering across the lower deck.

"Guess we won't need that transport boat after all," I said aloud, suddenly realizing no one was within range to hear it.

Fresh screams of terror and the sounds of metal colliding were almost deafening. The rapid fire plunked the surface of the upper deck now, offsetting the rhythmic patterns from their long-range guns. I peeked out from the metal structure where I huddled, grateful that it didn't seem like anyone was physically injured. Sebastian and Julian were a few feet away, shouting ideas on how to proceed. Luca and Hope crowded together in an uncomfortable position close to the heavy door that Felix crossed moments prior.

The shots increased in number, and Julian hollered instructions for a counterattack. I grabbed ahold of my automatic weapon, casually slung around my shoulder if it were a mere accessory, and readied it for firing.

"Luca!" I screamed, and his eyes snapped to mine. "Get the hell out of here when we fire back."

His eyes were full of confusion, rimmed with dark circles from too little sleep. He shouldn't be here, for his own safety and everyone else's. I shifted my gaze to Hope, not having the patience to repeat myself or wait for my words to register.

"You got him?" I said, and she nodded.

"Now!" Julian and Sebastian called in unison.

We all moved together. The power of our weapons provided an outlet to retaliate for entire lives' worth of damage. It was kind of mesmerizing. I kept my finger on the trigger, only breaking the concentration to see Hope and Luca slip through the door and into temporary safety. Everyone fired at rapid speed, but too many of the bullets were landing short of the enemy ship, not causing any serious damage. At least, not the kind that was being inflicted on our own ship.

We were burning through ammunition too fast, and I noticed it a few beats before Julian and Sebastian. I tried to get their attention, but they were too preoccupied, patiently looking through the scopes of their weapons and aiming.

Nico half rolled, half ran over to Sebastian and Julian, where they gave him instructions, and he scurried away to delegate to the others. This would be so much easier if we had the walkies.

The General's ship was close enough that I could make out all the details, even with the smoke and rain of bullets clouding. Most of their fire was coming from an out-of-reach tower-like structure. We'd never be able to reach that with our array of weapons and cause maximum damage.

I sat back, needing a moment to right my mind and movement, and I noticed the platform above the doorway. My breath caught at the sight of the intimidating weapon sitting there untouched. The Guard assigned to that weapon was not in sight. I hoped he'd moved to a different strategy by choice — instead of a gruesome alternative. I'd be able to find out if I got to it without being killed in the process.

The climb up to the heavy artillery would leave me

vulnerable. I would have to crawl around until I reached the bottom of the ladder, swing around off the side of the ship, feet dangling over the sea, and climb up.

I was desperate to get Julian and Sebastian's attention and advise them of my plan, but they didn't hear me over the noise. Once I moved, maybe they'd pick up on what I wanted and help cause a distraction.

I eyed the ladder, thin rails, and steps. I could make it in about thirty seconds — an easy bet to battle against the elements on the island, but here, I was under pressure of getting killed. I just had to get across the deck on my hands and knees and scurry up the ten rungs of the ladder, and we could win this. We could take down the General and start over.

Sebastian, Julian, and the others coordinated firing of their weapons. It was causing some problems, but the others stepped up their efforts, too. I could feel the impatience of both sides growing exponentially.

The holes were created in random patterns across our deck but were slowly turned into sizable gaps in the floor. I was grateful that all of our people were mostly unscathed, that the only damage was to our ship. It was better, obviously, to hit metal than skin, but soon, the bullets would reach the area below where the Elite, other crew members, and Luca were trying to support without directly being in the line of fire.

With a rush of determination, I slid my gun over to a volunteer in my proximity. His eyes, radiating with fear and confusion, propelled me forward. I crawled to the ladder, stopping momentarily to collect my breathing behind a small metal structure. Gunfire narrowly missed me, and I couldn't stop my hands from shaking.

Sebastian and Julian stared at me in disbelief. Julian seemed to be rolling over emotions of equal parts shock and anger, but Sebastian's expression cracked in helplessness for a second before transforming into something I could hold onto — pride.

"Cover me!" I cried, and I swung my body over the side of the ship to begin my ascent.

My sacrifice hadn't gone unnoticed by everyone on our deck, who began firing in unrelenting uniform waves, causing the General's ship to momentarily halt their attack. I looked down, and my heart dropped when I realized Sebastian led the charge.

He stood, fearless, an automatic weapon in his hands, waving it slowly back and forth. Too much of him was exposed in his stance. I imagined enemy fire cutting through him, and it took everything in me not to jump down to push him away. Yells of encouragement pounded in my ears, reminding me of my purpose.

My arms and legs dragged, growing heavier with each movement. I pushed forward, unsure why I felt the weight of my own body in addition to everyone else's as I continued upward. The sky, a beautiful, tranquil shade of blue, was almost too peaceful to witness this chaos.

The ship rocked violently. The metal was cold beneath my fingertips, but my palms were sweaty and hot, making it difficult to grip the ladder. I had three, maybe four, rungs left until I reached the top to fight back or they started firing again, tearing through my delicate skin as I tumbled to my death. I wasn't sure what would happen first.

Expletives carried up from the fight below me, just as common to my ears as the steady clanging of firefight. I panicked, realizing the sound wasn't just from our guns —

the enemy resumed their side of the fight, and a few bullets zoomed past me. I pressed my body against the side of the ship, climbing the last few arduous feet.

I pulled myself up toward the steel wall, and a bullet cut through my chest. I keeled over, falling behind the thick barrier. I screamed from the impact, not prepared for the searing white hot pain, then succumbed to the encroaching blackness.

I forced my eyes open, biting down the overwhelming urge to pass out. The roaring below me increased tenfold, and I glanced at the wound. Blood gushed out a few inches below my shoulder and on the top part of my back. The bullet, hitting right below my clavicle, must have gone straight through.

I was lucky, and I knew it, but like everything else in this situation, it hurt. I gritted through the pain, forcing the weakness to transform into strength. I climbed up onto the seat, expelling precious energy, and rested my weakening upper body against the gun. My lungs couldn't drag air in and out fast enough. My arms, exhausted from the climb, burned. I forced them up against the sides of the weapon.

I felt immense satisfaction as I aimed then put my fingers on their respective triggers. With one last look at the enemy ship, I pulled them back.

Disappointment prevailed when nothing came of my effort. Looking around frantically, I discovered a box of cartridges at my feet and dumped them in the empty shell box attached to the weapon. This time, I didn't build up anticipation within myself — I immediately shot off a few rounds, then picked up the pace. I was pleased with myself for figuring it out, and a few cheers rose up from below.

Even with my lack of experience with this type of

weapon, I oddly felt at ease. It seemed like a natural motion to use the scope and aim. The rounds fired, shaking my entire body, and the other's stopped. I took out the tower then tore through the bottom layer of their ship.

Our anchor lifted out of the water, and we moved toward Fernandina at top speed. A hard tap on my foot caught my attention. A Guard gestured for me to let him take my place. I complied, begrudgingly releasing the trigger.

The climb down was excruciating, and I was acutely conscious of the amount of blood loss from my shoulder. I counted the rungs back down. With only a few steps left, I swung and jumped. Sebastian steadied me, locking his arms around my waist and pulling us both into the stairwell.

He roughly pulled my shirt aside, eager to see the wound. "It went straight through," he exhaled, relief washing away the lines of concern that dug into his forehead.

"Yeah," I agreed. "The blood makes it look way worse than it is."

"Still, I want a Medic to patch that up."

"No time," I replied. "Here—"

I ripped the other sleeve of my shirt with my teeth. A makeshift bandage would have to do. Sebastian's hands took over, freeing the material and moving to tie it around my shoulder.

"Who was supposed to man that weapon?" I asked.

His jaw was clenched, and I swallowed his lack of response. He moved methodically, not letting any affection flow through his fingers.

"That'll do for now, Sebastian," I said, gently. "Thank you."

He dropped his hands to his side, and his eyes met mine.

"Where did they get that thing?" I asked, gesturing to the ship that was now following us.

"The ministers, if I had to guess," he answered with a scratchy voice.

"They're as good as dead," Julian said angrily, storming in to look at my blood-soaked shirt.

23

I WOULD TRADE ANOTHER BULLET, another blindsiding, burning piece of fire cutting through my skin and muscles than be subjected to this silence.

It was unsettling against the previous moments, which were overwhelming with the sound of yelling, the screeches of metal, and the groans of physical activity as everyone departed the ship. The beach was beautiful and covered in the whitest, softest sand I'd ever seen, but I barely acknowledged it as we took off for the trees.

Hope, Luca, and Felix led those avoiding the fight deeper into the jungle to find cover, but most of us picked up weaponry and stayed on the outskirts. I felt vulnerable even with the protection among the trees.

"What do you advise here, General?" Sebastian asked.

Julian spouted off plans, and Nico chimed in occasionally. They recommended a few strategies from their training in warfare, but the General, as drunk and useless as he'd been, knew all of them.

I was getting a headache from the planning. Everything seemed so confusing and intense. I wondered if blood loss could cause someone to lose the ability to focus on strategy. I looked up, searching for the sun among the dense branches, and an idea struck. I'd climbed up coconut trees on Island Seven, and I managed to do well on the deck — minus getting shot.

Turning away from the group, I picked a tree with a thicker trunk and began to climb. It was wide enough to support my weight, and I used my thighs and one arm to push upward. I tried to hold my injured side steady, but I couldn't contain the grunts of discomfort that spilled out of my mouth. Finally, I reached thick enough branches that shielded me from the ground and settled on one of the wider ones.

The ship was getting closer to the beach, and I sadistically smiled at the half of it that was submerged under the water. It would continue to crumble with each stride they made toward land.

"Hey, up here!" I yelled. No one noticed my voice against the increasing ground volume, and I wondered what else I'd have to do to get their attention. "Look up!"

It wasn't like they were expecting someone to shout at them from above, but clearly, I wasn't the only unobservant one. I didn't have anything I could throw at them to get their attention — no fruit or coconuts, just the clothes I was wearing and a set of double pistols I hastily strapped to my sides. My spare pocket knife was hidden in my boot, which could possibly cut down a branch.

I stared at the group, all serious in tone and stature. They were following Julian's lead. He was starting to get anxious, eyeing the ship and their position. I whipped out one of the pistols and fired one shot straight up into the sky.

"What the hell, Mol?" Julian said, exasperated while waving his arms. "Now they know where we are!"

I rolled my eyes. "They can probably hear you yelling all the way on Island Seven." The group of armed, trained men and volunteers stared at me, stunned.

Now, with the group of fighters perched in the surrounding trees and branches, everything was quiet and still. Nervous anticipation buzzed once again, this time throughout the treetops. We watched the ship halt a few hundred feet from the beach. The defectors from our ship and the General covered the remaining distance by transport boats.

They were all decorated in pristine protective gear, their heavy boots splashing in the shallow water. They looked properly shielded and armed, a uniformed threat against us. Most of us wore a mismatch of dirty and torn gear, and I cringed at the comparison. There wasn't enough to cover everyone — one of crates the General made off with the night he left was packed full of gear, so what remained was spread across everyone. We looked like a group of children, and they looked like an efficient operation.

Sebastian, Julian, Nico, and I forewent protection to give everyone else more. I felt exposed now, but when I made the decision, I was all confidence — no helmet or a bullet-proof vest needed, just raw determination.

With us being outnumbered and outmatched, Julian set forth a more defensive tactic. It would be easy to pick off people with our guns from so far up with the element of surprise on our side, but it felt dirty. It was like something the General would have happily planned, and I knew Julian felt the same way. There was no way of knowing who shot at us earlier and whether people were following the General out of loyalty or fear.

The others reached the trees, and my heart pounded. The General remained on the beach, standing tall with a smug look on his face. He seemed satisfied with his own personal protection enough to walk confidently, decked out in the best gear, ready to watch the chaos unfold.

My pistol trembled as I shook in anger, wondering if he was out of range. Sebastian, sensing this from across the group, signaled to Julian then jumped off the branch. We all followed him, landing softly a few feet below. The men clearly hadn't expected to be attacked from overhead — or at all.

It provided a brief advantage to us. We rendered several people unconscious with blows to the head. For a few minutes, the strategy of knockout over kill worked too well. Some in our group were getting cocky, laughing at the easy takedowns, and it became detrimental to our strategy.

Those on the beach with the General began firing in our direction, hitting people on both sides of the fight. I dove for cover and landed hard on my shoulder, shooting a jolt of nausea through me. I rolled over and moved forward slightly.

I propped up onto my elbows and clutched a pistol tightly. With a limited number of rounds in each of my guns, I needed to use them carefully. I peeked out from behind the tree. From the angle, I could see a few of the General's men, standing without cover and blindly discharging their automatic weapons.

I was about to cause people pain, something that would leave a scar or cause lasting damage, and I couldn't help but feel guilty. I inhaled deeply, and on the exhale, I fired three shots, hitting a trio of enemy Guard members precisely in the upper thigh, through the gap in the gear, causing them to collapse.

While deciding my next move, a force from behind grabbed at my ankles and flipped my body over. It was my turn to be shocked, and I dropped the pistol I just fired and landed hard on the other. Ray's heavy boot came down to rest on my neck, applying increasing pressure. One hard step from him into my windpipe could kill me. I looked up, defiantly, completely submitting to my disadvantage.

"Not going to fight back, Mol?" Ray asked, leaning down closer to my face. "I always liked the fire in you. Such a shame to see it put out."

A bullet whizzed by his head. In the second he turned to see who fired it, I twisted out from underneath him. I swung my leg, kicking his out, and climbed on top of him, pressing the barrel of my pistol against his forehead. When our positions were reversed, I was tense and rigid under his strength, but under mine, he was relaxed.

"Do it, Mol," he said, licking his lips. "Let them see how their little experiment in distraction turned into a killer."

I tried kept my face blank, channeling Sebastian, but something gave away my ignorance. He laughed again, and I pressed the barrel harder into his skin

"You haven't figured it out have you? The special treatment in these past few weeks? The dress up? The dinner last night? It was all to show you off to the Authority, give them ideas about collecting their own special pet projects from islands."

My disgust for Ray wavered as I processed his words. No doubt he was exaggerating, trying to stop me from pulling the trigger, but it surfaced doubt deep down inside me. I didn't question why my presence last night was so important or even necessary at all. Is that what Sebastian needed me for? To make an example of me? I shook that notion out, knowing that people tried to rob me of any devotion to Sebastian in more emotional ways. Still, that didn't mean everyone else tangled up in this Authority web was innocent.

"I hope it all works out for you Mol," he said, his voice low and menacing. "I really do."

He shifted his hips a little, and I readjusted my hold on his arms and my hips on his body. I felt him, hard and eager, pressing into me. I drew up my arm and brought the butt of the gun down to hit his temple, knocking him out cold. I stared at his motionless figure for a few seconds, feeling a mixture of pity and repulsion.

The General was still away from the fighting, flanked by six Guard members. Succumbing to anger and the memories of the injuries he inflicted, I ignored all logic. Standing up in the open, I fired. My bullets found a few legs, and my last round hit a Guard on the torso. I reached for my other pistol, which was hanging off my belt, giving them enough time to run. I chased after them, firing along the way.

Sebastian, Julian, and another Guard member flew past me, making a move on the General. I turned to join them but was held up by someone on the General's side. He caught my jaw with a few jabs. I shot his shoulder at close range, somewhere near the same spot I'd been hit earlier. He roared but didn't falter, so I shot him again in the leg and made my way to the beach.

The fights and training with Julian prepared me for this. I felt grateful for it, knowing that our bickering and hours of sparring made me stronger. We'd get through this, and I'd get a chance to hurt the General. I was tough, my wounds and bruises attested to it, and he wasn't. I imagined the satisfaction of making him beg for mercy and stopped at the edge of the trees.

My optimism, so welcome and adored, vanished. It dissolved, leaving behind no trace, and I fell to my knees.

The Guard member who accompanied Sebastian and Julian to the beach was either dead or close to it, face down in the sand with his neck was twisted at an odd angle. Two men held Sebastian back from the General, who pushed up his sleeves in preparation. Julian was fighting — and losing — to another Guard who had four inches and about sixty pounds on him.

"Tell me Sebastian, my Commander," the General purred in a mocking tone, "do you want to die now or watch my replacement die first? I'm looking for a direct order here."

Like Julian, Sebastian didn't look good. His stomach was victim to a few knife wounds and a fair amount of bleeding. I couldn't tell how deep they were from my position thirty feet away, but I was in slight disbelief at how they were both in such bad shape so quickly.

"Killing me accomplishes nothing," Sebastian said stoically, not bowing to the threats. "This is a waste of precious lives for nothing. The changes in place are irreversible, and if I'm not here to carry them out, someone else will."

"To that end, my Commander, we agree."

The General tilted his head, and his two men raked their knives across Sebastian's skin. The blades moved deeper and deeper into his abdomen. I raised a hand and shot to Sebastian's right and left. Both Guards fell into a sickening thud beside him, but he remained upright. I kept my hand raised as I stepped onto the beach, meeting the General's eyes.

Blood pounded throughout my system. It pumped quickly, pushing me forward, and everything around me froze. There was no sound — only a ringing echoing in my ears — until Sebastian slumped to the ground in my peripheral vision.

"Nicely done," the General admitted. "Playing with something new?"

Even with a pistol aimed straight at his face, the General was fearless, even upbeat.

"I'm better with a gun than a knife," I promised.

He raised a finger in my direction and shook it. "I wouldn't use if I were you," he warned.

"I've never been afraid of a bit of blood," I said. "I believe you're familiar?"

"I'm sure you've dreamed about spilling blood," the General said, laughing. "But his—" he gestured to Sebastian, who clutched his stomach. "Or his—" I turned to see the other Guard walk up with Julian in a chokehold and a gun pressed to his temple.

"Clearly you're quick with a gun," he mused, glancing at the two fallen men next to Sebastian. "But are you quicker than my trusted Guard here, who has spent the past decade training every day with firearms? Are you willing to gamble, little girl?"

I cocked my head to the side, narrowing my eyes at the General. The sun, now high in the sky, beat down. Perspiration formed in a layer on my body, collecting in my palms under the pressure of the decision. My eyes moved from the General to Sebastian, who looked vulnerable as I'd ever seen him, and finally, to Julian, who was bruising and bleeding at a few different points — there was even a small blade lodged into his upper leg.

They both looked bad. Bad enough that I wasn't sure how long they'd live even if I decided to save them. The Medic team was led far into the jungle, and if they made it back here, I didn't know if they were even skilled enough to repair this kind of damage. Island Seven was a long ride away for the transport boats.

Julian encouraged me with a nod, hoping to make it easy on me to choose death for him and the General, but I remained still. When I didn't fire, he mouthed "Shoot!" between short gasps of air. But I'd decided long ago I wasn't interested in anyone's opinion — not Julian's and certainly not the General's.

"Okay," I said and dropped my pistol to the ground, kicking it away.

"No," Julian hissed, baring his teeth.

I suddenly felt light and very unarmed, put off by how dependent I'd been on weapons. I motioned to the Guard for him to release Julian, who gasped for air when he obliged. The Guard upheld the bargain, but the General wasn't interested in fairness — only destruction.

He reached behind his back for his own gun, preparing to fire it at one of us, and I reached down, grabbing my knife. The General fixed to pull the trigger at Sebastian. I threw the blade, slicing deep into his hand, which caused his aim to shift to the left. The bullet intended for Sebastian hit Julian in the chest — too close to his precious, stubborn heart. He fell, and I screamed. In a blur, I grabbed the General's dropped gun and fired it in his direction until there were no bullets left. I turned my attention to Julian, rushing to his side to put pressure on the wound.

The Guard stood there, somewhat dumbfounded by the turn of events. I scrambled to stop the bleeding or do anything else useful, cursing myself for not asking for Medic training.

I looked up at the Guard, and he raised both of his hands in surrender. "Go now," I shouted at him, without stopping the movement on Julian's chest. "Go get help. Tell them you've changed sides. Tell them you were forced to help the General. Tell them anything. Just go get help. Now."

He ran off, and I released my buried emotion. I didn't have the willpower to hold it in any longer, and tears poured down my cheeks. Julian closed his eyes, and Sebastian crawled over next to me, laying beside him. They both looked weak and helpless, beautiful and broken. There was so much blood, so little breathing, and nothing I could do.

I sat back, finally acknowledging the tugging prickly feeling that moved up and down my spine. I turned to see the General alone, in a transport boat, speeding away on the open sea and staring at me.

24

────────

ONE OF THE machines on Island Seven backfired a week ago, injuring a few Engineers. The mishap mostly caused minor cuts, but two men fell victim to third-degree burns, so the Authority brought in a Doctor from Island Two. He had just completed a final round of checkups on the patients when Nico and a few others arrived on a transport boat, demanding his assistance and supplies.

It took a few hours, the longest of my life, for them to arrive back. I was right — the Medic team on the ship was too inexperienced to handle these types of injuries. Their Placement brought them patients with the occasional headache, strained muscle, and hand injury from training. Bullet and knife wounds weren't really their thing.

The Doctor examined Sebastian and Julian quickly, while they faded in and out, and shouted for someone to retrieve vials of liquid and tools from his bag. I begrudgingly relinquished control to him and the Medic team.

Hope and I jumped into action to help how we could and set up a camp. The distraction was welcome. We gave out directions and stepped in to help set up a makeshift medical bay, choosing to bring it out of the ship and onto the beach instead of trying to move Julian and Sebastian. They were the most critical, but there were other patients, too. People on both sides of the action — or maybe we were all just one side now — came back with various injuries.

It took the entire afternoon for us to unload furniture and supplies from our ship, which was anchored in an awkward tilt too close to the beach. On some level, I appreciated it. Seeing the ship that caused me all spectrums of pain immovable and useless reflected how I felt.

Along with our efforts, Nico questioned the opposing Guard. Unsurprisingly, most of those who defected did so under the threat of harm to the lives of their families or loved ones. The General's decades of threats and fear-inciting still held up from his cell onboard. Ray was the exception, admitting he found the General's motives interesting, and Felix led the charge in tying him up to a nearby tree.

The moon, full and round, was high in the sky, providing a decent amount of light to finish up the camp setup. Luca rigged one of the ship's generators into providing a light source inside the medical bay, then he immediately took off down the beach in search of solitude when he saw Julian's condition.

His expression, one screaming of unnecessary self-deprecation, alerted some nagging sibling concern. I grabbed his arm, trying to stop him from spiraling into melancholy.

"Luca, don't do this to yourself," I pleaded with him.

"I'm not doing anything to myself," he answered unconvincingly.

I could see the guilt on his face, and I knew he regretted not putting himself in the fight. Coupled with not being able to help Julian, it would be easy to fall into a deep, dark hole of anguish. Julian would need weeks or months to recover from his injuries — if the Doctor was able to help him at all — and I refused to let Luca spend one second longer blaming himself for any part of what happened.

"It's not your fault," I assured him. "You being here would have been a distraction for Julian, and it probably would have turned out way worse."

"Worse?" Luca said in disbelief. "Julian is helpless in a bed while some stranger with close ties to the Authority tries to pull a bullet from his chest. How does it get much worse than that, Mol?"

He was shaking with anger, gnashing his teeth together like a rabid dog, ready to spring it all on me. My instincts to soothe flared up, hoping to bring him back down to coherent truths.

"It's not your fault," I repeated, both my voice and resolve lowering.

"Then whose fault is it? Yours?"

"No, I don't know," I stuttered, suddenly feeling defensive.

He moved closer, and I readied myself for a full serving of his rage.

"All I know is that up until a few weeks ago, we were boring. We were normal, and I had a plan. Then you got us caught up in a mess, and this is where we ended up."

He hated that version of normal too, but somehow, he had the audacity to decide I was at fault. It was pathetic.

We both changed in the past few weeks. People we cared about were in hospital beds. The only difference between him and I is that I fought. I served my penance, and I was prepared to face the consequences. He was willing to hide behind his notebooks and his secrets, shielded from any true struggle.

"You're a coward, Luca," I said, simply, unable to find additional words to voice my understanding of his thoughts.

I saw the flash of hurt in his eyes, and I immediately regretted my words, which in a moment of self-awareness on a different day I could cop to being merely a projection of my own insecurities. He turned away, grabbing the canvas where the recovered walkies were laid out, and stomped down the beach.

"I'll let you know when there is news," I called after his figure.

He found a place to settle down and resume his work, pulling a screwdriver from his pocket and angrily unscrewing one of the walkies. I watched him for a few moments then took off toward the pile of supplies.

I recognized many of the items in the group — decorative pillows from Sebastian's quarters, sets of hangers from the Elite, assorted pans from the kitchens, weight sets from the Guard training quarters. I rolled my eyes at the group's choice of prioritization in what they removed from the ship as I searched for a small crate that held the only thing I knew would help at this moment.

I could hear Hope, Nico, and Emilia collaborating on the beach setup. I didn't plan on returning to life onboard in the near future, at least not on this particular ship, and was pleased to find that no one else did either. Cooks, Elite, and Guard came together to line up the beds under canopies, build bonfires to prepare dinner, and organize the rest of the items being unpacked from crates.

I turned away, not wanting to disturb something so organically perfect, and tears formed in my eyes.

"Can I help you find something, Mol?"

"No thanks, Isabel," I said, graciously, not wanting her to see the emotion on my face. "I'm on a personal mission."

I felt her scrutiny, but she didn't press. "Okay, well let me know."

"Will do," I whispered a few moments after she stepped away.

When I finally located it, I smiled a big, teeth-baring grin. I'd seen the picture on the General's bottle enough to know I'd found the right box among the crates from the cargo area, and I almost jumped around in a fit of happiness. I carried it to the main bonfire where the crowd was gathered. The clanking of glass and the noise from the weight hitting the sand got everyone's attention.

"Does anyone have a crowbar?" I called out.

One was quickly recovered and thrust into my hands. I pried open the crate, not caring that the motion caused blood to spill out from both sides of my shoulder wound. I plucked a full bottle out for myself, loving the excitement that fell over the group, and moved away to find my own secluded spot, settling between the water and the medical bay.

I tore open the protective cover, twisted the cap off, and took a long, hard swig. The alcohol tore through the stress of the past twenty-four hours and, somehow, the past eighteen years. It burned as it moved down my throat. A hot, delicious sensation eased over me, not unlike the one Sebastian fired up under my skin. The thought of him surfaced anxiety I wasn't ready to process, so I drank more.

I appreciated the irony of drinking the General's personal stash of alcohol, something that set these events in motion. I looked at the water, where hours earlier he sped away, and closed my eyes to concentrate on the hopeful dialogue of those on the beach. The contrast was overwhelming, so I took another drink, noting the burning wasn't so bad anymore.

My senses were heightened, more definite, but I could feel less control over my muscles. I almost relaxed when I heard the canvas slap open from the medical bay. I told myself to avoid that area because I'd been in the way, but really, I couldn't be in the room where some stranger was attempting to save two important people in my life.

I placed the bottle on the ground next to me and put my face in my hands.

I could handle the blood, and probably even a look at their organs, but I couldn't handle the uncertainty. That, and all the lies. Ray, a traitor by most definitions, was more straightforward with me than most. I'd been able to put my trust in Sebastian, and now, without another option, this mysterious Doctor from Island Two, but I couldn't trust anyone else. Including two people I thought I'd known better than anyone.

I was even willing to play a part in the Authority's games. I was a pawn in a dress, the picture of Authority perfection for them. I did it thinking I was somehow fighting for a better future, a cause I understood. But I wasn't sure I understood anything anymore.

I rubbed my eyes and reached to take another swig, opening my eyes with the bottle at my lips, and wasn't surprised to see the Doctor standing above me. I mentally calculated how much of the liquid moved and gave him my most challenging look.

"You know you should really get that looked at by a Doctor," he said, gesturing to my shoulder.

"Probably," I shrugged, offering him the bottle. "But the only one I know has been kind of busy."

He chuckled and sat down beside me, ignoring my outstretched hand.

"As a person who cares deeply about the health of those in the Network, I don't recommend this form of medicating."

I rolled my eyes. "Not in the market for another lecture from someone in the Authority, thanks, though."

"How many lectures have you gotten?" he asked, good-naturedly.

He leaned back into the sand, remaining propped up by his palms.

"Enough," I admitted, taking another sip.

"As I was saying before I was interrupted," he said, pausing for emphasis. "On a medical level, bad idea. On a personal level, fantastic idea."

I nodded in approval then handed the bottle to him. "I'm Mol, by the way," I said, watching him take a long pull.

"I know," he coughed, wincing slightly at the burn. He dragged his hand across his lips as if that would help it go down easier, and I watched the motion, unsure of why I was fascinated by his fingers.

His hands shifted to run through his dark hair, which was a few inches longer than Julian's, and turned to face me. His eyes were green, rare just like my own blue, and offset by structured cheekbones. He looked vaguely like some of the people from Island Seven, with their almost-black hair color and tanned skin.

My cheeks burned under the realization that I'd been watching him for far longer than appropriate. I doused my embarrassment with more liquor.

"You know, typically, when a person makes an introduction, it's polite to return the gesture," I explained to him, aiming to sound condescending. "At least that's how us common non-Authority folk do it."

"You're anything but common, Mol," he said, smiling in way that made my heart flutter. I felt sick, recognizing this feeling.

It had to be the bourbon.

"So I guess I'll just call you 'The Good Doctor from Island Two,' then?" I asked, deflecting his compliment. At least, I thought he meant it that way — my brain teetered on labeling it an insult.

"Everett," he said, finally, picking up on my discomfort. "I'm surprised you're here drinking and bantering with me instead of hammering me with questions about a prognosis. That's how things usually go for us non-common Authority folk."

He smiled, and I forced myself to look away, digging my hands into the sand beside me.

"Getting drunk was kind of an accident," I admitted, choosing my words deliberately to avoid any slurring. "But I figured you would have delivered bad news first thing if that was the case."

He nodded. "The young General's surface wounds are cleaned and stitched, but the bullet wound caused a lot of bleeding," he said, his hands moving while he spoke, mimicking the actions. "We were able to stop it before it caused too much damage to his internal organs, and after much debate, we decided to leave the bullet inside him."

"What did you just say?" I snapped. "It's still in there? What the hell kind of Doctor are you?"

"It was too risky to remove it," he explained slowly. "We're not exactly in the cleanest of locations, and the chances of infection or causing more damage was too great to dig in and try to remove it. The bullet wedged itself back, and it's too close to the spinal cord and heart for us to feel comfortable—"

"Well I'm glad that you're comfortable," I almost shouted, not wanting to believe that there was a piece of metal lodged into Julian's chest.

He grimaced, and I realized my ignorance.

"Sorry," I offered, reminding myself that he was the expert here, not me.

He filled me in on some of the details, but it was getting difficult to process. My brain was suddenly very fuzzy.

"So he's going to be okay?" I interrupted.

"We won't know until he wakes up, but the prognosis is good."

"And Sebastian?"

He stared at me, expression puzzled.

"The Commander?" I asked, after too long of a pause. "Is he going to be okay?"

"The blades went in much deeper than we would have liked, but we were able to repair all of the damage to his intestines through few tiny incisions. He'll definitely be sore for a few days, and he most likely won't be able to tolerate solid foods for a week or so, but as with the General, we'll have a better idea once he wakes up."

I paused, debating on whether to show how grateful I felt toward him. Most people probably threw themselves at him, stroking his ego. I shuddered at the thought.

"Who is 'we?'" I asked.

"Pardon me?"

"You keep saying 'We were able to' and 'We're not' — who is we?"

He laughed, and I noticed, even in the slight cover of darkness, that it went all the way up to his eyes. "I got into the habit early on of not taking credit for miracles," he admitted.

I bit my bottom lip, not expecting that response. "That's probably for the best."

"Oh?" Everett asked, not expecting my agreement.

"I'm not sure this medical bay could fit your ego along with Julian's," I admitted. "Once he wakes up, of course."

"Well, it'll be a few hours," he said, playfully. "Plenty of time to offer up compliments and praise then insult me. It'll even the score."

I smiled unwillingly, and he leaned forward, closing the distance between us. I drew back immediately, my spine sticking up straight.

"Mol, just going to have a look at your shoulder," he said while undoing the tie of the sleeve-turned-bandage.

I winced at his touch. He moved closer, and my body trembled. I focused on my own respiratory system and not on his breath on my bare back. I'd never drink alcohol again.

A gunshot rippled in the distance, and I sprang to my feet, knocking Everett over in the motion. My head whipped around, trying to figure out who, what, or why there was firing.

And then I heard laughter.

Everett, no longer surprised at my movement, apparently found my reaction hilarious and pointed to the sky.

The most fascinating display of lights rippled across the black night, making the moon and stars seem dull in comparison. Every explosion brought new beauty to the evening — circles of purples and blues mixed with vibrant reds. It was incredible, and I was nearly speechless.

"Fireworks," I breathed.

Everett stood next to me. I turned my head, not expecting him to tower over me. He sidestepped closer.

"Your shoulder needs a thorough cleaning," he said, watching me.

I heard his words but was too captivated by the flashes of color. I'd dreamed about fireworks, hoping to one day witness the bursts of magnificence with my own eyes. I kept my eyes upward as I moved slowly but deliberately toward the water.

When my toes hit the warm waves, I stopped and watched the dazzling display intensify into something so amazing that I tried to burn it into my memory. It stopped suddenly, and I was left empty with just a smoky sky and the water in front of me.

After one longing glance above, I dove in.

25

"You know there are more efficient ways to clean a wound, right?"

Water dripped from the tangled mess of my hair, and my clothing stuck to my skin. I shook off what I could, the droplets flying around me and falling into the sand. I was suddenly grateful we were under the cover of darkness.

"I guess I'm an 'all or nothing' kind of girl," I deflected.

He opened his mouth to respond, but quickly closed it, watching Nico and Emilia approach. They stood closely, but I could see the wedge of distance driven between the two, heightened by the bickering that immediately quieted when they stepped within earshot.

"Mol, we should talk about what's happening," Nico said, in a very serious Guard tone.

"Go for it," I said, more confused than excited.

"Word spread of what happened today," he explained, as if I should already understand the repercussions. He stared at me expectantly, and I could see similar expressions on Emilia and Everett's faces.

"Okay," I nodded. "And?"

"And this is a big deal, Mol," Emilia said. "News of the General's defeat and Sebastian's changes to the Authority are spreading throughout the islands."

"But isn't that what we hoped would happen?" I asked, feeling a concrete wall build up between what they were inferring and what I was understanding.

"Yeah, well, that's not all," Nico frowned, and I prepared myself for bad news.

"It seems the Guard and the people on the islands have taken a particular favor to your part in all of this," Emilia continued. "Your bravery is inspiring them, Mol."

"Those fireworks — they were in celebration of you," Nico said, finally.

They stared at me with some enthusiasm that I knew should be surfacing, but instead, I only felt horror. I wasn't supposed to be a main part in all of this. Sure, the tipping point of this situation was spurred by my actions defending Emilia, but I didn't mean for anything unusual to happen or for me to be shoved into conversations across the islands.

Everything was so fuzzy, and my limbs swayed in the breeze.

"It's time to get that shoulder disinfected, Mol," Everett asserted, taking his time to interrupt the conversation. He seemed to be enjoying my discomfort. "We can't have a hero be defeated by neglecting to have a wound cleaned and properly stitched."

Any gratitude for his interference was shrouded by my irritation that he didn't do it sooner. "Let me get changed into something dry and tell Luca what's happening then I'll—"

"I'll get your clothes, and Nico can update Luca," Emilia offered.

Nico tilted his head and then turned to follow her,

walking quickly to catch up and resume their argument. It wasn't the friendly, light kind; it was the type of argument between two people with something to lose. I smiled, knowing how stubborn Emilia was and how much Nico cared for her.

"Well then," Everett said, clearing his throat. "Shall we?"

I sighed. "Sure."

I did feel better once I changed into my own dry clothes, even under the harsh, artificial light Luca created. Everett's hands worked with innate precision as he attended to the wound and stitched me up.

"This will help fight off any infection," he said, pulling the plunger to fill the syringe.

"A shot?" I asked, stupidly.

"A small ceftriaxone injection."

"You're going to give me a shot?"

He stared at me, and I burst into laughter. "I was already shot!" I exclaimed, laughing at his seriousness and the absurdity of it all.

A bullet made its way through my body and exited. I killed people today. The General killed people today. And here I was, getting drunk and watching fireworks.

I clutched at my stomach, trying to remain still as the needle pierced my skin. Once the it was discarded and the bandage covered both sides of my shoulder, I tugged my shirt on and laughed, loud and hard. Tears streamed down my face, and I laid down on the bed, sprawling out.

He watched me with amusement and cleaned his tools. "You need coffee."

"Probably," I admitted.

I reluctantly stood up, ready to go off in search of ways to make it with the dying embers of a bonfire. The blood in my head fell to my feet, and I felt woozy. I sat back down.

"Whoa," I mumbled. "This is new."

He laughed. "How about I get that coffee for you?"

"No, I've got this," I promised. I stood up again, this time slowly, and felt normal doing so.

"Mol, you've been through a lot today," Everett said, sternly. "Whether you're ready to process it or not, there will be plenty of time to fight and push yourself. But for now, you need rest."

"All right," I agreed, watching him get up. "And, hey, thanks."

"Anything for the one who gave us all of this," he mocked, swirling his hands in the air.

"No, really," I said sincerely. "Thank you."

After a wink, he was gone.

I slowly moved to the other side of the medical bay where Julian and Sebastian were sleeping. They looked battered, like they'd been stabbed, shot, and beaten nearly to death, but they also looked peaceful. I was dying for them to wake up, to confirm that they were still alive and more or less okay, but their bodies healed as they remained unconscious.

Sebastian's cot, while not overly large, looked inviting. In the early hours of yesterday, we were wrapped up in each other's arms, and I was craving the feel of his skin against mine again. I sighed, wishing I could lay down next to him, and instead sat down in the sand. I faced him, dropping my head next to his hand, and drifted off.

I woke up hours later completely disoriented. Hot sun streamed directly onto my skin, making the morning sticky and uncomfortable. I opened my eyes to see a methodically arranged tray of bread, jam, and fruit sitting on top of the folding chair next to me, and I reached out for the cup of black coffee. It was cold to the touch, but I took a long sip.

Sebastian's fingers moved to lightly trace his thumb on my skin, and I jumped in surprise. Words failed me when I met his gaze, and his face contorted in his attempt to adjust his position. The bag of pain medicine flowing directly into his veins through clear tubes was almost empty. I moved to get up and tell someone.

"Don't," Sebastian said, his voice scratchy. "Please, stay."

"How are you feeling?" I asked, tenderly brushing my fingers against his cheek.

"Amazing," he whispered.

I chuckled. "No, really."

"I've been better," he admitted. "But I'm glad you're here."

"Me too."

I looked at his bare chest and stomach, covered in bandages like the ones on my shoulder. His beautiful, perfect skin now would have scars and reminders of what happened on the beach. We were both marked forever, just in different ways. I would have holes marking the entry and exit wound below my shoulder — its severity would likely depend on how often I wore the sling Everett set out for me. Sebastian, he'd have slashes across him, healed into thin lines with help from the stitches holding him together.

He pressed a kiss against my forehead, something he meant as a gesture of affection to me, but instead, it was a reminder on what was on the front of my mind. It was the equivalent of someone smacking me on the forehead to not forget.

"Sebastian, I need to talk to you about something," I said, sitting up to put some distance between us.

He looked me over, mouth closed tightly, and grasped my hand in his.

"What's wrong?" I loved the sound of his voice, even its

hoarseness. I glanced over to make sure Julian was still out. The steady sound of snoring floated through the medical bay. Still, I kept my voice low.

"When I was fighting with Ray, he said something upsetting. Well, I know he was trying to rile me up, get me angry so that I'd hit him or something, but I actually think he said something true."

Sebastian's eyes narrowed, but he remained silent.

"You know that I've been a willing participant in fighting the General and challenging the Authority," I continued. "I'm actually glad to have been included in the planning and helping out how I can, offering whatever degree of usefulness, but Ray was saying that I'd been misled. That I was some sort of example for a sick islander makeover or something."

My eyes dropped to our interlaced fingers.

"And what did you say to that?"

"Well, I didn't respond specifically to that," I shuddered, remembering the sickening feeling of his arousal. "He said some other stuff and then I knocked him out."

"Of course you did," Sebastian smiled, and I returned it.

"But for what he said," I pressed. "I kind of think he was telling the truth."

Sebastian's thumb traced mine.

"I don't know who to trust at this point," I admitted, then chewed on my bottom lip.

"Do you trust me?" He was genuinely curious, and I realized I'd set up him to believe I thought he could be tangled in this mess of deception.

"Yes," I said, without hesitation.

He pulled me down to him. His lips caught mine in urgency, and I met his pace.

"Ugh, Mol, this is worse than death," Julian croaked out.

272

I sprung apart from Sebastian, and ran to the opening of the medical bay.

"Luca!" I yelled, causing a Medic to jump. "He's awake."

He ran in while I was helping a very stubborn Julian drink some water, and they had a reunion not all that different from mine and Sebastian's. I sat on the edge of Sebastian's bed, trying to not get emotional at the relief I felt that Julian was awake and talking.

Luca was kneeling next to Julian's bed, speaking softly into his ear, when Everett, a Medic, Hope, Nico, and Felix walked in. Everett and the Medic started pelting Julian and Sebastian with questions, flashing a light into their eyes and taking tedious notes.

"Well, I hate to talk business at a time like this," Hope said with a sigh.

"Hope, please don't start lying to us now," Nico joked, watching the Medic adjust one of Julian's tubes. "You never hate to talk business."

"All right, you've caught me," she said, blushing slightly. "But we are going to need a new home base now that our ship is temporarily out of commission."

"We have a few options," Felix exclaimed, clapping his hands excitedly. "We couldn't have picked a better island, to be honest, location-wise. We are fairly close to all of the facilities on Island Seven and Island Five."

"Some of the bullets cut through key areas on the ship, but I have some ideas on how to cut down on repair time," Luca added.

Hope moved in closer, eyeing Sebastian's bare chest in a way that made me inexplicably angry.

"Everett, how long until the Commander and the General have recovered enough to hike a few miles?"

He looked at Hope like she was a lunatic, making me

273

feel slightly better. "The General will need to have the surgery first to remove the bullet, followed by weeks of close monitoring. All patients will need to stay off their feet and focus on recovery."

Somehow, I knew that last line was a warning to me.

"Okay, I'll bite, Hope, why do Julian and Sebastian need to go on a hike?" I asked, suspiciously.

In the middle of asking the question, I realized that Sebastian and I were the only two who were giving her our full attention — everyone else seemed to already know the answer. I instinctively reached for Sebastian's hand.

"It's not just the two of them," she explained. "It's all of us — we're a part of this future together."

I stopped myself from laughing out loud, and Sebastian squeezed my hand.

"It's time that you and Sebastian were introduced to the Refuge."

EPILOGUE

I COULD SEE THE BEACH, with our expansive camp sprawled out for a few hundred feet, from my viewpoint. Everyone scurried across the sand like little ants, distributing supplies, making repairs to the makeshift buildings, or just wandering around participating in idle chit chat. I squinted slightly, attempting to make out the background, Island Seven, and a few of the others.

I was surrounded by dense trees, and the natural smell of the wood and plants was almost overwhelming. Wildlife was everywhere. Birds chirped and other animals moved throughout the brush, seemingly unfazed by the presence of a group of sweaty, panting humans, making their way to the top.

"Keep up!" Hope shouted from twenty feet or so above me. "We're almost at the top."

"You said that fifteen minutes ago," Julian groaned, walking past me with Luca at his side.

"Having trouble, General?" I teased, and he responded with a middle-finger gesture.

The rest of the group continued, but Sebastian waited

for me, and I begrudgingly turned away from the scene below.

In true poetic nature, we, the de facto leaders of what's ahead, forged on to understand more of our past and set up for the future. In the medical bay, six weeks ago, with plenty of raw emotions not even twenty-four hours after the General's disappearance, Hope opened up to Sebastian and me.

She gave us a general understanding of the Refuge, a group of people with views not so different from my own, who banded together in the final decade of Sebastian's father's command. The group of people were grossly unhappy with the Authority, and they found solace in the abandoned islands — Fernandina housed their head-quarters.

Toward the end of the former Commander's reign, the General stumbled upon some of the members and made it his personal mission to have everyone tortured for information then killed. My parents were included in that. The night of their death, one of the other members came to tell Luca everything, cementing his membership into the secret society, but they agreed they wouldn't tell me until it was absolutely necessary.

And then when I created my own path and Sebastian made his, everything changed.

The Refuge, which struggled for years to make any measurable impact due to their need to stay unnoticed, seemed unnecessary now — especially with the changes over the last few weeks. The headquarters had been aban-doned for years, but Hope thought it would be the perfect place for the new chain of command to begin.

Sebastian and I didn't take the news well. He was passive, angry that they didn't trusted him sooner when he was on the path for making changes that aligned with their agenda. He was polite and asked many questions. I, however, made my unhappiness clear, letting everyone know how much I hated the decisions they'd made on my behalf, like leaving me in the dark, and how angry I was. Then, I refused to speak to anyone for days.

If he wasn't so fragile in the midst of recovery, I would have slapped Julian. I got some shred of satisfaction now, though, climbing up the mountain measurably faster than him.

We trekked for another five minutes before coming to a halt to watch Nico pull branches away, revealing a metal door. He yanked at the handles, and the hinges creaked. One by one, we made our way down the steps, pulling out small lights Luca recovered from one of the ship's crates.

When we finally reached the end of the hall, another metal door, this one giant and somewhat impenetrable-looking, greeted us. Next to the handle, there was a square with the numbers one through ten, and Hope stepped forward to press several in a row. The door accepted the numbers and swung open.

"Electricity?" I asked, surprised at the sophisticated technology available in the middle of a mountain.

"Solar panels," Luca explained, pointing upward when we entered the room.

I expected a dark, swampy headquarters, but it turned out to be more like the ship — grandeur mixed with sheer necessity. The biggest difference, however, was the light. The ceiling was covered in windows, letting the sunshine stream in and the clouds reflect. I saw what Luca meant by the panels — there were so many of them sticking out of the random equipment in the room, but there was also a neat row angled up on the roof.

"Wow," I muttered in slight disbelief.

"We were able to find comfort here," Hope said. "There's no aerial technology left, and the transport boats were so limited. There was no chance, really, of anyone finding it accidentally, but we still factored in some precautions."

We all wore awed expressions smattered across our faces, which surprised me. Sebastian and I were the last to be looped into the Refuge, but everyone else prepared for this for years.

"Please feel free to explore," Hope encouraged. "Quarters are down that hall, with the bathrooms attached. The kitchens are farther down, and you'll eventually stumble upon a medical bay and some private meeting rooms."

Everyone took off, splitting up to explore at their own pace.

"Actually, Mol, can I have a minute?" Hope asked, gesturing for me to sit at a desk. I obliged out of mere curiosity, not respect. Things were never easy between the two of us, and the recent revelations only made things a bit more challenging — from my perspective, at least.

"If you open the bottom drawer of the desk, you'll find a box. I'm not sure what is inside, but I have been tempted many times to open it and find out for myself. Admittedly, it just didn't feel right."

She paused, collecting herself in a very solemn way.

"Giving you this opportunity now feels like the most logical way to move forward. I do hope you'll forgive me for hanging onto this for so long."

Hope opened her palm, and I gasped. My mother's necklace, gold, polished, and exquisitely beautiful, was clutched in her grasp. She set it on the desk in front of me, gently, and left the room.

"Bottom drawer, Mol," Hope called out in a reminder.

My vision tunneled, only seeing the necklace. I picked it

up and held it close to my heart. I swallowed emotion down my throat, and I fought back the tears. I opened the bottom drawer, pulling out the box.

It was locked, but it wasn't a normal one with a keyhole — it opened with a shape pressed against it that happened to be the same as the necklace. I took a breath and pushed it in, embarrassed that I yelped when a pop indicted it unlocked.

I emptied the contents on the desk, eager to sort through it all. There were stacks of papers in my mother's handwriting, random tools, a collection of torn notes, and, most notably, a large drawing that was folded up. I traced my mother's loopy cursive, but didn't pick up any of the envelopes. Somehow, I wasn't ready to read her thoughts quite yet.

I fingered the drawing, which intrigued me in an unexplainable way. I stood up and unfolded it, gasping immediately. The map was mostly a light shade a blue, with oddly shaped circles labeled "Island One," "Island Two," all the way up to "Island Seven," in green. It even included "Isla Fernandina" and a few other of the uninhabited islands.

I studied it further, trying to angle it perfectly under the light. I'd never considered how the islands were laid out, and I was fascinated by it. Island Seven was huge in comparison to the rest. Pride swelled inside me.

All the way to the right of the drawing was a large island, judging by the color pattern, but it didn't end. It wasn't surrounded by water on all sides like the islands — at least, not within the drawing. It appeared to be ten times the size of all the islands put together, with water only on one side.

Sebastian came back into the main room, finding me hunched over the desk, but I couldn't tear my eyes away from the map. He stood next to me, mirroring my position, and was likely drawing the same conclusions. I picked up the looking glass from the discarded pile of tools and moved it across the tiny letters.

"Bosque de la Rosa roja," I said, noting that the word "Rosa" was underlined a few times, with a small note next to it. "'Para el futuro.' I don't know what these words mean."

I looked up at Sebastian, surprised to see his facial expression was a blend of horror and confusion.

"What is it?"

He sat down on the edge of the desk, crumpling the edge of the map.

"My father," he breathed, rubbing his jaw roughly. "He used to call my mother his 'red Rose' — or 'Rosa roja' in the old language."

I gulped. "These are my mother's things. It can't be a coincidence, can it? This stuff has been locked up here for years."

We stared at each other, only interrupted by the sound of someone coming back down the hallway. I moved quickly, folding the map and tucking it back into the box, pretending to be interested in some of the random items on the desk.

"Oh good, you're both here," Hope said, innocently. "Find anything interesting, Mol?"

Sebastian put a reassuring hand on my back. I looked down at the box and its contents once more.

"Nothing worth sharing," I answered, and Sebastian kissed my temple.

ABOUT THE AUTHOR

Jennifer Ann Shore is a journalist, writer, and marketer.

40367137R00159

Made in the USA
Middletown, DE
26 March 2019